The thrilling novel of a love
born in a utopian ice eden—
and thrust into the frightening
world of the future . . .

THE ICE PEOPLE

THE ICE PEOPLE

By RENÉ BARJAVEL

Translated from the French by
CHARLES LAM MARKMANN

PYRAMID BOOKS • NEW YORK

To André Cayatte,
the begetter of this fantasy
and the inspiration of this book,
I dedicate both with affection.
                                   R.B.

THE ICE PEOPLE

A PYRAMID BOOK

Published by arrangement with William Morrow and Company, Inc.

Pyramid edition published February 1973
Second Xerox Education Publication published September 1974
Translation published in the United States in 1971

Translation published in Great Britain in 1970

French edition published in France by Les Presses de la Cité under the title *La Nuit des Temps*. Copyright © 1968 by Les Presses de la Cité

ISBN 0-515-02913-0

Library of Congress Catalog Card Number: 78-135150

Printed in the United States of America

Pyramid Books are published by Pyramid Communications, Inc.
Its trademarks, consisting of the word "Pyramid" and the portrayal of a pyramid, are registered in the United States Patent Office.

Pyramid Communications, Inc., 919 Third Avenue, New York, New York 10022

His hands in his pockets, his forehead pressed against the windowed wall of his room, Dr. Simon watched the day break over Paris. He was a tall, slim, dark-haired man of thirty-two. He was wearing a heavy toast-coloured turtle-neck sweater, slightly out of shape and worn at the elbows, and a pair of black corduroy trousers. His face was half hidden by a short, curly, dark beard. Because of the sunglasses he had worn during the polar summer, the hollows around his eyes seemed pale and fragile, as vulnerable as the fresh skin over a wound. His forehead was broad and creased by long squinting against the sun. His eyelids were swollen and the whites of his eyes were bloodshot. He could no longer sleep or cry or forget: it was impossible. . . .

The adventure had begun as a routine assignment. Years ago, technicians and administrators had replaced heroes as the explorers of the Antarctic continent. Technology had made it possible to combat the problems of climate and distance, even to guarantee comfortable accommodation for the explorers. When the wind howled too hard, they burrowed in and let it howl; when it abated, they went out again and everyone continued with his assigned tasks. The continent had been divided into pie wedges on the map, and the French mission, solidly established at Camp Paul-Émile Victor, had subdivided its wedge into little rectangles and trapezoids which it explored systematically one after another. The men of the mission knew that there was nothing to be found but ice, snow and wind, and rocks and soil below that, the same as everywhere else. But they were far removed from carbon monoxide and traffic jams; and they could imagine that they were small-scale heroic explorers braving great danger. The men of the camp shared a great comradeship.

The mission had just completed its exploration of Trapezoid 381; the file had been closed, a copy had been dispatched to the expedition's headquarters in Paris, and it was time to go on to the next task. Bureaucratically speaking, the mission should have proceeded from 381 to 382, but things did not happen that way.

A new device for sub-glacial probes had just been delivered to Camp Victor. It was revolutionary in its conception and, according to its inventor, it was capable of revealing the finest details of the earth's surface beneath several miles of ice. Louis Grey, the expedition's 37-year-old glaciologist, could hardly wait to give it a field test.

So it was decided that a task force would be sent to make a survey of the soil beneath the ice at Square 612, which lay only a few hundred kilometres from the South Pole. The big helicopter had to make two trips in order to convey the force, its vehicles and all its other equipment to the base of operations.

The area had already been roughly probed with the customary equipment which had revealed areas of ice between eight hundred and a thousand yards in depth existing side by side with ice-filled abysses more than two and a half miles deep. In Louis Grey's opinion this was an ideal site on which to test the new device. He thought that this was why he had chosen the area, but now no one would think of believing that. In the light of what had happened since, how could anyone think that chance alone, or any "reasonable" reason, had brought these men and their equipment to precisely the right spot in that vast desert of ice.

It was the beginning of December; in other words, the peak of the austral summer, when the sun did not set at all. It hovered over the men and the vehicles and circled the boundaries of their little world as if to keep them under observation from a distance. At about nine o'clock at night the sun slipped behind an ice mountain; perhaps an hour later it reappeared at the other end of the mountain; toward midnight it seemed to be about to give up and vanish below the horizon that was beginning to swallow it. But it fought back by inflating itself, changing its shape; it turned red, won the battle, and slowly went back to its former transit and its sentry round. It established a tremendous white and blue circle of cold and solitude round the task force.

Dr. Simon should not have been there at all, and he was homesick. He was coming to the end of a three-year tour of duty among the various French bases in the Antarctic, and he was more than weary. He should already have boarded a plane for Sydney, but instead he had remained at the request of his friend Grey, because an outbreak of measles at the base had prevented Simon's replacement from accompanying Grey's force.

This invasion of measles was amazing. Virtually no one ever becomes ill in the Antarctic; it is as if the microbes were afraid of the cold. Physicians assigned to expeditions as a rule have only accident victims to treat, or occasionally new arrivals who suffer from exposure before they have learned how to avoid rash risks. Furthermore, measles had virtually disappeared from the face of the earth since the perfection of the oral vaccine that newborn babies now received with their first feedings. In spite of all this, measles had broken out at Camp Victor. Approximately a quarter of the expedition was in bed shaking with fever and covered with spots. The glaciologist, Grey, had hastily assembled a handful of uninfected men including Dr. Simon, and packed them off to Square 612, hoping that the virus would not follow them. If it had not been for the measles . . .

———————————

Sitting on one of the treads of the snow-dog, Dr. Simon was dreaming of a *croissant* dipped in creamy coffee: dipped, soaked, softened, slurped up with all manner of ill-bred noises. By a slob, but a slob standing at a Paris bar, sawdust round his shoes, elbow to elbow with the early-morning grumblers, sharing their first pleasure of the day: coming fully awake in the warmth and the marvellous smell of *caffé-espresso*.

He could not take any more of the ice and wind. The wind never stopped pounding against him, against everyone in the Antarctic, its great paws steeped in the cold of hell and pounding all of them, their shelters and their aerials and their vehicles, to make them clear out of the continent and leave the wind alone with the lethal cold to consummate their loathsome ice-bound nuptials.

One had to be really stubborn in order to hold out against such persistence, and Simon had reached the end of his own stubbornness. Before he sat down he had placed a blanket folded into quarters on the track of the snow-dog, so that the cold would not be able to glue the skin of his buttocks to the metal through his woollen underwear, his trousers and his coat.

He sat facing the sun and scratching his face through his beard, trying to convince himself that the sun was warming him, although it was giving him almost as many calories as an oil lamp hanging two miles away. The wind was trying to bend his nose back towards his left ear. He thought of the sea breeze in the evenings at Colioure: so warm and soft, so cool-seeming because the whole day had been so hot. He thought of the inconceivable pleasure of undressing, immersing himself in water without turning into an iceberg, stretching out on a red-hot boulder. Red-hot! That seemed so unbelievable that he snickered.

"You getting high all by yourself now?" Brivaux asked. "That won't help you. Are you coming down with measles?" Brivaux had come up behind Simon: his depth-gauge hung against his chest on a broad strap that went round his neck.

"I was just thinking that there are places in the world where it's warm," Simon said.

"You haven't got measles, you've got meningitis. Don't sit there like that, you'll freeze your balls off. Here, take a look at this."

Brivaux pointed to the recording dial of his depth-gauge, which had already been marked by the stylus. The depth-gauge was the current model, and he had just used it to explore his assigned area. Simon got up and looked. He did not know very much about technology. But over the past three years he had had ample time to become familiar with the patterns traced on magnetic paper by the sensitive styluses of the portable probes. Mostly they looked like vague outlines of an empty lot, or a trash heap, or anything else that didn't really look like anything specific. But what Brivaux was showing him *looked like something that made sense*.

Like what?

Like nothing familiar, but . . .

The straight line does not exist in nature nor does the regular curve. Beaten, tortured, kneaded and stirred together through the ages by powerful geological forces, the earth's surface is completely irregular. But Brivaux's needle had transcribed a succession of curves and straight lines—interrupted, broken, but completely regular. It was thoroughly improbable and in fact impossible that the natural surface could look like this. Simon drew the obvious conclusion: "Something must be jammed in your depth-gauge."

"And is something jammed in your head, too?" Brivaux tapped his gloved index finger against Simon's forehead. "This gadget runs like a watch. I only wish I could function as well. *Down there* is where there's something screwy." He tapped the heel of his fur boot against the ice.

"A profile like this is impossible," Simon said.

"I know, I'm not sure I believe it myself."

"What about the others? What have they found?"

"I have no idea. I'm going to blow the whistle for them," Brivaux entered the snow-dog that served as a laboratory and a second later the howl of a siren summoned the members of the task force back to their base.

In fact they had already begun to return. First came the two walking groups with their conventional equipment. They were followed by the snow-dog that carried the receiver-transmitter of the new depth-gauge. The instrument was mounted in a metal case at the front of the vehicle between the treads, and a red cable connected it with its controls and recording dial inside the snow-dog. The vehicle's cabin held Eloi (the driver), Louis Grey, the glaciologist, who was impatient to see what the new instrument could do, and the engineer sent from the factory to demonstrate its use.

He was a tall, thin lad, on the blond side, with very delicate ways, and his natural elegance was such that his polar clothes seemed to have been made for him by

Lanvin. The old hands couldn't help grinning when they looked at him.

He got out of the snow-dog without a word, listening reservedly to Grey's evaluations of his "device". According to the glaciologist, the new machine was completely off its rocker; he had never seen even the most ancient piece of junk produce such a profile.

"You've got more surprises coming," Brivaux said. He was standing near the mobile laboratory.

"Was it you who blew the whistle?"

"It sure was, baby."

"What's going on?"

"Come on in and take a look."

And they saw.

———

They saw the four outlines, the four profiles—all different and all alike. The new probe's record was photographed on a three-millimetre film. Grey had watched it take shape on the monitor screen. The other members of the task force studied it on the big screen in the mobile laboratory.

What the three other probes had hinted at was made abundantly clear by the new instrument. Leaving no room for doubt, it produced on the screen a succession of profiles of tumbled stairways, broken walls, shattered domes, twisted spiral ramps—details of an architecture uprooted and smashed by a giant's hand.

"It's showing us the ruins of a city," Brivaux said.

"It can't be possible!" Grey's voice hardly dared to make itself audible.

"And why not?" Brivaux asked calmly.

He was the son of a peasant from the mountains of

Haute-Savoie, the last man in his village who went raising cattle instead of milking the Parisian tourists who
came crowding in, a dozen to the square yard. Old man
Brivaux had enclosed his bit of mountain in barbed
wire studded with signboards reading NO ADMIT-
TANCE and inside this prison he lived in freedom.

His son had inherited his light blue eyes, his black
hair, his reddish beard, his even temper and his sense
of proportion. Like everyone else in the laboratory who
knew how to interpret the profiles, Brivaux saw the
ruins of a city. The others didn't believe in what they
saw. He did. If he had seen his own father under the
ice, he would have been surprised for an instant; then
he would have said, "Look, there's Dad."

But the members of the task force eventually had to
accept the evidence for the four tracings fitted together
and corroborated one another.

Bernard, the draftsman, was ordered to make a synthesis of them. An hour later his first sketch was ready.
It looked like nothing that any of them had ever seen:
huge, strange architectural shapes torn apart by some
colossal force.

"How far down are these things?" Eloi asked.

"One thousand yards, or maybe twelve hundred,"
Grey said angrily, as if he were responsible for the figure's improbability.

"How long does that mean they've been there?"

"No way of knowing. We've never penetrated so
deeply."

"But the Americans have," Brivaux said equably.

"True. So have the Russians."

"Were they able to date their samplings?" Simon
asked.

"One can always try, but that doesn't mean it's accurate."

"Accurate or not, what figure did they arrive at?"

Even before he spoke, Grey shrugged at the absurdity of what he was about to say. "Approximately nine hundred thousand years, give or take a few centuries."

There were one or two exclamations of amazement, and then a stupefied silence.

The men in the mobile laboratory made repeated comparisons between Bernard's sketch and the last segment of the profile, now motionless on the screen, becoming aware of the enormity of their ignorance.

"That can't be right," Eloi said. "This stuff was made by men. Nine hundred thousand years ago there were no men, there were just monkeys."

"Where'd you get that?" Brivaux demanded.

"What we know of man's history and the evolution of life on the earth," Simon said, "amounts to no more than a flea's turd on the Place de la Concorde."

"So?" Eloi said.

"Fr. Lancieux, I apologize to your instrument," Grey said.

"This device is miraculous," the glaciologist said. "But there's something else that they didn't notice. Show it to them. And tell them what you think about it."

Lancieux pressed the rewind switch and then a red button. The screen brightened and once more it showed the slow procession of the silhouette of the ruins. "*There* is where you have to look," Grey said, pointing his finger toward the top of the screen. Above the tortured profile of the subsurface there was a barely visible straight line, just perceptibly wavy and perfect in its regularity. Indeed no one had noticed it at all, perhaps on the assumption that it was a reference line, certainly nothing of importance.

"Tell them," Grey repeated. "Tell them what you told me! At this point . . ."

"I should prefer to make a counter-experiment first,"

Lancieux said in an embarrassed tone. "None of the other instruments has recorded—"

"They're not sensitive enough!" Grey interrupted.

"Perhaps not," Lancieux said in his soft voice. "But it isn't certain. . . . Perhaps it's only because they weren't set on the right frequency. . . ."

The technicians plunged into a discussion of the modifications that should be made in the older equipment. Dr. Simon filled his pipe and went out of the laboratory.

———————

I am not a technician, Dr. Simon reflected. I do not measure my patients or, at any rate, I measure them as little as possible, I prefer to try to understand them. But one has to have the ability. So, I am lucky . . . .

My father who was a physician in Puteaux, used to see more than fifty patients a day go through his examination room. How could he ever know who they were and what was wrong with them? A five-minute examination, punch and punch-card, diagnostic machine, prescription form, social-security papers, receipts, a couple of rubber-stamp impressions—all right, go put on your clothes, next, please. My father hated the medical profession as he and his colleagues were obliged to practice it. When the opportunity arose for me to come here, he pushed me into it as hard as he could. "Go! go! You'll have a mere handful of patients, a village! You'll be able to get to know them!"

He died last year, worn out. His heart let him down. I didn't even have time to get there before he died. Undoubtedly he'd never found the time to perforate his own personal little card and shove it into the slot of his

*electronic diagnostician. But he had taken the time to
teach me certain things that he had learned from his
own father, a doctor in the Auvergne. For example,
taking the pulse, or examining the tongue or the whites
of the eyes. It's amazing how much the pulse can tell
about a man's insides: not only the state of his health
at that moment but his temperament, and even his
character—whether he is aggressive or inaccessible,
easygoing or irritable, arrogant or submissive. There is
the healthy man's pulse and the sick man's pulse, but
there is also the wild boar's and the rabbit's.*

*Like every doctor, of course, I have an electronic di-
agnostician with its little punch cards. What physician
doesn't? But I use them only to reassure those patients
who have more faith in machines than in men.*

After Brivaux had left his father's farm to study in
Grenoble, he had placidly disregarded the traditional
sequence of courses and skipped various intermediate
stages in his education. He graduated from the school
of electronics a year ahead of time and at the head of
his class. His engineer's diploma could have been a
golden bridge into any of the great industrial corpora-
tions in the world, but he had chosen Camp Victor,
without a golden bridge. Because, as he explained to
his friend, Dr. Simon: "Doing electronics here is a ball.
... We're practically on top of the magnetic pole,
ionized particles are skittering around in the teeth of
the solar wind, and there're a thousand other gimmicks
that no one knows anything about yet. That makes an
interesting combination. A man can tinker here."

He flung his arms out wide and his fingers beckoned

to the mysterious currents of creation to infuse him. Simon smiled, imagining him a Neptune of electronics, standing erect at the pole, his hair lost in the shadows of the sky, his arms outstretched in the perpetual wind of the electrons, distributing through all nature the living flux and reflux of the planet-mother. But it was "tinkering" in which Brivaux demonstrated a kind of genius. His thick, hairy fingers were unbelievably skilful, and his technical knowledge was combined with an infallible intuition. He *smelled* electric current as animals smell water. And then his fingers fashioned the snare that would capture it. A couple of bits of wire, a circuit, three semi-conductor devices—he would twist, assemble, solder; then a puff of smoke, a smell of resin, and there it was: a dial began to live, a curve pulsed on a screen.

The problem that Lancieux had posed was no real problem for him; in less than an hour he had modified the three conventional instruments, and the teams set out again. But the evidence they were seeking was so awe-inspiring that they expected to come back empty-handed. Except for Lancieux, who knew his equipment thoroughly, they were sure that the little wavy line was the product of some whim of the new instrument—what television people call a "ghost".

The sun was slipping behind the ice mountain when they returned. Everything was blue—the sky, the clouds, the ice, their faces and the vapour that came from their nostrils. Bernard's red cover-all was the colour of a plum. But they had not come back empty-handed. The wavy line was engraved on all the instruments. It was less detailed and it had lost its little curl, but it was there. They had indeed found what they had gone to seek.

Comparing their charts with Lancieux's, Grey had been able to determine the precise location of their quarry on the surface beneath the ice. He showed its profile on the screen inside the mobile laboratory. It resembled a fragment of a huge staircase that had been overturned and broken. "Boys," Grey said in a small voice, "there . . . there there is . . ."

A piece of paper shook in his left hand. He stopped speaking and cleared his throat. His voice refused to obey him. He tapped the screen with his piece of paper. Then he swallowed his saliva and burst out, "My God! It's insane! But it exists! The four probes can't all be crazy! Not only are there these inexplicable ruins, but in the middle of all this muck there's an ultrasonic transmitter operating!"

The mysterious little line was the record of a signal sent out by that transmitter and by all the laws of logic, the transmitter had been operating for more than nine hundred thousand years. It went deeper into the past than history and pre-history, it knocked every scientific credo to pieces, and it was on a scale beyond the grasp of all these men. The only one who accepted the fact with equanimity, apparently, was Brivaux, the only one who had been born and brought up in the country. The others had grown up in cities, where landmarks are only temporary, and all things bow to the forces of construction and decay, of change and destruction. He, in the school of the Alpine rocks, had learned to see far and to understand eternity.

"They're going to think we're insane," Grey said.

He called the main base by radio and asked for a helicopter to take his group back to the base at once. But he had forgotten the measles. The last healthy pilot had just taken sick and gone to bed.

"André's getting better," the base radio added. "In three or four days we'll be able to send him out for you. But what do you want to come back for? Are the icebergs on fire?"

Grey broke the connection. That stupid joke had gone a bit stale.

Ten minutes later Pontailler himself, the base commander, called back in great anxiety to ask why the task force wanted to return. Grey tried to reassure him that there was no trouble, but refused to be more specific. "Telling you wouldn't be enough," he said. "I'd have to show you. Otherwise you'd think we've all gone out of our minds. Just send someone out for us as soon as you can." And again he signed off.

When, five days later, the helicopter arrived at Square 612, Pontailler was aboard, and he was the first to hurry out.

Grey's team had spent those five days in mounting excitement and joy. Once the first shock dissolved, they had accepted the ruins and the transmitter and adopted them. They had gathered many more profiles and recordings. On the basis of the coordinates provided by the instruments, Bernard was working on a kind of bird's-eye view, full of gaps and blank spaces, which nevertheless were already beginning to look like a fairy-tale landscape, all mineral and empty and broken and unknown, yet *human.*

Brivaux had improvised a microphone and connected it with the recording apparatus of the new instrument to produce a tape recording which he played for his colleagues. They heard nothing. Then Brivaux smiled. "It's all in the silence," he said. "You can't hear ultrasonics. But they are there, I guarantee you that, although we would need a frequency reducer to hear them. I don't have one, and there's none at the base. Someone is going to have to go to Paris."

Someone would have to go to Paris. That was Pontailler's conclusion when he was brought up to date, when he had gone through the process of rejecting and then finally accepting the evidence of the find. It could not even be reported by radio, when any ear in the world might be listening at any time. All the documents had to be taken to headquarters in Paris where the director of Polar Expeditions would decide what should be done with them. Meanwhile everyone was to keep his mouth shut. As Eloi said, "This could be something red-hot."

When I finally took the plane to Sydney, beginning my leave two weeks late, I was already impatient to return to the Antarctic. I was no longer tormented by the yearning for a croissant *and coffee. Really not. There was something under the ice much more exciting than the early-morning smell of unwashed Parisians.*

The plane soared up on its own breath like a plastic bubble on a stream of water, pivoted on its axis in search of its proper direction, then let out a scream and shot off in a fifty-degree climb toward the north and the sun. In spite of the balancing mechanisms of the heavily padded seats, it's a funny feeling to climb at such an angle and with such acceleration. But this was a plane that carried only hardened old hands, and it was in no danger of breaking windows on the ground with its supersonic bangs. So the pilots made the most of the situation.

The briefcase I carried with me contained not only my toothbrush and pyjamas but also microfilms of the profiles and of Bernard's bird's-eye view, the tape recording, and letters from Grey and Pontailler authenticating all these things. (Though I had not the faintest idea of the fact, I was also taking along the measles virus which was about to make a world tour under the name of Australian measles. The pharmaceutical laboratories had to develop a new vaccine in great haste, and they made a fine profit.)

I didn't arrive in Paris until two days later. I had forgotten that it had become very difficult to cross oceans.

In our icy insulation we had grown away from the world's shabby, stupid hatred. Now I read the Australian newspapers. There were little brush fire wars almost everywhere in the world. They had spread since my departure for the Antarctic. And they had multiplied. On every border, as customs barriers fell, police carriers took their place. Arriving at the airport in Sydney, I was authorized neither to enter the city nor to leave the country. God knows which military visa was missing from my passport. It took me thirty-six hours of hectic negotiation to be able to board the jet for Paris. I was afraid that they would want to stick their noses into my microfilms: what would they have thought they were? But no one asked me to open my briefcase. I might as well have been carrying plans for nuclear bases. That didn't matter to them. It was the visa that was needed. Those were their orders. It was stupid. It was an organized world.

As soon as Simon had unpacked the contents of his briefcase, Rochefoux, the director of French Polar Expeditions, took matters in hand with his customary vigour. He was almost eighty years old, but this didn't keep him from spending several weeks each year in the neighbourhood of one of the poles.

Today he had summoned television reporters and other members of the press to a news conference after the meeting of the commission of the United Nations Educational, Scientific and Cultural Organization. He had concluded that secrecy had been maintained long enough, and he meant to shake UNESCO as a fox terrier shakes a rat, to get the help his organization needed.

Workers from the *Centre National de Recherches Scientifiques* were completing the installation of various apparatus in a large eighth-floor office. Standing at the big window, Rochefoux and Simon watched two officers on horseback in the courtyard of the École Militaire. The Place de Fontenoy was filled with men playing *pétanque,* a Provençal bowling game not unlike Italian *bocce*; at each turn the players blew on their fingers before picking up the bowl.

Rochefoux muttered something and turned away. He had no great respect either for idlers or for soldiers. The engineer who had been supervising the installation of the communications equipment announced that everything was ready. Then the members of the commission began to arrive and take their places along the table.

Two hours later they knew everything that Rochefoux could tell them, they had seen everything the microfilms could show, and they had asked Simon a hundred questions. Rochefoux began his concluding remarks, indicating a point on a map projected on a screen in front of them.

"Here on the Antarctic continent, at the eighty-eighth parallel, under more than three thousand feet of ice, there are the remains of something that was constructed by intelligent creatures, and it is sending out a signal. For nine hundred thousand years this signal has been saying: 'Here I am, I am calling you. . . .' This is the first time that men have heard it. Will we hesitate? We rescued the temples in the Nile Valley. But the waters of the Aswan Dam were rising around our knees and forcing us into action. Here, obviously, there is something greater: the obligation to know and to understand. Something is calling us. We must go to it. This requires substantial means, and France is unable to do it all by herself. She will do her part, but she must call on the other nations to join her."

He went on, "So far, you have seen the signal in the form of an ordinary line drawn on graph paper. Now, thanks to my friends of the CNRS, who have listened to it in every possible way, you will be able to hear it."

He motioned to the engineer, who activated another circuit.

First an oscilloscope screen showed a luminous line as rigid as a violin string, while the air shivered with a high-pitched whistle. Then the CNRS engineer slowly manipulated a rheostat. The pitch became lower and less painful. Muscles relaxed, jaws unclenched, a delegate removed his fingers from his ears. The pitch became still lower, and the whistle turned into a trill. The straight line on the oscilloscope screen was now wavy.

Slowly, very slowly, the engineer's hand brought the signal down through the whole scale of frequencies. When he reached the realm of the infrasonic every pulsation sent a shiver into flesh and bones and objects, vibrating the walls of the UNESCO building to their very foundations. It was like the beating of a gigantic heart, the heart of some unimaginable animal, the heart of earth itself.

Typical headlines from French newspapers: THE GREATEST DISCOVERY OF ALL TIME ... A FROZEN CIVILIZATION ... UNESCO PLANS TO

MELT SOUTH POLE. Headline from an English newspaper: WHO OR WHAT?

A French family at dinner—the Vignonts. Father, mother, son and daughter were seated around the outer circumference of a crescent-shaped table while the television screen on the wall facing them showed the evening news. The elder Vignonts managed a retail store belonging to the European Shoe Manufacturers. The daughter was a student in the School of Decorative Arts. The son was midway between his second and third attempts at the baccalaureate.

On the screen a Russian ethnologist was being interviewed live; the programme was being relayed by a satellite. The Russian scientist spoke in her own language with a simultaneous translation:

"You have been invited to become a member of the expedition charged with solving what has been called the mystery of the South Pole. Do you hope to find traces of human beings under twelve hundred yards of ice?"

The ethnologist smiled. "If there is a city there, it was not the great auks who built it." There are no auks in the Antarctic, there are only penguins. But an ethnologist is not required to know this.

Next, the television presented an interview with the secretary general of UNESCO, who announced that the United States, the Soviet Union, England, China, Japan, the African Union, Italy, Germany and several other nations had let it be known that they would offer material assistance toward the de-icing of Square 612. Rapid preparations would be made, and everything would be on an operational basis by the beginning of the next polar summer.

Strollers on the Champs-Élysées were interviewed:

"Do you know where the South Pole is?"

"Well . . . uh . . ."

"How about you?"

"It's in the south!"

"Excellent. Would you like to go there?"

"Well, since you ask, no."

"Why not?"

"It's too cold."

At the crescent-shaped table Mother Vignont shook her head. "It's stupid to ask questions like that!"

Father Vignont had his own comment: "The money that's going to be spent on that! It would make more sense to build some new parking lots."

Bernard's bird's-eye projection appeared on the screen.

"Still, it's pretty odd to find such a thing in a place like that," Mother Vignont observed.

"There's nothing new about it," the daughter said. "It's pre-Columbian."

Her brother was not even looking: as he ate he was reading the comic-strip adventures of Big Billy. His sister nudged him. "Have a look, at least! It's pretty exciting, isn't it?"

He shrugged. "It's stupid," he said.

———

A monstrous machine thrust its muzzle into the flesh of the mountain of ice and hurled out a cloud of transparent shreds that the sun transformed into a rainbow. More than thirty tunnels had already been dug inside the mountain, and all around them supply dumps and radio and television transmitters had been established by the International Polar Expedition (known by its French initials—EPI, for *Expédition Polaire Internationale*). The little town built inside the mountain was called EPI 1, and the settlement that was sheltered beneath the ice of Square 612 was EPI 2. EPI 2 was the central installation. It contained the atomic pile that supplied power, light and heat to the two sub-surface villages and to the surface settlement, EPI 3, which was composed of hangars, vehicles and all the other machinery to be used against the ice. Never before had there been an international undertaking on such a scale. Men had turned to it eagerly as though it were the long-awaited chance to put aside their hatreds and to reach brotherhood in a totally unselfish endeavour.

France being the host nation, her language was chosen as the working language. But in order to facilitate communication, Japan had set up a short-wave universal translating machine in EPI 2. It could simultaneously translate all the conversations that were fed into it, regurgitating them in seventeen languages on seventeen wavelengths. Every scientist, project captain and important technician had been given an adhesive receiver no bigger than a pea, tuned to the wavelength of his own language; he kept this receiver constantly in his ear. He had also received a transmitter in the form of a pin that he could wear on the chest or the shoulder of his outer clothing. A pocket switch, as flat as a coin, enabled him to insulate himself against the thousand different conversations in their seventeen translations that swirled together in the air and to hear only the person with whom he was speaking.

The atomic pile was American, the cargo helicopters were Russian, the heavily lined outer clothing was Chinese, the boots were Finnish, the whiskey was Irish and the cooking was French. There were British, German, Italian and Canadian machinery and instruments, Argentine meat and Israeli fruit. The climate control and accommodations inside EPI 1 and 2 were American, and they were extraordinarily comfortable.

The Shaft.

Perpendicular to the point at which the ultrasonic transmitter had been located, the shaft was biting into the translucent ice. It was thirty-five feet in diameter, dominated by an iron tower not unlike a derrick, vibrating with its power plants and giving off vapours that the wind turned into scarves of snow. Two elevators carried men and equipment to and from the bottom of the excavation. Each day the bottom of the shaft moved a little nearer to the core of the mystery.

In two weeks the ice explorers at the bottom of the shaft had reached the ruins.

Professor João de Aguiar, Brazil's representative in UNESCO and its current chairman, mounted the podium and faced his audience. He was in evening dress. Tonight the great lecture hall was crowded with scholars and diplomats and reporters, with every Frenchman or foreigner who was anyone in Paris.

Above and behind Professor de Aguiar's head, the world's largest television screen almost completely covered the wall. It had been installed to display a live broadcast from the bottom of the shaft as transmitted by the antenna of EPI 1 and relayed by the Trio Satellite.

The screen was illuminated, and against it an enormous silhouette of the chairman stood out in soft, somewhat muted colours and perfect detail. The two chairmen, the little flesh-and-blood one and his tremendous image, gestured in a friendly fashion and began to speak. They talked for seven minutes, and this was the conclusion:

". . . Thus it has been possible to hollow out a large chamber in the ice, in the very centre of the remarkable ruins that the ice still holds in its grasp. Except for the few heroic pioneers of science whose skill and courage have created the shaft, no one in the world has seen the ruins. And in a moment the entire world will discover them. Through the miracle of electronics, this switch which I will press will turn on floodlights at the other end of the world, and we shall see the image of what was perhaps the world's first civilization as it speeds into every modern household. It is not without great emotion . . ."

In his little booth a control engineer was watching the chairman's image on his monitor screen. With the chairman, the engineer thrust his thumb home.

At the other end of the world the ice chamber was illuminated.

The first thing that the viewers saw was a flight of huge stairs, or yellow tiers, that came down out of the night and disappeared in another night below.

To the right there was a section of broken wall, the colour of grass, in some unknown material that was not quite opaque. Below this, the beginning of a wide spiral ramp made of a metal that looked like steel. The ramp disappeared in the milky mist of the world of ice.

Then the next phase began. An air hose was turned on the slab of ice that contained the fragment of wall. As the entire world watched, the first shard of the entombed past was about to be freed from its matrix. The warm air rushed out of the hose and struck the ice, which began to melt as exhaust hoses drew off the vapour and the water to the surface.

The slab of ice grew thinner as it melted, and finally it had shrunk back flush with the green wall. Then the undulating image on the television screens, distorted by the dripping lenses of the armoured cameras, showed the green wall and the ice melting together.

The hot air had filled the entire ice chamber. All its walls were dripping. Cataracts poured from the ceiling on the men in their diving suits. At last the warm air reached the summit of the spiral ramp of steel, and the steel melted.

Newspaper headlines: BIGGEST FLOP OF CENTURY . . . BURIED CITY JUST A PHANTOM . . . BILLIONS SPENT ON MIRAGE.

Rochefoux attempted to clarify matters in a television interview. He explained that the tremendous pressure to which they had been subjected during nine hundred millennia had broken down the hardest bodies into their component molecules. But they were preserved in their original shape by the ice. When it melted, it released the molecules, and the water dissociated and dispersed them.

"We are going to employ a new technique," Rochefoux said. "We will cut away the ice with the objects contained in it. We have not abandoned our efforts to discover the secrets of this civilization that has come to us from the abyss of time. The ultrasonic transmitter is still putting out its signal. We will continue to dig down to it."

At a depth of one thousand seventy-three yards below the surface of the ice, the shaft made contact with the soil of the continent. The signal came from below the soil.

Having bitten through the ice, the shaft drilled into the soil and then into rock. Right from the start the rock seemed unusually hard; it was vitrified, as if it had been heated and compressed, and it became progressively harder as the shaft descended. Soon its density perturbed the geologists. It was a kind of granite, but it seemed as though the molecules of which it was composed had been "pre-selected" and deployed in a minimum of space to afford a maximum of cohesion. After a number of mechanical tools had been broken, the bottom of this rock stratum was finally reached, and about a hundred twenty yards below the bottom of the ice, the shaft encountered sand. This sand was a geological heresy; it should not have been there. Therefore, according to Rochefoux, who was incorrigibly optimistic, someone must have placed it there. It was proof that the expedition was on the right track.

Below them, the signal continued to be audible. They would have to go on digging.

Drilling into the sand could not begin until a metal sleeve had been lowered for the preservation of the shaft, for the sand was dry and smooth as the inside of an hourglass and as free-running as water.

Fifty-five feet beneath the rock floor, one workman in a crew linked to one another by ropes like Alpinists began to make frantic motions and shout something unintelligible through his anti-dust mask. He was trying to say that he felt something hard beneath his feet.

Suddenly the suction dredge began to whine and quiver. Its hose collapsed. Higgins, the engineer in charge, cut off the motor of the dredge, climbed down from the platform on which he had been standing and set the workmen to clearing away the sand, first with shovels, then by hand, and finally with brooms.

When Rochefoux went down to the bottom of the shaft, accompanied by Simon, Brivaux, Leonova, the anthropologist who headed the Russian mission, and Hoover, the chemist who led the American group, they found an unbroken metal surface convex in shape and yellow in colour emerging from the fine sand.

Hoover requested that all motors be shut off and that no one speak or move. The silence that followed was protected from the noises of the earth by more than a hundred metres of rock and more than a half mile of ice. When Hoover knelt down to test the surface with his fingers, everyone could hear the cracking of his left knee. He tapped the metal surface with his gloved index finger. There was only a muted sound. He took a copper hammer from his pocket and struck it against the metal, first lightly and then harder and harder. There was no resonance.

He muttered something and lowered his face closer to the surface, which showed no sign of the hammer blows. He tried to cut away a fragment with a tungsten-steel chisel, but the chisel skidded over the metal and could not bite into it. Then he poured various acids on the metal and examined the treated areas through a portable spectroscope. He stood up again in perplexity. "I can't understand what makes it so hard," he said. "It's practically pure."

"What are you talking about?" Leonova demanded edgily.

Hoover was a huge potbellied, red-faced giant of a man with an easy temperament and slow movements. Leonova was dark, slender, and volatile; she was the prettiest woman in the expedition. Hoover looked at her and smiled. "What? You didn't recognize it? You, a woman? It's gold!"

Brivaux had turned on his recording apparatus. The paper unwound on its reel and the familiar thin line appeared there. The signal was coming from below the golden surface.

A larger area was cleared: the golden surface still curved off into the sand in every direction. It seemed as though the drilling shaft had arrived somewhat to one side of the pole of a vast sphere.

The pole of the sphere was cleared and exploration continued beyond it. Then a discovery was made. Concentric circles of sharp, short teeth were found in the metal; they were positioned so as to enable them to engage as gears. The largest had a diameter of about ten feet.

"This looks like the tip of a drill," Hoover said. "To make a hole to get out of here!"

"Do you think it's hollow? Is there someone inside?" Leonova asked.

Hoover raised his eyebrows. "There was once." Then he added: "Before they could worry about getting out they had to get in. There's a door somewhere!"

Two weeks after the initial contact with the golden sphere, the various exploratory instruments had accumulated enough information to make it possible to draw provisional conclusions.

The sphere was apparently resting on a pedestal and both were embedded in a sand-filled pocket within a layer of artificially hardened rock. The sand was probably intended to insulate the sphere against seismic shocks and any other earth movements. The sphere and its pedestal seemed to be a solid unit. The diameter of the sphere was eighty-nine feet ten inches, the height of a ten-story building. It was hollow. Its outer skin was nine and a half feet thick.

Workmen began to clear away the sand, intending to empty the hollow in the rock at least as far as the equator of the sphere.

Then the door was found. It was a circle, the diameter of which was slightly more than the height of a man, and it was traced in the skin of the sphere by what seemed to be a weld. As soon as the door was found, a temporary floor was laid on the sand for the accommodation of scientists and technicians who were lowered to it by an elevator.

Brivaux went over its entire circumference with a little instrument with several dials. "It's welded all the way through," he said.

"Once the pot was full, the lid was welded on," Hoover said. "It seems more like a grave than a shelter."

"What about the drill?" Leonova replied. "Is it there just to make an exit for the cat?"

"My dear girl, there were assuredly no cats in those days." Hoover made as if to thrust his index finger under her chin. His finger was the size, shape and colour of a small sausage, with reddish freckles and red hairs. In a fury Leonova knocked his hand aside.

"She'd bite me!" Hoover smiled. "All right, beautiful, we're going back topside. After you."

The elevator could hold two persons, but Hoover took up the space of three. He lifted Leonova as if she were a feather and sat her on the iron bench, shouting, "Up!" The elevator started to move immediately. Suddenly there was a crash, followed by shouts. Something caught Hoover at the back of the knees; he fell backward and his head struck something hard and rough. He heard a snap inside his head and fainted.

He regained consciousness in a bed in the infirmary. Simon was leaning over him and watching him with a smile. Hoover blinked two or three times trying to clear his head and asked abruptly, "What about the girl?"

"She's all right," Simon answered.

Then Hoover asked, "What happened?"

"A landslide. The ice above the corridor collapsed."

"Anyone hurt?"

"Two men killed."

Simon said this in a low voice, as if he were ashamed of it. These had been the first two deaths in the expedition. One was a miner from Reunion Island, the other a French carpenter. Four other men had been injured, including a Japanese electrician who was still in critical condition.

The corridor was a roughly rectangular cut in the rock wall. It was cluttered with a jumbled mass of mortar and twisted metallic shapes that had regressed to their mineral origins. The same sort of rubble had been found mingled with the sand between this opening and the door of the sphere, and it had been carefully bagged and sent to the surface for examination and analysis.

The corridor had been given that name because the scientists thought that it was the terminus of a passage, but its dimensions were more reminiscent of a large hall. It was undoubtedly the place from which the men of the past—if they were men—had hollowed out and hardened the rock, brought in the sand, and built the sphere. It was the umbilical cord from which the sphere had developed in its rocky placenta. The corridor came from somewhere, and it could lead to somewhere. The next step was to clear it, enter it and go see.

But before or after the sphere? The scientists held a meeting in which they decided that the sphere should be explored first.

The next day Hoover attended an informational meeting in the conference room. When he mounted the platform to take his seat among the executive committee of EPI there was a brief surge of laughter. He had got out of bed for the meeting, wearing only a dressing gown over his pyjamas. It was the colour of crushed raspberries and decked with rows of blue and green crescents. His big belly gave its cord an absurd angle, and one end hung down to his boots which were lined with white bearskin. His round, turban-shaped bandage was the finishing touch; it made him look like the Grand Panjandrum in a Greenwich Village production of Molière's *Malade Imaginaire*.

Rochefoux, who was chairman, rose and embraced him. The wave of laughter was drowned in a greater wave of applause.

The room was filled. Besides the scientists and experts from every country, there was a pool of a dozen journalists representing the world's most important news services.

The big screen behind the podium showed an overall view of the floodlighted excavation in the rock where some thirty men were busy, helmets on their heads and masks suspended round their necks ready for instant use. The upper half of the sphere, looming out of the sand and the scaffoldings, had a soft glow; it seemed tranquil, yet also threatening in its mass.

In a singsong voice Leonova described the work that was being done, and the simultaneous-translation machine began to whisper its seventeen different languages into all the ears in the room. Leonova paused, meditated a moment, and then resumed, "I don't know what this sphere reminds you of but to me it suggests a seed. The seed should have sprouted in the spring. The drill is a stem that should have grown and found its way into the light, and the hollow 'pedestal' was a receptacle for whatever it displaced. But the spring didn't come. And the winter has lasted nine hundred thousand years. And yet I won't, I can't believe the seed is dead!" She was almost shouting: "There's the signal!"

A journalist rose to demand, "Then why are you waiting to open the door?"

Leonova stared at him in surprise, and her voice was cold when she replied, "We are not going to open it."

There was a murmur of astonishment in the audience. Rochefoux, smiling, rose to explain.

"We are not going to open the door because it may trigger some defensive or destructive device. We are going to enter here."

With a bamboo pointer he indicated a site at the pole of the image on the screen.

"But," he continued, "there is one difficulty. Our diamond-tipped drills have broken on this metal, and it will not yield to the oxyhydric torch. It melts, but immediately reseals itself, as if cut flesh were to heal immediately behind the knife. This is a phenomenon the mechanics of which we do not understand, but we know that it takes place on the molecular level. To open a path for ourselves into the metal, we must attack it at the molecular level and dissociate the molecules. We are waiting for a new torch that will utilize laser and plasma at the same time. As soon as it arrives, we will launch Operation O, the Opening . . ."

The tunnel of ice and rock had now become a tunnel of gold. A hole six and a half feet across was made in the skin of the sphere. At the bottom of the hole, in a golden glow, a white knight was assailing the metal with a lance of light. The man in the asbestos armour and the steel-and-glass helmet was Lister, an English engineer, armed with his "plaser". (The word had been formed from *plasma* and *laser*; the device was the product of both British and Japanese industry.)

In a Japanese house the traditional print on the wall had been replaced by the television screen. The kneeling hostess was serving tea. The commentator's voice was low as he reported that the bottom of the tunnel, now only a few inches thick, was about to be pierced. A television camera introduced into the interior would allow the honourable viewers of the entire world to enter the sphere and learn its mysteries at last.

Leonova, wearing an asbestos cover-all, had joined Lister at the bottom of the shaft, but Hoover, because of his size, had had to remain on the platform with the technicians. Now he was lying on his belly at the edge of the hole and shouting advice to Leonova, who could not hear him.

She was kneeling beside Lister behind a protective shield. The jet of red flame thrust into the gold, which bubbled and dissolved into waves of light.

Suddenly there was a fearful shriek. Flame, sparks

and smoke were sucked violently downward. The heavy shield tumbled on to the golden surface, Leonova lost her balance, Hoover shouted and swore, Lister clung to his plaser. A technician had already cut off the plaser's power. Leonova picked herself up, took off her mask and spoke into her microphone. She announced calmly, "The sphere has been pierced. Contrary to what we expected the temperature inside the sphere must have been colder than it is outside. This collision of temperatures created a violent implosion, but a balance has now been established."

Simon was on the surface of the sphere with Hoover and Lanson, the British television engineer who was superintending the lowering of a thick cable. The tip of the cable contained two lenses, one on top of the other: a miniature floodlight and a minicamera. Leonova, at the bottom of the shaft, seized the cable in her gloved hands and fed it into the black hole. When she had introduced about a yard of it, she raised her arms, and Lanson stopped feeding cable.

"Ready to go," he told Hoover.

"Wait for me," Leonova said. She climbed back to the platform where she could watch the monitor screen.

"Let's go!" Hoover called.

Lanson turned to a technician. "Lights."

Below the golden floor the floodlight's eye opened and the camera's eye began to record. The image rose up along the cable, leaped from the top of the antenna of EPI 1 to Trio whirling on its axis in the black emptiness of space, bounced off the other satellites and fell like rain onto every television screen in the world.

It showed nothing.

Nothing but a lazy spiral of greyish dust that the light of the tiny lamp tried in vain to pierce.

"Dust!" Hoover grumbled. "How could that damned dust have got into the hermetically sealed sphere?"

An amplifier interrupted Hoover's perplexity. The voice was that of Rochefoux, speaking from the conference room. "Break the whole shaft through at once," he said, "and find out what's inside the sphere."

The floor of the shaft was opened and the platform bearing a scout group was ready to be lowered. The group consisted of Higgins, Hoover, Leonova, Lanson and his camera, Shanga from Africa, Lao from China, Hoi-To from Japan, Henckel from Germany, and Simon. The platform was dangerously overloaded, but the sensibilities of all the delegations had to be considered. Rochefoux, who was feeling extremely tired, had given up his place to Simon.

Since he was the youngest, Simon had the privilege of being the first to descend. He was wearing a stifling yellow cover-all, grey felt boots and an astrakhan cap. The temperature inside the sphere was $-34°F$. Simon was wearing a miner's lamp on his head, an oxygen mask on a strap, and a revolver in his belt. He had tried to refuse the revolver, but Rochefoux had insisted that he take it: one never knew what might be ahead.

A metal ladder, which would also serve as a broadcast antenna, had been affixed to the edge of the shaft, and hung down into the unknown. Simon settled his cap and descended. The others watched him disappear in the golden glow and then the darkness.

"What do you see?" Hoover yelled.

There was a silence and then the loudspeaker replied, "I've got a footing. There's a floor—"

"For God's sake, what do you see?" Hoover insisted.

"Nothing. There's nothing to see."

Hoover yelled, "I'm coming down!"

He started down the metal ladder in his pink cover-all and his heavy green woollen cap topped with a tuft of many colours. "You're going to bring the whole thing down!" Leonova said.

"I don't weigh anything," he replied. "I'm just a big snowflake." He adjusted his mask and started down. Lanson, with a smile, aimed the camera at him.

———

I was standing on a floor of gold in an empty round room. There were wisps of dust along the metal surfaces. The circular golden wall was pitted with thousands of little niches that seemed to have been made to contain something and now held nothing.

The others came down, looked, and said nothing. The almost invisible dust modulated the shafts of light from the lamps on our caps and ringed our masked profiles with haloes.

Then the two electricians arrived with their batteries of floodlights. An area of wall opposite me was smooth, without niches. It was trapezoidal in shape, somewhat broader at the base than at the top, with a slight narrowing at mid-height. I thought that this trapezoid might be a door, and I went towards it.

That was how I took my first step toward you.

———

There was no visible means of opening this door, if it was a door: neither knob nor keyhole. Simon raised his gloved right hand and pushed against the right-hand edge of the door. The door opened part way. Simon removed his hand. Without a sound, and without even the click of a mechanism, the door went back to its former position.

"Well," Hoover demanded, "what are we waiting for? Let's go."

He pushed against the left side of the door. It remained open. Simon gestured to one of the electricians, who adjusted his light and aimed it into the doorway.

The door opened onto a corridor several yards long. The floor was of gold and the walls were of some porous-looking green substance. A blue door made of the same material blocked the end of the corridor. There were two other doors on the right hand and one on the left.

Simon entered, followed first by Hoover and Higgins and then by others. When he came to the first door, he stopped and pushed at it with his hand.

His gloved hand sank into the door and went through it.

Hoover muttered in surprise and tried to move closer. He was unintentionally crowding against Higgins, who in order to keep his balance, backed against the wall.

He went through it.

He shouted, and the universal translator relayed his shout to everyone's earphones. There was a heavy thud a few yards away and Higgins was silent.

The shock had jarred the walls. They shook, visibly telescoped, folded in on themselves, and quietly collapsed into soft heaps of dust, revealing a dark chasm. The floodlights pierced the darkness, illuminating other walls which were falling noiselessly and disclosing a whole world in the act of dissolution—objects, machines, unknown shapes all losing their forms, vanishing into themselves, falling in heaps onto floors that crumbled in their turn.

From the very base of the sphere, where all these amorphous masses were tumbling together, the thick grey wreaths of a cumulus cloud of dust arose. The scientists and technicians had barely time to see Higgins lying with his arms crossed, a golden stake driven through his chest. Then the cloud enveloped him and continued to mount.

They had barely put on their masks when the cloud reached them, enshrouded them and filled the sphere. They froze where they stood, not daring to move. They could see nothing now. The collapse of the walls and floors had left them on a gangplank without a rail, above eight stories of nothingness, imprisoned in an impenetrable fog.

"Kneel down!" Hoover shouted. "Slowly. Down on all fours."

And in this way, slowly, feeling the width of their plank with their hands, they made their way back to the round room and then to the outside of the sphere. One by one they emerged, trailing scarves of dust. The golden depth was filled with fumes.

Two men dressed in diving suits went down by the ropes to look for Higgins' body. They finally found it. His funeral service was held in the church that had been set up beneath the ice. A cross formed by lights was raised in the translucent ceiling. Then he was taken by airplane back to his South African home.

The papers had a holiday. CURSE OF SPHERE STRIKES AGAIN ... WILL SOUTH POLE TOMB KILL MORE SCIENTISTS THAN KING TUT'S?

In the restaurant of EPI 2 the newspapers that had just arrived by the latest plane were passed from hand to hand. Leonova stared contemptuously at a British weekly with the headline: WHAT GHOSTLY SLAYER STANDS GUARD AT THE GOLDEN SPHERE?

"The capitalist press is getting hysterical," she said.

Hoover, seated opposite her, poured a full pitcher of cream over a plate of cornflakes. "It's common knowledge," he replied, "that Marxists don't believe in the supernatural, but just wait until the ghost comes and tickles your toes one night." He gulped down a mouthful of cornflakes and went on, "There must have been something that pushed Higgins through the wall, no?"

"It was your big belly! Aren't you ashamed to carry such a monstrosity everywhere you go? It's not only unnecessary but dangerous!"

Hoover tapped his paunch lightly. "It's responsible for all my intelligence. When I lose weight, I become gloomy, and as stupid as anyone could be."

For a week a gigantic air hose had been drawing off the dust from the sphere. The air that it sent back to the surface was fed into bags in which it was screened, and the resulting dust was shipped off to laboratories throughout the world.

When no more dust could be found in the bags, the scouting party went back into the sphere. Floodlights were trained in all directions, and the interior was once more transparent. The light, reflected, refracted and diffused in every direction by the same metal, poured golden reflections over a mad, abstract golden architecture.

When the sealed area collapsed, everything that was made of the same alloy as the outer wall had survived. Floors without walls, stairways without rails, ramps leading nowhere, doors opening into emptiness, closed-off rooms joined to one another, supported and shored up by perforated girders of flying buttresses as delicate as a bird's bones, forming a graceful and inconceivably beautiful skeleton of gold.

Almost at its centre a vertical column ran through the sphere from top to bottom. It was, or more likely it contained, the drill. Resting against its base and apparently welded to it was a structure about thirty feet high, hermetically sealed and shaped like an egg, narrow end up.

"We've opened the pod," Leonova murmured. "This is the seed."

A staircase whose golden steps seemed to hover in the air led like an architect's dream from the site of the door in the sphere's wall to a point about a quarter of the way down from the apex of the egg.

By way of aerial gangways and stairs and paths the explorers made their way down to the egg, finding its entrance at the end of their path. The entrance was ovoid in shape, wider at the base. It was locked, of course, and there was no apparent means of opening it. But it was not welded.

It withstood every pressure. Simon, like a schoolboy, took out a pocket knife and tried to slip its blade into the almost invisible groove around the door. The blade slipped off without penetrating. Hoover took out his copper hammer and tapped. Like the wall of the sphere, the door gave off a dull thud.

Brivaux was sent down with his recording instruments. The ultrasonic line appeared again on the paper.

The signal was coming from inside the egg.

Television screens in the conference room enabled scientists and journalists to watch the labours of the teams inside the sphere. Carpenters were setting up scaffolds and shoring up stairways.

Standing on the stairs that led to the egg, Hoover was expounding on the details of his group's work. The reporters in the conference room followed everything on the big screen and took notes.

"We've got through it!" Hoover said. "Here's the hole." He pointed to a black thumb-sized opening.

"When the egg was pierced there was no current of air in either direction. The equalization of internal and external pressures could not have been coincidental. Somewhere there is a device that *knows* the outside pressure and regulates the inside pressures. I'd sure like to know where it is and how it works."

From the directors' conference table Rochefoux spoke into his microphone. "How thick is the door?"

"Eight and a quarter inches; it's made up of alternating layers of metal and another substance that seems to be a thermal insulator. There are at least fifty layers. Now we're going to measure the interior temperature."

A technical assistant inserted a long metal tube into the hole; the end that he retained held a dial. Hoover took a look at it, automatically looked away, and looked back in surprise. "Well, boys. It's going down, it's going down! It's at least eighty below, Centigrade. A hundred below. A hundred twenty." He stopped reading off statistics and simply whistled in astonishment. The universal translator whistled in all its seventeen languages. "Minus a hundred eighty Centigrade!" the replica of Hoover on the big screen said. "A hundred ninety-two below, Fahrenheit. It's almost the temperature of liquid air!"

Louis Deville, the correspondent for Europress, who was smoking a long black cigar as thin as a tube of spaghetti, said, "Good God, it's a deep freeze! It'll be full of frozen peas."

"We had planned to insert a steel hook through this hole," Hoover said, "and pull up on it to open the door. But this temperature would make the metal as brittle as a matchstick. We'll have to figure out something else."

Something else turned out to be three huge suction cups, attached to the outside of the door and linked to a mobile winch chained in turn to the system of metal girders and flying buttresses around the egg. A pump pulled the air out of the cups until they were almost empty. They could have lifted a locomotive. Hoover began to set the winch in motion.

"Aren't you afraid there might be some destruction device there?" a British journalist in the conference room asked Rochefoux.

"We found none behind the door to the sphere after we had got inside. There's no reason why there should be one in the egg."

Leonova, who was too impatient to watch from a distance, had gone below with Hoover and his technicians. Simon and two nurses were also present, ready to act in any emergency. On the screen the image of Hoover looked up toward his committee colleagues. The winch continued to turn.

In the television control booth Lanson switched on the transmission circuit. A German correspondent was broadcasting behind a soundproof glass partition. In the press section Louis Deville rose to ask whether he could put a question to Hoover. Rochefoux invited him to the platform to use the direct microphone. "Can you hear me, Mr. Hoover?" he asked.

The back of image-Hoover's head nodded affirmatively.

"Good. You've made a hole in the ice and found a pod. You've made a hole in the pod and found an egg. What do you think you're going to find today?"

Hoover turned around with a delightful smile on his face. "Nuts?" he suggested.

The universal translator hesitated only a millionth of a second before it told its French-speaking listeners, "Bolts?" One must not ask too much of an automatic brain.

Deville rubbed his hands as he went back to his seat. He had a good lead for tonight, even if . . .

"Watch it," Hoover said. "I think this is it."

The loudspeaker was suddenly filled with a sound like the ripping of velvet. A dark gap appeared at the bottom of the door.

"It's opening from the bottom," Hoover said. "Detach two suction cups, fast!"

Hoover worked the winch as fast as he could. There was a blood-chilling arpeggio, as if all the strings in a piano were breaking in quick succession. Then the door gave way.

In a few minutes the doorway was cleared. Leonova and Simon climbed into their cover-alls, the astronaut clothing that was necessary to protect them against the cold inside the egg. For the moment there were only the two outfits, and Hoover had had to relinquish the notion of getting into one of them. For the first time since his weight had gone over two hundred pounds he was sorry to be fat. But it was Hoover who finally opened the door. He put on asbestos gloves, thrust his hands into the gap at the level of the top step of the stairway, and pulled. The door came up like a lid.

Simon was the first to enter the egg. A blue light was shining from within and the stairway Simon stood on seemed to end somewhere in the blue. Its final steps stood out in black profile and stopped almost in the centre of the egg. Below, a great metal ring seemed to be suspended in the void. This was the source of the soft light. It was surrounded by strangely-shaped devices. A network of rods and wires connected them, and all were oriented toward the ring as if to receive something from it.

The big blue ring was turning. It hovered in the air, supported by nothing, in contact with nothing. Everything else was absolutely immobile. The ring was turning. But its surface was so smooth and its movement so regular that Simon sensed rather than saw the motion and could not tell whether it was slow or fast.

Lanson, who had come down from the conference room in order to check on his cameras, switched on a floodlight. The thousand-watt blaze engulfed the blue luminescence, blinding from view the spectral machines and reflecting off a glossy surface above them.

Simon was still standing on the stairway, five steps above the transparent floor, and Leonova was two steps above him.

They looked toward the top of the egg, a room with a vaulted roof. Two long, narrow golden pedestals rose from its floor, facing the stairway. Each of them supported a cube of transparent material, similar to very clear ice. And inside each of these cubes a human being lay.

The one to the left was a woman, the one to the right a man. They were naked. The man was tall and well muscled. His clenched left fist was on his chest.

The woman's legs were closed. Her hands lay one on the other, just below her breasts. From her shoulders to her flower-like feet, each curve of her body was a note in a perfect harmony.

Her face, like the man's, was covered by a golden helmet which stylized features of solemn beauty.

The transparent substance that enveloped the man and the woman was so cold that the air around it turned liquid. It made runnels that decked the two cubes with a lacework that danced and broke and fell, evaporating before it could reach the floor.

The figures lying inside these jewel boxes of shifting light were endowed by their very nakedness with a splendour of innocence. Their skin, with the smoothness and patina of polished stone, was of the colour of warm wood.

Although the man's body was less perfect than the woman's, it gave the same remarkable impression. Theirs was the youthfulness not of a man and a woman, but of the species.

Slowly Simon put out his hand.

In all the world, there was an instant of silence. Even the old and the children forgot to babble. Then the figures from Square 612 vanished and normal life resumed, somewhat more irritated, more bitter than before.

Leonova closed her eyes and shook her head inside her helmet. When she opened her eyes again, she did not look back in the direction of the man. She stared downward.

She took out a small dialled instrument from her equipment kit and placed it against the cube that held the woman. Leonova looked at the dial and said in an impersonal voice into the microphone inside her helmet: "The temperature on the outside of the cube is 457.6 degrees below zero, Fahrenheit."

A wave of surprise ran through the scientists watching from the conference room. This was only a shade off absolute zero.

Louis Deville leaped up in such excitement that he forgot his microphone. "Can you ask Dr. Simon while he's looking at them whether as a physician he believes that they are alive?"

"Don't stay close to the cubes!" Hoover's translated voice commanded into Simon's and Leonova's earphones. "Get back! Farther! Your outfits aren't made for that temperature."

They retreated toward the bottom of the stairway. Simon thought of Deville's question, which he had begun to ask himself a moment ago. At first he had not had the slightest doubt: this woman was alive, she could be nothing but alive. But this was only a wish. And now he was seeking objective reasons for believing or doubting. He ticked them off into his microphone, though he was really talking to himself.

"They were alive when the cold froze them. The condition of the man is proof of that." He moved his padded arm in the direction of the man's erect penis. "This is a phenomenon that has been observed among certain victims of hangings. It evidences a sudden sharp congestion and a rush of blood toward the lower body. This is the source of the legend of the mandrake: the magic root with a human shape that was born beneath gibbets where the soil was fertilized by a hanged man's seed. Possibly an analogous congestion may take place during quick freezing. It could occur only in a body that was still living. But it is possible that death followed a second later. Even if those two persons were in a state of suspended animation after having been frozen, how can we know what condition they are in today after nine hundred thousand years?"

The public address system in the conference room, which was carrying Simon's remarks live, bore witness in these last words to the young doctor's anguish, and then it was silent.

"We would have to ascertain their present temperature," Hoi-To, the Japanese physicist at the directors' table, said. "Our civilization has never succeeded in attaining absolute zero. But it appears that these people had access to a superior technology. Perhaps they did arrive at it . . . Absolute zero is the complete immobility of all molecules. It means that no chemical change is possible. Not even an infinitesimal change. Now, death is a change. If absolute cold prevails at the centre of these cubes, this man and this woman are in exactly the same condition in which they were when they were placed in this temperature. And they could remain that way for all eternity."

"There's a simple way of seeing whether they are dead or alive," Simon's voice said over the amplifiers. "And, as a doctor, I consider it to be our duty: we must try to revive them."

World-wide sentiment was divided. In huge headlines the newspapers demanded: WAKE THEM or LET THEM SLEEP. The former argued that there was an imperative duty to revive the sleepers, the latter that no man had a right to intrude on the peace in which they had waited for such an incredible time.

On motion of the Panamanian delegate to the United Nations, the General Assembly was convoked to discuss the question of reviving the sleepers.

New space suits had arrived at Square 612, but none was spacious enough for Hoover. He ordered one made to his measure. While he was waiting for it to arrive, he stood at the top of the golden stairway to observe the labours of his colleagues as they moved clumsily about inside the egg, their legs wide apart and their arms stiff. The dampness of the sphere penetrated into the egg and condensed into a fog. Frost had formed on the entire inner surface of the wall and a layer of powdery snow, as fine and soft as dust, covered the floor.

In spite of their protective clothing, the men who went down into the egg could not remain there more than a brief time, and this made it difficult to pursue their investigations. It had been possible to analyze the transparent substance which enveloped the man and the woman. It was solid helium: a substance that physicists specializing in research on cold had never been able to find, and one that they were theoretically convinced could not exist.

The frozen fog that filled the egg partly concealed the man and woman from the working parties that surrounded them. The couple seemed to retreat into this mist, to recover their remoteness, to withdraw once more into the beginning of time, far from the men who sought to reach them.

But the world did not forget them. Paleontologists were raging. What had been found at the South Pole *simply could not be true.* Or else the laboratories that had established the date had been mistaken.

Tests had been conducted on specimens of the crumbled ruins, fragments of gold, dust from the sphere. Their antiquity had been established through all known methods. More than a hundred laboratories had conducted a hundred tests apiece, resulting in more than ten thousand unanimous findings confirming the approximately nine hundred thousand years age of the discovery.

But this unanimity did not dent the paleontologists' convictions. They howled charges of exaggeration, error, distortion of truth. As far as they were concerned there was no doubt: less than nine hundred thousand years ago was virtually the beginning of the Pleistocene period. The only thing resembling man that could have existed at that time was Australopithecus, a sorry kind of primate to whom the chimpanzee would have seemed a tower of civilization.

Meanwhile, the UN's General Assembly suddenly lost interest in the two persons whose fate had been the reason for its convocation. The Pakistani delegate had just taken the floor to make a dramatic announcement.

His country's experts had arrived at figures on the quantity of gold represented by the sphere, its pedestal and its inside equipment. The total was fantastic: there were more than two hundred thousand tons of gold down there under the ice! In other words, more than all the gold in all the nations' reserves, all the private banks and all individual and secret holdings: more than all the gold in the world!

Why had this fact been withheld from public knowledge? What were the great powers plotting? Had they arrived at an agreement to divide this fabulous wealth among themselves as they had already divided everything else? This mass of gold could mean the end of suffering for half of the world's population. The starving nations demanded that this gold be brought to the surface, melted down and distributed among them in proportion to their respective populations.

The blacks, the yellows, and a few whites stood up and excitedly applauded the Pakistani. The poor nations made up a large majority in the UN and the great powers' right of veto was proving increasingly ineffectual in keeping them in their place.

The United States delegate requested and received permission to speak. He was a tall, thin man who bore the heritage of one of the most distinguished families of Massachusetts. In an emotionless, rather muted voice he declared that he understood his colleague's sentiments, that United States experts had just arrived at the same conclusions as the Pakistanis and that he had, in fact, been on the point of making a statement on the subject.

But, he added, other experts who had analyzed samplings of the gold from the Pole had reached a different conclusion: *this gold was not a natural gold* but a synthetic metal, created by some unknown process. Our atomic physicists, he said, also knew how to make artificial gold through the transmutation of atoms, but only with enormous difficulty, in small quantities and at a prohibitive cost.

The real treasure buried beneath the ice, he con-

The Ice People

cluded, was therefore not the quantity of gold, however great, but the skills locked into the brain of the man or the woman, or perhaps of both. This meant not only the secrets of the manufacture of gold, absolute zero and perpetual motion, but undoubtedly many others that were much more important.

"What has been discovered at Square 612," the American delegate said, "implies a highly advanced civilization imperilled by a cataclysm that threatened to destroy it completely. It provided a refuge from which a man and a woman could emerge when the scourge had passed. It is not logical to assume that the couple were selected on the basis of physical qualifications alone. One or the other, or both, must have had enough learning to be able to reconstruct a civilization equivalent to that into which they had been born. Our modern world ought to be thinking of sharing this learning. Those who possess it must be brought back to life and given their place among us."

"If they are still alive," the Chinese delegate commented.

The American made a fleeting motion with his left hand and a thin smile, both of which together meant, very politely but with the utmost contempt, *that goes without saying.* Then he looked around on the whole Assembly with an absent, bored air and continued, "Columbia University is ideally endowed with the scientists and the equipment to effect this reanimation. Therefore the United States proposes, subject to your consent, that it send an expedition to Square 612 to remove the man and the woman in their frozen blocks, transport them with every required precaution and the utmost rapidity to the laboratories of Columbia University, bring them out of their long sleep and welcome them in the name of all mankind."

The Russian delegate rose, smiling, and said that he

52

had no doubt of either the Americans' good faith or their scientists' competence. But in Akademgorodok the Soviet Union too had the technicians, the theoreticians and the equipment required. It, too, could undertake the task of reanimation. But in this vital moment for the future of mankind there could be no question of bickering over a treasure that belonged to all the peoples of the earth. Therefore the Soviet Union proposed that the couple be shared, one member being entrusted to it and the other to the United States.

The Pakistani delegate exploded. The conspiracy between the great powers was now out in the open! Right from the start they had intended to appropriate the treasure of Square 612. And by dividing the secrets of the past among themselves they would insure their mastery of the future. The nations that acquired a monopoly of the secrets locked under Square 612 would enjoy absolute power over the rest of the world. No country could hope to escape their hegemony. The poor nations must stand together against this abominable project, even if the two beings from the past must remain forever in their helium shells!

The French delegate, having gone out and telephoned his government, now asked for the floor. He pointed out that Square 612 was well within the slice of the Antarctic continent that had been allocated to France. In other words, it was French soil. And as a consequence whatever might be encountered there was French property. . . .

There was a great commotion. Some of the delegates protested; others snickered, or looked faintly amused.

The Frenchman smiled. When the flurry had subsided, he asserted that France was waiving her national rights and even her "finger's" right in the light of the universal importance of the discovery, offering everything that had been or hereafter might be found at

Square 612 on the altar of the United Nations. There was polite applause which he sought to still with a gesture.

But, he added, though she did not share Pakistan's fears, France felt that every means must be used to prevent them from being justified to however slight a degree. It was not only Columbia and Akademgorodok that were capable of carrying out the reanimation. Eminent specialists could be found in Yugoslavia, The Netherlands, India, not to mention the Arab universities and the highly competent group under Dr. Lebeau of Vaugirard Hospital in Paris.

This did not mean that France was ruling out Russian and American teams. She sought only to have the choice made by the Assembly as a whole and formalized in a vote.

The American delegate endorsed the proposal immediately. He suggested further that the meeting be adjourned until the next day in order to allow time for competent candidates to make themselves known. It was so voted.

The private negotiations began at once.

From beyond the atmosphere, Trio was sending pictures of the UN to the antenna of EPI 1. Scientists who were not engaged in more urgent work, as well as the correspondents, had been watching the session in the conference room. When it was over, Hoover pushed a button to darken the big screen. With a slight frown he looked around at his colleagues. "I think we have to have a discussion," he said. He asked the press to leave and used the public-address system to call all the expedition's scientists, technicians, skilled and unskilled labour to a meeting.

And when the General Assembly reconvened the next day its president was handed a communication from Square 612. At the same time it was made public by every medium of international communication. This was its text:

The members of the International Polar Expedition have unanimously taken the following decisions:

1. They refuse to admit the right of any nation, rich or poor, to claim any part of the gold in the sphere and its appurtenances for exploitation for profit.

2. They propose that, if such should be found to be useful to mankind, an international currency be established and based on this gold, provided that the gold remain where it is, inasmuch as it will be no more useful or "frozen" under twelve hundred yards of ice than in the vaults of national banks.

3. They do not recognize the jurisdiction of the United Nations, a political body, with respect to the decision—which is medical and scientific in nature—to be made on the subject of the frozen couple.

4. They will not entrust the couple to any one nation.

5. The whole of the scientific or other information of any kind that may be accumulated by the expedition will be placed at the disposition of all mankind.

6. They request that Forster of Columbia, Moissov of Akademgorodok, Zabrec of Belgrade, van Houcke of The Hague, Haman of Beirut and Lebeau of Paris join them immediately at Square 612 with all the requisite equipment for initiating the reanimation.

It was as if a Molotov cocktail had been thrown into the UN. The windows of the glass palace rattled right up to the top floor. On behalf of the children who were dying of hunger, the Pakistani delegate denounced the arrogance of scientists who sought to rank themselves above humankind and succeeded only in outlawing themselves from it. He talked about "technological dictatorship", declared that it was unthinkable and demanded sanctions.

After much heated debate the Assembly voted to dispatch a detachment of United Nations troops to Square 612 to take possession of everything there in the name of the United Nations. Two hours later the transmitter of EPI 1 asked for, and received, access to an international relay channel. Governmental and commercial stations interrupted their broadcasts in order to transmit the message from the Pole.

The first face that appeared was Hoover's. The solemnity of his eyes made one forget his round pink cheeks and tousled red hair. He said, "We are overwhelmed. Overwhelmed, but resolute."

He beckoned to the cameraman. The camera pulled back so that the picture included those who now stepped forward: Leonova, Rochefoux, Shanga and Lao Chang. They took their places on either side of Hoover, endowing him with the authority of their presence. Behind them one could see the entire staff of the expedition. Hoover spoke again:

"As you can see, we are all here. And we are all determined. We will never allow individual, national or international greed to monopolize a discovery which may determine the future of mankind, all mankind, not merely of some few.

"We do not trust the UN. We do not trust their troops. If they land on Square 612, we will drop our atomic pile into the shaft and blow it up."

For a moment he stood motionless and silent. Then he stepped aside and turned over his microphone to Leonova.

Her chin was quivering. She opened her lips but she could not speak. Hoover's big hand touched her shoulder. Leonova shut her eyes, took a deep breath and recovered something of her composure.

"We wish to work for all men," she said. "It would be easy to stop us. We do not have a single bolt or a crumb of bread that has not been sent to us by one nation or another. It would be enough to cut off our supplies, or simply to begin acting in bad faith. Our success thus far has been the result of concerted and unselfish effort by many nations. This effort must continue. You who are listening to us can compel it. I am appealing not to governments and politicians but to men and women, to all peoples. Write to your rulers, your chiefs of state, your ministers, your soviets. Write immediately—all of you write! You can still salvage everything!"

The camera moved in on her. Each drop of sweat on her face was magnified. A hand appeared on the screen, offering her a buttercup-coloured handkerchief. She took it and mopped both her forehead and her nose. Then she resumed, "If we have to give up, we will never release knowledge that, improperly employed, could produce irreparable evil. If we are compelled to evacuate, we will leave nothing behind us."

She turned away and raised the handkerchief to her eyes. She was weeping.

In almost every country where broadcasting was a state monopoly the explorers' appeal had been cut off before its conclusion. But for the next twelve hours the transmitter of EPI 1 continued to bombard Trio with the tapes of Hoover and Leonova. And Trio, a scientific artifact utterly devoid of opinion, relayed them for twelve hours to its brothers and sisters and cousins that girdled the globe. Almost two-thirds of them broadcast with sufficient power to be picked up directly on ordinary receivers. Each time that the tapes were rerun, the universal translator rendered the appeals into a different language. And each broadcast ended with two people out of the past, in their beauty and their immobile state of waiting, as they had appeared the first time on the screens.

The broadcasts introduced into the scheduled programmes, scrambled all the signals, and in the end got through in enough bits and pieces to be understood by those who chose to understand.

In the next twelve hours every postal system in the world was hopelessly bottlenecked. Mailboxes overflowed in the most remote hamlets of the Auvergne and Baluchistan. Sorting rooms were jammed from floor to ceiling in the smallest postal collection centres: at the next level the inundation was overwhelming. Public authorities and private contractors alike abandoned any thought of moving the mountains any farther. There was no need to read the letters. Their meaning lay in their number. And governments sent new instructions to their delegates in the United Nations, who voted enthusiastically and unanimously to cancel the orders for the dispatch of troops. Then they expressed their nations' confidence that the scientists of the International Polar Expedition would successfully, etc. . . . for the greatest public good, etc. . . . the brotherhood of nations, etc. . . . past and present, period.

The resuscitation experts summoned by the explorers arrived with their staffs and their equipment. Following specifications laid down by Lebeau, workmen set up a resuscitation chamber inside the sphere itself, above the egg.

Then the scientists had to decide whom to revive first. Risks would have to be taken with whoever was first; in a sense the scientists would be "feeling their way". On the other hand, the second would profit by their increased experience. So the less important of the two should be first. But which one was less precious?

To the Arab there could be no question: the only person who mattered was the man. To the American it was the woman with whom the most diffident precautions should be taken; the man's life could always be risked for hers. The Dutchman had no preference. The Yugoslav and the Frenchman, in spite of their resistance to the notion, tended to regard the man as the more valuable.

"You know as well as I, my dear colleagues," the Frenchman, Lebeau, observed in a meeting, "that men's brains exceed women's in both volume and weight. If the brain is what concerns us, then it seems to me that it is the man whom we must reserve for the second operation. Personally, however," he added, smiling, "having seen the woman, I could easily be inclined to believe that such beauty is more important than any amount of knowledge."

"There is no reason why we should favour either one of them," Moissov, the Russian, said. "Their rights are the same. I suggest that we form two teams and revive both at the same time."

It was generous but impracticable. There was neither enough room nor enough equipment. And the combined skills of all six experts might not be enough for the difficult moments of a single such operation.

Lebeau's argument was valid with respect to modern human brains. But who could say with assurance whether this difference of volume and weight had existed at the time from which the couple dated? Or whether, if it had existed, it might not have favoured the woman's brain? The golden masks that hid the two heads followed no possibility of even approximate comparison.

Van Houcke, the Dutchman, was an outstanding ex-

pert in the hibernation of the sea lion. For a dozen
years he had been keeping one in a frozen state. Every
spring he warmed it and revived it, fed it a few
herrings, and then, when it had digested them, froze it
again. But, apart from his speciality, he was a very un-
sophisticated man. He described his associates' uncer-
tainties to the reporters and asked them for advice.

The delighted correspondents laid the problem before world public opinion by way of Trio, putting the
question badly: "Who should be awakened first, the
man or the woman?"

Hoover, meanwhile, had finally received his custom-
made space suit. He put it on and went down into the
egg, where he vanished in the fog. When he went back
into the sphere, he urged the executive committee to
meet with the resuscitation specialists.

"We have to make a decision," he said. "The helium
blocks are shrinking. The refrigeration mechanism is
still functioning, but our entrance into the egg has im-
paired its efficiency. I have just inspected both persons
closely, the man and the woman. My God, she's beautiful! But that is not the problem. Above all it seemed to
me that she was in better condition than he. His chest
and other parts of his body show slight changes in the
colour of the skin, which may be signs of superficial epi-
dermal lesions. Or perhaps they mean nothing: I don't
know. But I think—I say honestly *I think*: it is an impression, not a conviction—that she is stronger than he
and better able to withstand any errors that you may
make. You are physicians; look at them again, study the
man, bearing in mind what I have just said, and then
make up your minds. In my opinion it is the woman
with whom the start should be made."

They did not go down into the egg. One had to begin
with one or the other, and they accepted Hoover's
view. So while public feeling mounted and the male

and female halves of the human race drew up their battle lines against each other the six resuscitation experts decided to start with the woman.

How could they have known that they were making a tragic blunder? If they had decided to begin with the man, everything would have been different.

A hot-air hose was aimed at the block on the left; it begin to emit air at the surface temperature, which was −25.6°F. The helium cube vanished in a few seconds, leaving the woman unharmed on her pedestal. Looking at her, the four heavily clothed men shivered. It seemed to them that now, stark naked on her metal couch and surrounded by whirling eddies of frozen mist, she must be in danger of death from the cold. But in actuality she was already visibly much warmer.

One of the four men was Simon. Because of his knowledge of polar problems and his familiarity with the sphere, the egg and the couple, Lebeau had asked Simon to become a member of the resuscitation team.

Simon walked completely around the pedestal. Because of his astronaut's gloves he found it difficult to carry his big pair of cutters. At a signal from Lebeau he gripped the cutters in both hands, bent down and severed the metallic tube that connected the golden mask with the back of the pedestal. With great gentleness Lebeau attempted to move the mask. It would not stir. It seemed to be part of the woman's head, even though it was clearly separated from her chin by a gap at least a centimetre wide.

Lebeau straightened, shrugged in defeat and set out for the golden stairway. The others followed him. They could no longer remain in the egg. The cold was penetrating inside their protective clothing. They could not take the woman with them. At her present temperature there was the strong possibility that she would snap like a piece of glass.

Directed by remote control from the resuscitation room, the air hose continued to move around her couch, bathing her in a flow of air that was now only four degrees below zero Fahrenheit.

After a few hours the four men went back into the egg. Synchronizing their movements, they slipped their gloved hands beneath the frozen woman and lifted her from her pedestal. The eight hands raised her, rigid as a statue, to shoulder height. Then the four men slowly began to walk, obsessed with the dread of stumbling. Huge and grotesque in their helmeted space suits, half concealed by the mist, they were like figures out of a nightmare bearing the woman whose dream had drawn them into another world. They mounted the golden stairs and went out of the egg through the luminous cavity of its doorway.

The air hose was withdrawn. The transparent block that contained the man, which had shrunk perceptibly during this undertaking, lost no more of its volume.

The four men entered the operating room and placed the woman on the resuscitation table.

At the surface the entrance to the shaft had been enclosed in a building constructed of huge blocks of ice. Its heavy door slid on rails. Inside were the blower machinery, the generators for the television, the telephones, the translation machine, the power supply and the separate lighting system, the passenger and freight elevator motors, their termini, and the emergency electricity source, a system of big dry-cell batteries.

Rochefoux, head of the EPI, was facing a horde of reporters, his back to the elevators. He had locked the doors of the elevators and put the key in his pocket. The press was protesting vehemently in a variety of languages. Smiling, Rochefoux informed them it was impossible for them to watch the woman being revived. No observers, not even himself, were permitted in the resuscitation chamber. He finally assuaged the reporters by promising that they would see everything on closed-circuit television.

Simon and six resuscitators, wearing sea-green tunics, surgeons' caps and masks, white cotton-and-canvas shoes and pink rubber gloves, surrounded the resuscitation table. The woman was covered to the chin by a warming blanket. The golden mask still hid her face. Various tubes and wires ran through slits in the blanket connecting the measuring instruments with the straps, electrodes, pressure cups and other devices attached to her frozen body.

Nine technicians, wearing yellow tunics and surgical masks, kept their eyes on the dials of these assorted instruments. Four male nurses and three women nurses, all in blue, stood by the physicians.

Lebeau leaned over the table and tried once more to remove the mask. It shifted a little, but it seemed to be held in place by a central axis.

"Temperature?" he asked.

"Plus five," a young man replied, using the Centigrade figure, the equivalent of forty-one degrees Fahrenheit.

"Blowers." A woman in blue held out the nozzle of a flexible tube. Lebeau inserted it between the mask and the woman's chin. "Pressure one hundred grams, temperature fifteen," he ordered. A young man turned two little knobs and repeated the figures. "Start it up," Lebeau said.

A faint hiss was audible as air at a temperature of fifty-nine degrees Fahrenheit flowed between the mask and the woman's face. Lebeau straightened and looked at his collegues. His expression was anxious. The woman in blue wiped the beads of sweat from his temples with a gauze pad.

"Try," Forster said.

"Wait a few minutes more. Just to minimize the risks."

They were endless minutes. The twenty-three men and women in the room stood tensely, listening to their hearts pound in their rib cages and feeling the weight of their bodies turn their calves to stone. Camera No. 1, focused on the golden mask, sent a giant replica of it to the big screen. Absolute silence gripped the conference room. The audio system brought the audience the over-rapid breathing behind the surgical masks and the hiss of the air blowing under the golden helmet.

"How long?" Lebeau asked.

"Three minutes seventeen seconds," a man in yellow replied.

"I'll try again."

Once more he bent over the woman, inserted his fingers under the mask and applied gentle pressure to the tip of the chin. Slowly the chin yielded. The mouth, which was invisible, must now be open. Lebeau gripped the mask with both hands and tried again to lift it very slowly. There was no further resistance.

Lebeau sighed, and beneath his thick brows his eyes were smiling. He continued his slow removal of the mask. "Exactly what we suspected," he said. "It's an air or oxygen mask. She had a tube in her mouth."

He pulled the mask completely away and turned it upside down. There was indeed a hollow extrusion at the mouth, with a lipped edge: it was made of a translucent substance that appeared to be elastic. "You see!" Lebeau said to his colleagues, showing them the interior of the mask.

But no one looked. They were staring at *her face.*

———

*First I saw the dark cavern of your open mouth and
the two almost transparent rows of your delicate teeth
almost hidden by your pale lips. I was beginning to
shake. I had seen too many such open mouths in hospi-
tals, open mouths of bodies whose life had abruptly
deserted them.*

*But Moissov made a cup of his hand and placed it
beneath your chin, gently closed your mouth, waited a
moment and then took away his hand.*

And your mouth remained closed.

———

Closed, her mouth, pallid from cold, was like the rim
of a frail shell. Her eyelids were two long tired leaves
the lines of whose lashes and brows were shapes of
golden shadow. Her nose was slender and straight, the
nostrils slightly flared and fully open. Her glowing
brown hair seemed to have been anointed with golden
light. It encircled her head in little waves like reflections of the sun and partly hid her forehead and
cheeks.

There was a deep male sigh, which was picked up by
a microphone and which left the translation machine
baffled. Haman bent over the woman, separated her
curls and began to attach electrodes for the encephalograph.

———————

The cellar of the International Hotel in London was proof against the A- but not the H-bomb, against fallout but not against a direct hit; solid enough to meet the requirements of a trade that demanded both safety and comfort. It was armoured enough to inspire confidence but not enough to guarantee protection, and by reason of its architecture, its insulation and its concrete walls, it possessed the ideal combination of cubic volume and sound-proofing needed for a "shaker".

That was the term applied to the increasingly enormous halls in which young people of all levels of society, wealth and intellect came together to dance. Boys and girls alike, driven by their instincts to seek a rebirth, huddled in hot, half-lighted wombs where, pounded by small-scale sonic booms, they lost the last shreds of prejudice and convention that might still have been clinging to their muscles, their genitals and their brains.

The cellar of the London International was the largest "shaker" in Europe, and one of the "hottest". It could hold six thousand people. There was only one orchestra, but a dozen ion speakers without diaphragms made the atmosphere vibrate like the interior of a tenor saxophone. And the proprietor of all this was sixteen-year-old Yuni, by his own admission the biggest wheel in all London, with his shaved head and his strange eyes, one crossed and the other bulging behind lenses as thick as sugar cubes. It was Yuni who had negotiated with the hotel's board of directors and taken a lease on the cellar.

Now Yuni stood in an aluminium pulpit emerging

from the wall above the orchestra, tending the controls of the sound system, one of his ears hidden beneath an earphone the size and shape of a cauliflower. He would turn ceaselessly back and forth among all the bands on the air waves and occasionally feed one of them into the loudspeakers instead of his own orchestra. His eyes were always closed as he listened, one ear beamed to the deafening roar in the cellar, the other savouring three bars, twenty bars, five bars culled from infinity. Now and again, his eyes still closed, he muttered a long, shrill cry that crackled above the all-embracing cacophony like vinegar in a frying pan. Suddenly he raised his eyelids slightly, cut off the amplifiers and shouted: "Listen! Listen!"

The orchestra broke off. Six thousand sweating bodies were suddenly plunged into silence and immobility. As consciousness began coming back, Yuni cried, "News of the frozen girl!"

The customers whistled and hooted and shouted insults.

"Scum!" Yuni shouted back. "Listen." He switched the sound system to the British Broadcasting Corporation. The announcer's voice filled the air.

"We are now broadcasting for the second time an announcement received and recorded from Square 612. . . ."

There was static, then silence. Then came Hoover's voice: "This is EPI at Square 612. It gives me great pleasure—very great pleasure—to read you the following bulletin just received from the operating room:

"The resuscitation of the female subject is continuing normally. Today, 17 November, at 2:53 p.m. local time, her heart began to beat again—"

The cellar exploded in a bellow. Yuni howled even more loudly. "Shut up! You're a bunch of slobs. Listen!"

They were silent again, and once more Hoover's voice was audible.

"—young woman's first heartbeats have been recorded. Her heart had not beaten for nine hundred thousand years. Listen to it."

This time the six thousand were mute. Yuni closed his eyes, and his face was radiant. He heard the same thing in both ears. He heard:

Silence
A dull throb: voom
Only the one
Silence . . . silence . . . silence . . .
Voom
Voom . . . voom . . .
Voom . . . voom . . . voom, voom, voom . . .

Very gently the drummer tapped out the rhythm with his foot. Then he began to use the tips of his fingers against his drum. Yuni began to mix the sound of the orchestra and the broadcast. The double bass joined the percussion and the heart. The clarinet wailed out a lo-o-o-ong note and then broke into a joyful improvisation. The six electric guitars and the twelve steel violins burst forth. The percussionist was smashing his drums with all his strength. As from a minaret, Yuni cried: "She's awake!"

Voom! voom! voom!

"She's awake!" chanted the six thousand faithful. "She's awake!" They sang and danced to the beat of the heart that had been restored to life.

This was the birth of the 'wake, the dance of awakening. Let those who want to dance, dance. Let those who can awaken, awake.

But she was not awake. Her lids were still closed in that interminable sleep. But her heart was beating with serene strength, her lungs were breathing regularly, and her temperature was slowly rising to the level of the living.

"Look!" Lebeau said, watching the encephalograph. "Irregular pulsations . . . she's dreaming!"

Dreaming! A dream had remained with her, crouched frozen somewhere in her head, and now, warmed back into being, it had just burgeoned. In what forms? Happy or unhappy? Dream or nightmare? The pulse rate went up suddenly from thirty to forty-five, the blood pressure gained a point, the respiration became faster and irregular, the temperature rose to 96.8°.

"Attention, please!" Lebeau said. "Pulse now at pre-waking rate. She's waking up! Turn off the oxygen."

Simon removed the oxygen mask and handed it to a nurse. The woman's eyelids trembled. A tiny sliver of shadow appeared at the bottom of the lids.

"We'll frighten her," Simon said. He snatched off the surgical mask that hid the lower part of his face, and the other doctors followed his example.

Slowly the woman's eyelids opened. Her eyes appeared incredibly large. The whites were very bright and very pure. The iris was large, somewhat hidden by the upper lid; it was as blue as a summer-night sky and seeded with gold dust.

Her eyes were fixed on the ceiling, which she probably did not see. Then, as if a catch had been released, her brows knitted and her eyes moved. She saw Simon, then Moissov, Lebeau, the nurses, everyone. A look of bewilderment spread over the woman's face. She tried to speak, opening her lips, but she could not control the muscles of her tongue and her throat. She made a kind of gasping noise. Then she made a tremendous effort to raise her head a little, and looked at everything. Moissov smiled at her. Simon was quivering with emotion. Lebeau began to speak very gently. He recited two verses of Racine, the most harmonious words any language had ever brought together in: *"Ariane, ma soeur, de quel amour blessée . . ."*

It was a hymn of language, perfect and comforting. But the woman was not listening. Horror was visibly enveloping her. Again she tried to speak, but without success. Her chin began to tremble. She closed her eyes again and her head fell back.

"Oxygen!" Lebeau ordered. "Heart?"

"Regular. Fifty-two," a young man in yellow said.

"Fainted," van Houcke observed. "We gave her a terrible fright. But what did she expect to find?"

"Suppose your daughter were put to sleep and then woke up in the middle of a coven of Papuan witch doctors?" Forster said.

The physicians decided to move her to the surface while she was unconscious: a comfortable room had been prepared in the infirmary. They wrapped her in a cocoon of transparent plastic with a double layer of insulation, into which air was fed by a pump. Four men then carried her to the elevator.

The press swarmed out of the conference room. The big monitor screen showed the men in yellow taking off their masks and disconnecting their equipment. Lanson switched off the camera in the operating room and activated the camera inside the egg.

Suddenly Leonova stood up. "Look!" she said, pointing at the screen. "Mr. Lanson, focus on the pedestal on the left."

The picture of the empty base swung around, grew larger and became clearer behind the wispy veil of mist. But one side of it was missing. A whole vertical panel had sunk into the floor, disclosing metal shelves containing objects of unfamiliar form.

The woman was no longer in the operating room, but

her place on the resuscitation table had been taken by the objects found in the pedestal, which had been restored to normal temperature. The physicians around the table had been replaced by scientists of other disciplines. Leonova cautiously picked up something that looked like a folded garment. She unfolded it into a rectangle of material that was neither paper nor fabric, of an orange colour with red and yellow designs. Absolute cold had kept it in a state of perfect preservation. It was flexible, light and free-flowing. There were several other objects like it, though varied in colour, shape and size. There were no sleeves, no openings of any kind, no buttons or hooks or snaps—absolutely no way of "putting them on" or keeping them on.

They were weighed and measured and numbered and photographed; microscopic samplings were taken for purposes of analysis, and then the objects in the next category were examined.

Cubes with rounded corners, each edge measuring something over eight and a half inches. A hollow tube set at an angle was attached to one face. The whole was solid, made of some light material of a very pale grey. Hoi-To, the physicist, picked up a cube, studied it for a time, then looked at the other objects.

There was a box without a lid, containing octagonal rods of various colours. Hoi-To chose one of them and inserted it in the hollow tube attached to the cube. It began to glow with a soft light. And the cube drew a deep breath. Hoi-To smiled a thin little smile. His fine fingers set the cube down on the white table.

Now it was speaking. A woman's voice speaking in a strange language, quite low. Then there was music, like the breath of a light wind through a forest peopled with birds and hung with harps. As if projected from within, a picture appeared on the uppermost surface of the cube: the face of the woman who was talking. She looked like the woman who had been found in the egg, but they were two different people. She smiled and disappeared, her place taken by a strange flower, which in turn dissolved into fluid colour. The woman's voice was still audible—not in a song, not in a recitation, but both, so to speak, at the same time, as simple and natural as the sound of a stream or of rain. And each face of the cube was illuminated, one by one or together, showing a hand, a penis, a bird, a breast, a face, an object that changed its shape and its colour, a form without meaning, a colour without form.

Everyone in the room watched and listened, fascinated. It was incomprehensible and totally strange; at the same time it touched them deeply and personally, in harmony with their own inmost, secret aspirations, regardless of conventions and barriers.

Hoover shook his head vigorously, cleared his throat and coughed. "It's a funny gadget," he said. "Shut the thing off."

Hoi-To removed the rod from the tube. The cube went dark and silent.

The woman lay in a room where the air was heated to a temperature of eighty-six degrees. Her protective covering removed, she was stretched out on a narrow bed. Electrodes, metal plates, clips, attached to her wrists, her temples, her feet, her arms, formed connections that zigzagged and spiralled between her and various pieces of equipment.

Two nurses were massaging the muscles of her thighs. A man was working on the jaw muscles. Another nurse was playing an infra-red lamp on her neck. Van Houcke was delicately palpating the abdominal wall. The physicians and nurses and technicians, perspiring in the overheated room and apprehensive over this prolonged unconsciousness, watched and waited and spoke in low voices. Simon looked at the woman and at those who surrounded her and touched her. He clenched his fists and his teeth.

"The muscles are responding," van Houcke said. "One might say she was conscious."

Moissov went to the head of the bed, bent over the woman and raised first one and then the other of her eyelids. "She is conscious!" he said. "She is closing her eyes deliberately."

"Why?" Forster asked.

"Because she's afraid!" Simon almost shouted. "If you want her to stop being afraid, you'll have to stop treating her like a laboratory animal!" He threw out his arm as if it were a broom to sweep out the five persons standing around the bed. "Get away from there. Let her alone!"

Van Houcke objected but Lebeau said, "He may be right. He worked in psychotherapy under Périer for two years. He may be better qualified than we are at this point. Take all that stuff away."

Moissov was already removing the electrodes for the encephalogram. The nurses released the outstretched body from its web of wires. Simon grasped the sheet that had been folded back to the foot of the bed and tenderly opened it over the woman as far as her shoulders, leaving her arms free. On the middle finger of her right hand she wore a large gold ring, the stone of which was shaped like a truncated pyramid. Simon took her left hand, which was unornamented, into both of his and held it as one might hold a frightened bird.

Without a sound Lebeau sent the nurses, the technicians and the masseurs out of the room. He moved a chair close to Simon, stepped back to the wall and gestured to the other doctors to do the same thing. Van Houcke shrugged and departed.

Simon sat down, letting his hands, which still held

the woman's hand, rest on the bed, and began to speak, almost in a whisper, very affectionately, very calmly.

"We are friends," he said. "You do not understand what I am saying to you, but you do understand that I am talking to you as a friend. You can open your eyes. You can look at our faces. We don't wish you any harm. Everything is all right. You can wake up now. We are your friends. We want to make you happy. We love you."

She opened her eyes and looked at him.

Down below, others had been busy examining, weighing, measuring and photographing various objects; in some instances their use was immediately clear, in others it was a mystery. Next in line was a kind of combination glove and mitten with three partitions: one for the thumb, one for the index finger, and a wider one for the three other fingers. Hoover picked it up. "Glove for the left hand," he said, holding it out to be photographed. He looked around for its right-hand mate. There was none. "Correction," he added. "Glove for one-armed man."

He thrust his left hand into the glove and tried to flex the fingers. The index finger was rigid, the thumb moved, and the three other fingers bent inward toward the palm. There was a muffled explosion, a flash of light and a cry. Ionescu, the Rumanian who was working opposite Hoover, was thrown into the air by some tremendous force and crashed down again.

Hoover, stunned, raised his hand to examine it. With a blood-curdling crash the top of the opposite wall and half the ceiling were reduced to dust. Just in time, barely avoiding blowing up the rest of the ceiling and his own head, he did the right thing: he straightened his fingers. The red glow faded from the air.

"Oh!" Hoover remarked. He held out his left arm at

full length, and stared at his gloved left hand. It was trembling. "A weapon," he said, and in seventeen languages the Translator repeated: "A weapon".

The woman had closed her eyes again, but now it was because of exhaustion.

"She must be fed," Lebeau said. "But how can we guess what her people ate?"

Simon raged, "You've all seen enough of her to know she's a mammal! Milk!" Suddenly he was quiet, and everyone tensed: the woman was speaking.

Her lips were moving. Her voice was very weak. She stopped, then began again, repeating the same sentence over and over. She opened her blue eyes and it was as if the sky had flooded the room. She looked at Simon and repeated her phrase. Confronted with the obvious fact that there was no possibility of making herself understood, she closed her eyes again and said no more.

A nurse brought a cup of warm milk. Simon took it and very gently held its warmth against the back of the woman's hand where it lay on the sheet.

She looked up. The nurse raised her upper body and supported her. The woman tried to take the cup but the fine muscles in her hands had not yet regained their strength. Simon raised the cup toward her. When the smell of the milk reached her nostrils, she grimaced in revulsion and pulled away. She looked around and repeated her earlier sentence. Obviously she was trying to ask for something.

"It's water! She wants water," Simon said.

It was indeed water that she wanted. She drank the whole of one glass and half of another.

When she was lying down again, Simon placed his hand against his own chest and spoke his own name softly: "Simon." He repeated the action and the word twice. She understood.

Looking at Simon, she raised her left hand, placed it on her own forehead, and said: "Elea". Never taking her eyes from him, she repeated the action and said again: "Elea".

The men who picked up Ionescu's body in order to remove it had felt as if they were lifting a rubber bag filled with sand pebbles. There was only a little blood at the nostrils and the corners of the lips, but the bones were shattered and the flesh reduced to pulp.

All this was now several days in the past, but Hoover still occasionally caught himself looking furtively at his left hand and bending three fingers toward the palm. If at such times he was in the neighbourhood of a bottle of bourbon or scotch, or even brandy, he took from it the reassurance that he badly needed. And he needed all his infinite optimism to be able to live with the destiny that had made him a killer twice in a matter of weeks.

The weapon and the objects that had not yet been studied were very cautiously returned to the pedestal. The workmen rebuilt the resuscitation room and the technicians repaired whatever was reparable, but much of the equipment was totally destroyed. Work couldn't begin on the other occupant of the egg until replacements arrived.

The woman—Elea—refused every kind of food offered to her. An attempt was made to get broth into her stomach through a tube. She struggled so violently that she had to be placed in restraint. But no one could manage to make her open her jaws. The tube was introduced by way of one nostril. But the broth had barely got to her stomach when she vomited it.

At first Simon protested against this outrage, but then he had become resigned to it. The outcome convinced him that he had been right. While his colleagues were coming to the conclusion that the digestive system of the woman out of the past was not adapted to modern nutrition, Simon was asking himself again and again, "How are we going to *communicate*? Talk to her, listen to her, understand her, learn what she needs: how?"

Her body in a straitjacket and her arms and legs strapped, she no longer reacted at all. Motionless, her eyelids again shutting out the vast sky of her eyes, she seemed to have reached the very limits of fear and resignation. A hollow needle thrust into the artery of her right arm slowly fed nutritive fluid from a vial suspended above her bed. Simon looked on this barbarous device with loathing; yet, however atrocious, it delayed the day when she would die of starvation. He couldn't stand it any longer. Something must . . .

He rushed out of the room and out of the infirmary.

Carved out of the ice, Amundsen Avenue, a thoroughfare thirty-six feet wide and almost a thousand feet long, was the spinal column of EPI 2, a tribute to the first man to have reached the South Pole. Doors and minor streets opened to right and left off the avenue. Simon found himself in the centre of the thoroughfare and started to run on the rough ice. The Universal Translator was almost at the other end of Amundsen Avenue.

He entered the Translator's premises, trying six wrong doors before he chose the right one. Finally he arrived in a narrow room with two walls of glass and a third of metal. On the metal wall was a huge console, a mosaic of dials, knobs, switches, gauges. Lukos, the Turkish philologist, presided here from a big-wheeled chair in front of the console.

He had the mind of a genius and the body of a longshoreman. Even seated he gave the impression of enormous strength. It was he who had designed the translation machine's brain. The Americans had been sceptical, the Europeans had been incapable, the Russians had been distrustful, but the Japanese had accepted him and given him everything he needed. The machine at EPI 2 was his twelfth and the most highly perfected.

Lukos had two sources of Elea's language with which to work, and both were in front of him now: the singing cube and something else, no longer than a paperback book. A luminous strip covered with regular lines appeared on one of its flat sides, each line composed of a series of signs that seemed to be writing. Three-dimensional pictures completed the object's resemblance to an illustrated book.

"Well?" Simon said.

Lukos shrugged. For two days he had been covering the translation machine's recording screen with groups of symbols that seemed to have no connection with one another.

"Something keeps eluding me," Lukos grumbled. "And eluding her too." He caressed the metal of his console with his great paw, then inserted a rod in the tube of the musical cube. This time the sing-song voice that was activated was a man's, as was the face that appeared—clean-shaven, with large light blue eyes and black hair that fell to the shoulders.

"The solution may be there," Lukos said. "My machine has recorded all the rods—there are forty-seven of them. Each one contains thousands of sounds. There are more than ten thousand different words in the script—if words are what they are! When I've fed them all into her, she'll have to compare them one by one and in groups, each sound and each group of sounds, until she can form a general idea, a rule, something to follow. I'll help her, naturally, by going over her hypotheses and suggesting others to her. And the pictures will help us both."

"How long do you think it's going to take you?" Simon asked anxiously.

"A few days, perhaps. A few weeks if we get lost."

"The woman will be dead!" Simon shouted. "Or else she'll have gone mad. You must solve it at once! Today, tomorrow, in a couple of hours. Shake up your machine! Mobilize everyone on the base. There are plenty of technicians here."

Lukos looked at Simon as Menuhin would have looked at someone who urged him to "shake up" his Stradivarius in order to make it play a Paganini *prestissimo* "faster". He said, "My machine is doing what she knows how to do. It isn't technicians she needs; she's got enough of them. What she needs is brains."

"Brains? There's not another place in the whole world where you'll find better ones assembled than here. I'm going to request an immediate meeting of the executive committee. You will explain your problems . . ."

"Those are little brains, doctor—tiny human brains. They'd need centuries of haggling before they could agree on the meaning of a comma. When I say *brain,* I'm thinking of hers." Again he caressed the console's face, adding, "Hers and her sisters'."

A new SOS went out from the transmitter of EPI 1, a request for the cooperation of the world's best electronic brains.

Replies came in immediately. Every available computer was offered to Lukos and his staff. But those that were available were neither the largest nor the best. As far as these were concerned, EPI received promises: as soon as they had a free minute between programs nothing would give their owners greater pleasure and every effort would be made . . . And so on.

Simon had three cameras set up in Elea's room. One

was focused on the needle in her arm, another on her face with its closed eyes and hollow cheeks, and the third on her body, once more naked and now tragically emaciated.

These pictures he sent out over the antenna of EPI 1 to Trio and all men's eyes. And he spoke:

"She is going to die. She is dying of hunger, and we are letting her die because we don't understand her when she tells us what we could give her to eat. She is going to die because those who could help us don't want to divert a minute of their precious computers' time. They're too busy comparing the production costs of an octagon-headed bolt with the production costs of a hexagon-headed one, or finding the optimum distribution of retail outlets for paper napkins. . . .

"Look at her. Look at her closely. You will not see her again because she is going to die. We of this modern age have mobilized a vast force and the greatest minds of our time to seek her in her slumber far below the ice, and this only to kill her. We should be ashamed."

He was silent a moment and then, softly, he repeated, "We should be ashamed."

John Gartner, president and chairman of the board of Intercontinental Mechanical and Electronic, saw the broadcast aboard his private jet as he was flying from Detroit to Brussels. At this moment he was a hundred thousand feet above the Azores and eating breakfast. Having just finished ingesting, through a straw the yolk of a soft-boiled egg cooked in a sterilized transparent bag, he was working on his whiskey and orange juice.

"This boy is right," he said. "We ought to be ashamed if we don't do something."

He ordered that his cartel's computers be immediately made available to the EPI: the seven in America, the nine in Europe, the three in Asia and the one in

Africa. His appalled underlings pointed out to him the frightful disruption of the firm's operations that could result. It would take months to undo the damage, and some losses would be such that they could never be compensated.

"That doesn't matter," he said.

He was a man, and he was really ashamed. He was also an efficient man and a businessman. He ordered that his decision be made public at once. The consequences were these:

Intercontinental Mechanical and Electronic's popularity and sales rose by 17 per cent, which in turn set off a chain reaction. Within hours the world monopolies, the research centres, the universities, the ministries, even the Pentagon and the Russian Ballistics Centre had let Lukos know that their electronic brains were at his disposition. If only he would move as quickly as possible.

The exhortation was superfluous. Everyone at Square 612 knew that Lukos was battling against death. Elea was growing weaker by the hour. She agreed to try other foods, but her stomach would not keep them down. And all the time she kept repeating the same series of sounds, two or perhaps three words.

From the bottom of the world Lukos attempted and achieved the most incredible agglomeration. In accordance with his instructions the computers were interconnected by wire, by short wave, by light beams, by relays by all the stationary satellites. For a few hours the great brains in servitude to competing companies, enemy generals, conflicting ideologies, vengeful races were united in a single intelligence that girdled the entire earth and filled the sky with the web of its communications. With its unimaginable sources it laboured toward the microscopic and unselfish goal of deciphering three words.

In order to understand these three words it was necessary to analyze the whole language. Exhausted, unwashed, their eyes red with lack of sleep, the technicians assigned to the Universal Translator gave battle to time and the impossible. Unceasingly they injected data and problems into the circuits of the Total Brain—everything that had already been examined by the Translator and the new hypotheses elaborated by Lukos. His incredible mind seemed to have grown to the dimensions of its giant electronic counterpart. He communicated with it at unbelievable speed, limited only by the capacity of the transmitters and relays, which roused him to fierce rages. It seemed to him that he could have dispensed with them and communicated directly with The Other. Those two fantastic intelligences—the one that was alive and the other that seemed to be alive—did more than communicate. They moved on the same level, above everything else.

Simon impatiently shuttled between the infirmary and the Translator, nagging at the weary technicians who cursed him, and at Lukos who did not even notice him. But at last came the instant when everything became clear.

Then the brain dissolved. The links were severed, the nervous system established around the world broke up into its component parts. All that was left of the Total Brain were the independent ganglia, reconverted into what they had been before—socialist or capitalist, commercial or military, working to further profit and prejudice.

Within the four aluminium walls of the big hall in the Translator's building there was absolute silence as Lukos adjusted the little spool containing Elea's words on the receiving platen. A microphone had caught them in her room as she spoke them, with less frequency and decreasing strength.

There was a sharp click as everything fell into place. Simon leaning with both hands on the back of Lukos' chair, began to nag once more. "Well?"

Lukos threw the starting switch. The spool seemed to make a quarter turn, but it was already empty and the printer was clacking. Lukos was still looking at the printout when Simon snatched it out of his hand.

Simon read the French translation. Utterly confounded, he looked at Lukos, who had had time to read it in Albanian, English, German and Arabic. Lukos shook his head. He took the paper back and read it through. It was the same absurdity in seventeen languages. It made no more sense in Spanish than in Russian or Chinese. In English it said:

FROM EAT MACHINE

Simon no longer had the strength to shout. "Your brains," he said, his voice almost a whisper, "your great big brains—what a joke." His head bowed, his back bent, he dragged himself over to the nearest wall, knelt down, then stretched out, turned his face away from the light and went to sleep.

He slept for nine minutes and then woke with a shout: "Lukos!" Lukos was there, busy feeding the Translator fragments of the text found in the reading-thing and deciphering the translations disgorged by the printer. They were fragments of a story in an astonishing style, taking place in an alien, fantastic world.

Simon said, "Lukos, have we gone through all this for nothing?"

"No," Lukos replied. "Look." He held out the printed sheets. "This is sensible stuff, not gibberish. The Brain was not a fool and neither was I. It understood the language and my Translator learned it. She's translating it faithfully, accurately: from eat machine."

"From eat machine?"

"That means something! If we don't understand, we're the idiots."

"I believe you. I believe you." Simon's tone, as his hopes revived, was euphoric. "Could you put this language on one of your channels?"

"I don't have any available."

"Make one available! Eliminate some other language."

"Which one?"

"What's the difference? Korean, Czech, Sudanese, French!"

"They'll go raving mad."

"To hell with their raving madness! Do you think this is any time to care about their nationalism?"

"Ionescu!" Lukos cried. Simon looked baffled, and Lukos explained, "Ionescu—he was killed. He was the only one here who spoke Rumanian. I'll throw out Rumanian and take over its channel." Lukos stood up and his steel chair creaked with relief. He picked up an intercom and shouted into it, "Hello! Haka! For Christ's sake, are you asleep?" He began to roar insults in Turkish.

A drowsy voice replied. Lukos issued his instructions in English and then turned to Simon. "A matter of two minutes." Simon rushed for the door. "Wait!" Lukos called. He opened a closet, took out a tiny transmitter and an earphone bearing the Rumanian colours and gave them to Simon. "Here, she'll need these."

Simon took the minuscule instruments. "Be careful," he warned, "not to let your damned machine start howling into her ear."

"Promise. I'll keep my eye on it. A whisper, just a whisper." His hands, as hard as jointed bricks, gripped those of the man who had become his friend in these hours of superhuman effort, and the grasp was gentle. "I promise you. Go!"

A few minutes later Simon walked into Elea's room.

The nurse sitting beside Elea's bed was reading a romantic novel. She rose when she saw the door open, and she motioned to Simon not to make any noise. Her face assumed an expression of professional concern as she looked toward Elea's. Actually she was completely indifferent: she was still absorbed in her book, the heart-rending confession of a woman deserted for the third time, with whom the nurse-reader suffered and damned all men, including the one who had just arrived.

Simon bent over Elea, whose face, in spite of the gauntness born of starvation, had still retained its warm colour. Her nostrils were almost translucent. The eyes were closed. The breast barely moved with her breathing. Softly he said: "Elea ... Elea ..." Her eyelids fluttered slightly. She was conscious and she understood.

Leonova came in, followed by Lebeau and Hoover, who was carrying a sheaf of photographs. From a distance he held them up for Simon to see; Simon nodded agreement and turned all his attention back to Elea. He placed the tiny microphone on the blue sheet close to her emaciated face, lifted a lock of her soft hair to reveal her left ear, like a pale flower, and very carefully inserted the receiver in the pink shadow of the auditory canal.

She sketched a reflexive attempt to shake her head and get rid of what might be a new torture. But in her exhaustion she abandoned the effort.

In a very low voice Simon said in French, "You can understand me. Now you can understand me." And in Elea's ear a man's voice said in her own language, "Now you can understand me."

The others in the room saw her catch her breath a moment, then relax. Overflowing with compassion, Leonova went up to the bed, took Elea's hand and began pouring out the fullness of her heart to Elea in Russian. Simon raised his head to glare at Leonova and gestured at her to go away. Rather shocked, she obeyed. Simon reached out his hand for the photographs, which Hoover gave him.

First Elea's left ear was flooded with a torrent of sympathy rushing out in a feminine voice that she understood; her right ear was assailed by a gravelly clamour that she did not understand. Then there was silence. And then the man's voice spoke again.

"Can you open your eyes? Can you open your eyes? Try." He stopped speaking, and everyone looked at Elea. Her eyelids were quivering. "Try. Again. We are your friends. Don't be afraid."

And her eyes opened.

They were amazing. It was impossible to grow used to them. No one had ever seen eyes so big, of so deep a blue. They had lightened a little and they were no longer the blue of midnight but rather the blue that follows the twilight, the blue of night that follows a storm, when a heavy wind has washed the sky with its waves. And there were still glints of gold in the blue.

"Look!" the voice said. "Which is eat machine?" In front of her two hands were holding a picture, then replacing it with another and another and another. All the pictures were of things that were familiar to her. "Eat machine? Which is eat machine?"

Eat? To live? What was the point?

"Look! Which is eat machine?"

Sleep . . . forget . . . die . . .

"No! Don't close your eyes! These are the things that we found with you. One of them must be eat machine. Look! I'm going to show them to you again. If you see eat machine, close your eyes and open them."

At the sixth photograph, Elea closed her eyes and re-opened them. "This one!" Simon said. "Hurry!" He thrust the picture toward Hoover, who snatched it from him and ran out with the speed of a cyclone.

The picture showed an object that had not yet been studied but had been put back into the pedestal with the weapon.

It is worth a moment to summarize what made it so difficult to decipher and understand Elea's language. It was actually not one language but two: one feminine and one masculine, each completely different from the other in syntax and vocabulary. Men and women understood each other, but the men spoke the masculine language, which had its own masculine and feminine genders, and the women spoke the feminine language, which had its own feminine and masculine genders. In writing, sometimes one and sometimes the other was used, depending on the time and season of what was being described, the colour, the temperature, the degree of excitement or tranquility, the mountains or sea. And occasionally the two languages were mixed.

It is difficult to furnish examples of the differences between the male and female languages because two equivalent terms would be translated only by the same word. The man would say "it must be without thorns" and the woman would say "petals of the setting sun", and each would know that the other was talking about a rose. The illustration is approximate: when Elea lived man had not yet invented the rose.

"From eat machine". These were indeed three words, but according to the logic of Elea's language, they were also a single compound definable as "what is produced by the eat machine". The eat machine was "the machine that produces what is eaten".

It had been placed on the bed facing Elea, who had

been helped into a sitting position supported by pillows. In order to prevent her from contracting a chill, Simon had had the temperature of her room raised. Hoover was dripping like an icicle on a stove. He had already sweated through every one of his garments; the shirts of the others in the audience were wringing wet. A nurse periodically distributed white towels for their faces. The cameras were also in the room; one of them was focused on the "eat machine" in close-up. The machine was green, more or less hemispherical, dotted with a great number of buttons which spiralled from its summit to its base and reproduced all the colours of the spectrum in hundreds of different gradations. At the top there was a white button. The base stood on a small cylindrical support. The whole thing was equal in volume and weight to about half a watermelon.

Elea tried to raise her left hand. A nurse moved to help her, but Simon brushed the nurse aside and took Elea's hand in his own.

Close-up: Simon's hand supporting Elea's and guiding it toward the body of the "eat machine".

Close-up again: Elea's face, and then her eyes. Lanson could not tear himself away from them. One or another of his cameras was always coming back to focus on those eyes from the dawn of time. He did not broadcast this picture to the world: he reserved it for a monitor screen—for himself.

Elea's hand came to rest at the top of the hemisphere. Simon was guiding it like a bird. Elea had the will power, but she lacked the strength. He sensed where she wanted her hand to go, what she wanted it to do. Now she was guiding him and he was supporting her. Her long middle finger touched the white button and then brushed over variously coloured knobs in a random fashion.

Hoover wrote down the names of the colours on a

limp envelope that he had taken from his pocket. But he could find no names to differentiate the three kinds of yellow that she had pressed one after another, and he gave up.

Her hand went back to the white button, rested on it, tried to press it and could not. Simon pressed it. The button barely yielded; there was a slight hum, the cylinder opened and a little golden tray slid out. It held five tiny spheres of a transparent pinkish substance and a minuscule two-pronged golden fork.

Simon picked up the fork and thrust it into one of the little spheres, which offered very slight resistance before it yielded like a cherry. He raised it to Elea's lips.

She opened her mouth with an effort. It was difficult for her to close it again on the food. There was no movement of chewing; the observers supposed that the sphere was melting in her mouth. Then, clearly visible in her thin throat, her larynx rose and fell.

Simon mopped his face and offered her the second sphere.

In a few minutes she was using the food machine without help. She pressed various knobs, received some blue spheres, ate them, rested a little, and then returned to the machine.

Her strength was returning swiftly, as though she was asking the machine for more than mere food. Each time she pushed different buttons and got a different number of spheres in a new colour. She ate them, drank water, took deep breaths, rested a few minutes, and started again.

Everyone who was in her room or who was following her actions on the screen in the conference room saw life literally filling her out again, her body putting on flesh, her cheeks losing their hollows, her eyes regaining their deep colour.

"Eat machine": it was a feeding machine. Perhaps it was also a healing machine. The scientists were seething with impatience. The weapon and the eat machine were maddening to their imaginations. They were burning to question Elea and to open the machine: it, at least, was not dangerous.

As for the journalists, for whom Ionescu's death had provided a sensation, they found the eat machine and its effects on Elea to be a new and no less fantastic source for copy. There was always something unforeseeable, a contrast of joy and pain; this expedition was a journalistic gold mine.

At last Elea pushed aside the machine and looked at all the persons who were watching her. She made an effort to speak; her voice was barely audible. She began again, and everyone heard, in his own language: "Do you understand me?"

"Oui ... Yes *... Da ..."* They all nodded their heads to emphasize that they understood.

"Who are you?" Elea asked.

"Friends," Simon replied.

But Leonova could contain herself no longer. She was thinking of the universal distribution of food machines to all the poor nations and all the starving children. "How does that machine function?" she asked. "What do you put into it?"

Elea apparently either did not understand or regarded these as infantile questions. She was absorbed in her own concerns. "There were supposed to have been two of us in the Shelter," she said. "Was I alone?"

"No," Simon said, "there were two of you—yourself and a man."

"Where is he? Is he dead?"

"No. He hasn't been revived yet. We started with you."

She was quiet for a moment. It was as if the news

had reawakened some sombre apprehension in her rather than given her pleasure. She took a deep breath and said, "He is Coban. I am Elea." And again she asked, "You—who are you?"

Once more the only reply that Simon could offer was, "We are friends."

"Where do you come from?"

"Everywhere in the world."

This seemed to amaze her. "Everywhere in the world? I don't understand. Are you from Gondawa?"

"No."

"From Enisor?"

"No."

"What countries do you come from?"

"I'm from France, she's from Russia, he's from America, he's from France, he's from The Netherlands, he's—"

"I don't understand. . . . Is there peace now?"

"Hmm." This was Hoover.

"No!" Leonova declared. "The imperialists—"

"Both of you shut up!" Simon ordered.

"Certainly we are compelled," Hoover said, "to defend ourselves against—"

"Get out!" Simon ordered. "Get out! Leave us doctors alone here."

"We were stupid. I'm sorry. But I'm staying," Hoover said.

Simon turned to Elea. "What they were saying is meaningless," he told her. "Yes, there's peace now. You have nothing to fear."

Elea breathed a great sigh of relief, but there was fear in her next question. "Have you any news from the Mass Shelters? Did they hold out?"

"We do not know," Simon answered. "We have no word."

She uttered a syllable and stopped. There was a

question that she wanted to ask but she was afraid of the reply. She looked around the room, and then turned her gaze back to Simon. Very softly she asked him: "Paikan?"

There was a brief silence. The neuter voice of the Translator—neither a man's nor a woman's—said into the seventeen channels in seventeen languages, "The word *Paikan* does not appear in the vocabulary with which I have been programmed and does not correspond to any plausible neologism. I take the liberty of supposing it to be a proper name."

Elea too heard this, in her own language. "Of course," she retorted, "it is a proper name. Where is he? Have you had any news of him?"

Simon looked at her soberly. "We have heard nothing of him. How long do you suppose you have been asleep?"

She looked back at him anxiously. "A few days?"

"More."

Once again Elea's eyes swept over the setting and the people that surrounded her. Once again she felt the uprootedness of her first awakening, its alien, nightmare quality. She tried to get a grip on the impossible. "How long have I slept? Weeks? Months?"

"More. Much more. You have slept—"

"Careful, Simon!" Lebeau interjected.

Simon paused, watching Elea with deep concern. Then he turned to Lebeau. "What were you thinking?"

"I'm afraid."

Anxiously Elea repeated her question. "How long have I been asleep? Do you understand my question? I wish to know how long I have been asleep. I wish to know—"

"We understand you," Simon told her, and she was silent. "You've been asleep—"

"I don't approve!" Lebeau interrupted again. He

92

covered his microphone with his hand so that the Translator would not hear him. "You're going to give her a terrible shock. It would be better to break it to her gradually . . ."

Simon's face was dark and his brows were knitted obstinately. "I have nothing against shocks," he said, also covering his microphone with his hand. "In psychotherapy, the shock that purges is preferable to the lie that poisons. And I think that she's strong enough—"

"I wish to know—" Elea began, again.

Simon swung around to her and said brusquely, "You were asleep for nine hundred thousand years." She looked at him in stupefaction; he did not allow her time to think. "This may seem remarkable to you. It does to us too. Nevertheless it is the truth. The nurse will read the report of our expedition to you: we found you at the bottom of a frozen continent, and our laboratories employed a variety of methods to measure the time that you had spent there."

He was speaking to her in a tone that was impersonal and schoolmasterish, and the Translator's voice modelled itself on his, calm and unconcerned in Elea's left ear.

"Such a period of time," he continued, "has no common measure with the life of a man or even of a civilization. Nothing is left of the world in which you lived, not even the memory of it. You have to accept this idea, accept the facts, accept the world into which you have awakened and in which you have only friends."

But she was no longer listening. She had withdrawn from the voice in her ear, from the face that was speaking to her, from the other faces that were watching her. There remained only the certainty of the chasm across which she had been hurled, far from everything that had been her life. Far from . . . *"Paikan!"*

As she screamed the name she rose naked and savage in her bed, superb and taut like an animal hunted to the death. The nurses and Simon tried to restrain her. She evaded them, and leaped from the bed, shouting *"Paikan!"*

She ran straight for the door through the ranks of the onlookers. Zabrec tried to throw his arms around her. He got her elbow in his face and spat blood as he let her go. Hoover was knocked against the wall; Forster thrust out his arm to stop her and was punched so hard that he thought a bone had been broken. She jerked the door open and ran out.

The reporters, who had been watching on the screen in the conference room, swarmed into Amundsen Avenue. The door of the infirmary swung open and Elea ran like an antelope with a lion at its heels. She ran straight ahead, straight toward them. They formed a road block and she did not see them. Flashbulbs exploded along the line of photographers. Elea knocked over three men and their cameras; then she made for the exit. She reached it before anyone could catch her, just as the sliding door was opening to admit a snow-dog bearing supplies.

The outside air was white with a 125-mile an hour blizzard. Crazed with grief, blind, naked, Elea hurled herself onto the knives of the wind. It thrust into her flesh, swept her up and carried her toward death. She struggled, regained her footing, fought back at the wind with her fists, tore it out of her lungs with a shout fiercer than its howl. The storm poured into her mouth and stifled her cry in her throat.

She fell.

A second later her pursuers picked her up and carried her back inside.

"I warned you," Lebeau said to Simon.

Simon gloomily watched the nurses kneading and massaging the unconscious Elea. "Paikan," she murmured.

"She must be in love," Leonova said.

Hoover snickered. "With a man she left nine hundred thousand years ago!"

"She left him yesterday," Simon said. "And during one night all eternity came between them."

"Poor woman," Leonova murmured.

"I didn't know," Simon said in a low voice.

"My boy," Lebeau replied, "in medicine one must always assume what one doesn't know."

———

But I had known.

I watched your lips. I had seen them tremble with love when you spoke his name.

Then I wanted to tear you away from him all at once, brutally, to make you know that there was nothing left of him, not even a grain of dust that had been shifted over the world a thousand times by tides and winds . . . to make you see that your memories were drawn from the void. That behind you there was only the dark, and that your light, hope, and life were here in our time, with us.

I did you harm.

But you first, when you spoke his name, you crushed my heart.

The doctors had anticipated pneumonia and severe frostbite at the very least, but Elea suffered no ill effects at all: no coughing, no fever, not the slightest redness of skin.

When she returned to consciousness it was apparent that she had absorbed the shock and mastered her emotions. Her face had taken on an expression of utter indifference. She asked to have the expedition's report read to her. But when the nurse began to read it, Elea shut her off with a gesture and asked, "Where is Simon?"

He was not in the room. Ever since his stubbornness had almost turned out so tragically, the resuscitation team had deemed him a dangerous individual and had forbidden him to have anything to do with Elea.

Her eyes scouted the room for him. She had become accustomed to his face, his voice, the solicitude of his movements. And it was he who had told her the truth. In this unknown world, at the conclusion of her frightening journey, he was already a familiar figure, a rock on the bank to which her hand could cling. "Where is Simon?"

"I think it would be best to send for him," Moissov said.

Simon came and began to read to Elea. Then he put down the documents and began to tell the story in his own words. When he came to speak of the discovery of Elea and her companion, she raised her hand to interrupt him. "He is Coban, the wisest man in Gondawa. Gondawa was our country." She paused briefly and then added in a very low tone, "I wish I had died in Gondawa."

As soon as Elea was amenable to answering questions, the scientists fought one another to be the first to ask the hows and whys of the eat machine.

"How does the food machine operate?"

"You've seen it."

"But what about the inside?"

"It manufactures food."

"But what does it use to manufacture it?"

"The Whole."

"The Whole? What's that?"

"You know very well. It's what made you too."

"The Whole . . . the Whole . . . isn't there any other name for it?"

Elea spoke three words, which were followed by the impersonal voice of the translation machines. "The words that have just been spoken on Channel Eleven do not appear in the vocabulary with which I have been programmed. By analogy, however, I think I can suggest this as an approximate translation: *universal energy*. Or, perhaps, *universal essence*. Or *universal life*. But I find these two latter suggestions somewhat abstract. The first is undoubtedly closest to the original meaning. But, for the sake of accuracy, the two others would have to be embraced in it."

Energy! The machine manufactured matter out of energy! It was not impossible in the current state of scientific knowledge. But a fantastic quantity of electricity would be necessary to produce an invisible particle that would vanish as soon as it had appeared. On the other hand, this first cousin to a half-watermelon, which looked like a rather stupid toy for children, pulled food out of the void with the utmost simplicity.

Lebeau had to curb the impatience of the scientists,

whose questions were tumbling over one another inside the Translator's brain.

"Do you know the mechanics of its operation?" Elea was asked.

"No. Coban knows."

"Do you know the basic principle of it, at least?"

"It makes use of Zoran's universal equation." Her eyes ranged in quest of something that would enable her to give a better explanation of what she meant. She saw that Hoover was making notes in the margin of a magazine, and she stretched out her hand toward him. He gave her the paper and pen. Leonova substituted an untouched memorandum pad for the magazine.

Elea tried to write, to draw, to sketch something with her left hand. She could not manage it. Beginning to be irritated, she dropped the pen and said to the nurse: "Give me your . . . your . . ." She imitated the act of applying lipstick, which she had so often seen the nurse perform. The astonished nurse complied.

Then, with broad, easy strokes, Elea drew the beginning of a spiral on the paper; then it was bisected by a vertical straight line; two short lines, one vertical and one horizontal, were drawn inside the spiral. Elea handed the paper to Hoover.

"This is Zoran's equation," she said. "It can be read in two ways. It can be read in ordinary language or in terms of universal mathematics."

"Can you read it?" Leonova inquired.

"I can read it in ordinary language. 'What does not exist exists.' "

"And in mathematical terms?"

"I don't know. Coban knows."

As they had pledged themselves to do, the EPI scientists had communicated everything that they themselves knew to everyone who had the capacity to understand it. The whole human race knew that it stood at the threshold of a fantastic upheaval. When the sleeping man had explained Zoran's equation, it would be possible to draw food for the hungry from the core of universal energy. No more savage wars for raw materials, no more conflicts over oil, no more battles for fertile plains. Zoran's equation would take everything necessary to men directly from the whole.

It was to begin the next day. The operating room had been rebuilt, the last of the equipment arrived to replace that which had been destroyed. The technical staffs were busy setting up and checking connections. Now the second resuscitation could begin.

Outside the storm had abated. The wind was still blowing, but in those latitudes it always blows, and when it does not exceed ninety miles an hour it is a gentle breeze. Now it was the middle of the night: the cloudless sky was the greyish blue of slate. The sun was crouching red at the horizon. Huge stars appeared in the sky.

The two men who had been working late in the sphere came out of the elevator: Brivaux and his assistant. They were the last to come up. They were extremely tired, and eager to stretch out and sleep. No one was left down below.

Brivaux closed and locked the elevator door. He and his assistant went out of the ice-walled building and swore as the wind caught them.

Then a round spot of light appeared in the dark, empty structure. Behind the pile of packing cases that had contained the new equipment, a man stood up, his teeth chattering. The flashlight in his hand was shaking. He had been hiding there for more than an hour, waiting for the last of the technicians to depart. In spite of his polar clothing, the cold had struck him to the bone.

He approached the elevator, took a collection of flat keys out of his pocket and began to try them, one by one. But his hands were shaking too much. He took off his gloves, blew on his stiff fingers, thrashed his arms against his body, and jumped up and down a few times. The blood began to flow again. He returned to his keys. Finally he found the right one. He entered the elevator and pushed the *down* button.

Simon, in the infirmary, was watching Elea sleep. Now he was never away from her. If he left for even a moment, she asked for him. The icy indifference in which she had enveloped herself was augmented, when he was not there, by a physical anxiety for which she demanded immediate relief.

He was there and so she could sleep. The nurse on duty was also sleeping on one of the two folding beds in the room. A blue bulb above the door gave off a very soft light. And Simon watched Elea as she slept. Her arms lay relaxed on top of the bedclothes. Her breathing was easy and slow and her face was serious. Simon bent over her and brought his lips close to the long hand with its long fingers, but then he went no farther and straightened up.

He returned to the empty folding bed, lay down, pulled up a blanket, sighed happily and fell asleep.

The man had entered the resuscitation room. He went straight to a small metal cupboard, which he opened.

One shelf contained various records. He leafed through them, separating pages here and there, photographing them with a camera slung over his shoulder and then replacing them. Then he went to the television monitor screen, which always showed the inside of the egg. The new camera, which was sensitive to infra-red rays, eliminated the mist. The interloper could clearly see Coban inside in his almost intact helium cube and the pedestal that had held Elea. The side of the pedestal was still open and the shelves contained objects that Elea had not requested.

The man worked the buttons guiding the camera by remote control. He focused it on the open pedestal, moved it in for a close-up and at last saw what he was looking for: the weapon.

He smiled with satisfaction and got ready to go down into the egg. He knew that its temperature was dangerously cold. He had been unable to obtain a space suit and he would have to work very quickly. He left the operating room. The interior of the sphere, weakly illuminated by a few light bulbs, was like the skeleton of a gigantic surrealist bird. To break the spell of the total silence the man coughed deliberately. The sound of his cough filled the sphere like an explosion, shattered against the armature of girders and flying buttresses, struck the inner wall and bounced back at him in thousands of fragments.

He pushed his cap down hard over his ears, wrapped a heavy scarf around his neck and put on his fur gloves as he went down the golden stairway. An electric mechanism had been installed to open the door of the egg. He activated it. The door rose like a window. He slipped inside, and already the door was beginning to close behind him.

He was taken by surprise by the mist, which the infra-red camera had not shown him. The light that came up through the transparent floor and the layer of powdery blue snow coloured the mist an unreal blue. Flashlight in hand, preceded by a circle of the white light, the man made his cautious way down the stairs. As he descended he felt the savage cold bite into his ankles, his calves, his knees, his thighs, his belly, his chest, his throat, his skull.

He had to work fast. His right foot rested on the floor beneath the snow. Then his left foot joined it. He took one step to the left and inhaled for the first time. His lungs froze solid, turned to stone. He wanted to cry out, and he opened his mouth. His tongue froze and his teeth popped out of his gums. The interior of his eyes dilated and solidified, pushing out the pupils like mushrooms. There was still time, before he died, to feel the claws of the cold crush his testicles and crack his brain. His flashlight went out. Everything was silent again. He fell forward into the blue snow. As he hit the floor his nose broke. The powdery snow rose for a moment in a fragile luminous cloud, then settled again and covered him.

When the helmeted men in their space suits removed the corpse from its shroud of fine snow, its upraised right arm snapped off, and shattered into four pieces.

Rochefoux called the reporters and photographers together in the conference room. He announced, "I regret to inform you of the tragic death of your colleague, Juan Fernandez, a photographer for *La Nación* of Buenos Aires. He had entered the egg clandestinely, undoubtedly to take photographs of Coban, and he died of the cold almost instantly. It is a horrible death. I cannot urge you strongly enough to be careful. We are not hiding anything from you. On the contrary, we want you to know everything we discover and to disseminate it as widely as possible. But I beg you not to engage in any more such ventures, which endanger not

only your lives, but the success of the resuscitation operations which will affect the fate of all mankind."

But a message from *La Nación,* transmitted by way of Trio, asserted that the newspaper knew nothing of Juan Fernandez and that he had never been a member of its staff. Fernandez's room was searched. He had three cameras—one American, one Czech, and one Japanese—a German radio transmitter and an Italian revolver.

The resuscitation team and the officials of the EPI held a conference out of range of the journalists' curiosity. They were staggered.

"It must be one of those idiotic secret services," Moissov said. "But which one? We'll probably never know. But the one thing they all have in common is stupidity, and the one thing they're efficient at is causing disasters. We have to find some way to protect ourselves against them."

"The bastards," Hoover muttered in English.

"Unfortunately," Moissov continued, "I'll have to use words that are less vivid and less accurate, and I don't much like that, because they're pompous. But one must after all speak with the words available to one—"

"Go on, then," Hoover interrupted.

"I'm a physician," Moissov said. "You're ... what are you?"

"I'm in chemistry and electronics. But what's the difference? There's all kinds down here."

"True. And yet we're all the same. We have one thing in common that's stronger than all our differences: the need to *know.* We come from every scientific discipline, every nation, every ideology. You don't like my being a Communist Russian. I don't like your being capitalist imperialists bogged down in the muck of a social past that's rotting away. But I know and you know that all this is far outweighed by our shared curiosity.

103

You and I alike want to *know*. We want to know the universe in all its secrets. And we already know one thing: that man is a miracle and that men are pitiful and that each one of us in his own way, in his own little area of knowledge and his own miserable nationalism, is working for all men. What is to be learned here is fantastic. And what we can derive from it for the good of mankind is beyond imagination. But if we allow our nations to get into it with their eternal imbecility, their generals, their ministers and their spies, the result will be tragic."

"It's easy to see that you take evening courses in Marxism," Hoover said. "You always have a speech on tap. But you certainly are right. You are my brother." He patted Leonova's bottom. "And you're my little sister."

"You're a fat filthy pig," she retorted.

"Allow the voice of Europe to be heard," Rochefoux intervened with a smile. "We have gold—the gold that we cut away when we broke the skin of the sphere. We can use it to buy arms and hire mercenaries."

Shanga, the African, rose like a shot. "I oppose the use of mercenaries!"

"So do I," Henckel, the German, said. "Though not for the same reasons. I simply think they'll be shot through with god-damned spies. We'll have to organize our own police force and our own defences—defences for the contents of the sphere: the weapon and especially Coban. As long as he is frozen he is in no danger. But the resuscitation process is about to begin. There will be a tremendous temptation to abduct him before we have given his knowledge to the whole world. There isn't one single nation that wouldn't try to gain exclusive possession of what's in that head. The United States, for instance—"

"Oh, sure," Hoover said. "Sure."

"The Soviet Union—"

"The Soviet Union!" Leonova shouted as she sprang to her feet. "Always the Soviet Union! Why the Soviet Union? China too! Germany! England! France!—"

"No then," Rochefoux smiled, "even Switzerland—"

"I can get my hands on machine guns, revolvers, mines . . ." Lukos offered.

"So can I," Henckel said.

They left for Europe that day, accompanied by Shanga and Hoover's assistant, Garrett. It was understood that none of them would at any time lose sight of the others. So the good faith of each, as to which no one had any doubt, would be guaranteed by the presence of the others.

Day and night guard patrols were set up at the elevator and Elea's room. Two men, technicians or scientists, were always on duty together. In the light of what was at stake, no one dared trust anyone—even himself.

The Egg.

Two floodlights attacked the mist. The air hose was playing on the helium block that housed Coban. The block hollowed, changed shape, sank into itself and vanished. In the operating room the resuscitation team was going through the process of making themselves sterile, putting on their aseptic tunics and gloves and tying their cotton shoes.

Simon was not with them. He and Elea were sitting on the platform in the conference room before an audience of scientists. On the table in front of them was a group of objects from the pedestal. Elea was calm and motionless. The waves of her brown hair with its golden reflections were like a quiet sea. She was wearing the garments found in the pedestal. Around her waist she had placed four reddish-brown rectangles of a flowing, heavy material. They reached to her knees and shifted when she walked, revealing and then again covering her thighs, like water flowing in sunlight. Around her upper body she had wound a long roll of the same colour; it outlined her torso and her shoulders and hinted at the contours of her breasts that were free as birds beneath the cloth.

All these garments were kept on by a knot, a twist, an over-and-under, a miracle. It was quite complicated and at the same time very simple and natural; the people who watched her as she took her seat had the wretched feeling that they were wearing flour sacks.

This was the first of the working sessions which would gather information on the men of the past. Elea had agreed to answer questions. Her face was set and her eyes were like gates opening on the night. She was silent. Her silence had spread to everyone in the room and seemed to be indomitable.

Hoover cleared his throat. "Well," he said, "shall we begin? The best thing would be to begin at the beginning. Suppose you tell us first who you are? How old? Your occupation? Your family status? Briefly."

Twelve hundred yards below, the naked man had lost his transparent armour and was waiting for the temperature to rise sufficiently to permit him to be moved. In the glowing mist, four men in close-fitting red clothing, boots, and spherical plastic helmets approached his pedestal and arranged themselves in pairs on opposite sides. Two men stood guard with automatic weapons at the entrance of the egg. The four men in the mist bent down and slipped their hands, in gloves of fur, leather and asbestos, under the naked man. They waited.

Forster watched them on the monitor screen in the operating room until he saw that they were ready. He spoke into his microphone. "Lift him on the count of three, but be careful. All right, one, two, three—up!" The order reached the four plastic helmets at the same time in four different languages. The four men slowly straightened.

A blinding blue light erupted under their feet, burned their eyes, filled the egg like an explosion, surged out through the open door, invaded the sphere, rose through the shaft like a geyser, and vanished.

There had been no sound, no real explosion. It was only light. The snow on the floor of the egg was no longer blue. The device that had been manufacturing cold for 900,000 years had stopped working or destroyed itself when its reason for being was gone.

"My name is Elea," Elea said. "My number is 3-19-07-91. And here is my key." She raised her right hand with all the fingers folded inward except the middle one, on which her ring with its truncated pyramid stood out. She hesitated, and then she asked, "Don't you have keys?"

"We have things that we call keys," Simon said. "But I'm afraid they aren't the same." He took his key-case from his pocket, shook it, and opened it for Elea. She looked at it without touching it, in a kind of uneasiness mingled with incomprehension. She made an impatient gesture. And she went back to answering Hoover.

"I was born in the shelter of Depth Five, two years after the last war."

"What?" Leonova demanded. Other questions came like machine-gun fire. "What war? . . . Between which nations? . . . Where was your country? . . . Who was the enemy? . . ."

Simon stood up in anger. "If you can't show a modicum of discipline, I as the physician in charge will be obliged to forbid these sessions. I suggest that you allow Mme. Leonova to speak for all of you and ask the first questions. Eventually each of you will have his turn. Do you approve?" He beckoned to Leonova to join him on the stage. As she did so, he picked up a large globe standing on the floor and lifted it to the desk.

"You're right, my boy," Hoover said. "Go on, let her speak for all of us."

Stretched out on the operating table, the man was still naked. Physicians and technicians, all masked, moved busily around him, attaching electrodes, straps, wires to link him with the various instruments.

"Look!" Moissov interrupted abruptly. He pointed to a place on the abdominal wall. "And there, on the chest. There too—the left biceps."

"Damn!" Lebeau muttered.

Elea stared at the globe and began to rotate it in bewilderment, as though she did not recognize it. Undoubtedly the geographical conventions of her time were different from ours. Perhaps she could not grasp what was represented by the blue oceans. Perhaps the maps of her day represented north as down instead of up, or at the left, or the right? She hesitated, stopped to think, reached out her arm and turned the globe again, and her face showed that at last she knew what it was and also that she had recognized its difference.

She grasped the stand of the globe and swung it off its perpendicular. "This way," she said. "It was like this."

In spite of their promises the scientists could not repress stifled outcries. Lanson had trained a camera on the globe, and now it appeared on the big screen. The globe as Elea had canted it still had the north toward the top and the south toward the bottom, but they had been displaced by almost forty degrees!

Olofsen, the Danish geographer, was gloating. He had always championed the much-disputed theory of the shift of the earth's axis. All his carefully collected evidence and each of his arguments had been called inconclusive. He had thought that the shift had occurred earlier in the earth's history and had been less dramatic, but now this was a minor matter. He was right! There was no further need of proof: *he had a witness!*

Elea pointed at the Antarctic continent on the globe that Leonova was holding. She said, "This was Gondawa." The change she had made in the tilt of the globe's axis had moved the continent to a position between the South Pole and the Equator, in the warmest part of the temperate zone and almost in the tropics.

But a sudden cataclysm had swung the earth from its axis, jumbling climates in a matter of hours, burning what had been cold, freezing what had been hot, and submerging the continent under unimaginable masses of ocean waters flung out of their inertia.

"Enisor," Elea murmured, searching the globe for something that she could not find. "Enisor was our enemy." The roomful of scientists stared at the globe revolving on the big screen. "Ah! Here it is." The rotation stopped.

The American continents filled the screen, but the shift in the earth's axis had placed them in an unfamiliar position. North America was now leaning downward and South America was pointing upward. "There is some land missing here," Elea said.

Her hand appeared on the screen holding a pointer that Simon had given her. The chalked tip of the pointer rested on the eastern extremity of Canada, then moved over Newfoundland, leaving a broad red line that ran out into the middle of the Atlantic and then turned back to follow a very irregular course until it met South America at the easternmost point of Brazil.

Then Elea filled the area between her tracing and the coast with closely set red diagonal lines. Filling the vast gulf that separated the two Americas, she transformed them into a single huge continent. Its eastern bulge filled half the North Atlantic. She put down the pointer, laid her hand on the Greater America that she had just created, and said, "All of this was Enisor."

Leonova set down the globe. A new current of excitement ran through the room. Was the cataclysm that had mutilated Enisor the same one that had thrown the earth's axis out of position?

To all such questions Elea replied, "I don't know. Coban knows. Coban was afraid of this . . . That was why he built the Shelter you found us in."

"What was Coban afraid of specifically?"

"I don't know. But I can show you what it was like."

She selected a golden circlet from the objects arrayed before her and settled it tiara-fashion on her hair. Two small plates rested on her temples. Another covered her forehead above the eyes. She picked up a second circlet.

"You wear this Simon," she said. He turned to her. She placed the second circlet on his head and with her thumb lowered the forehead plate, which now hid the young doctor's eyes. "Just relax," she told him.

She placed her elbows on the desk and rested her head on her hands. Slowly she dropped her lids over her night-blue eyes.

Every face and every camera was turned toward Elea and Simon seated side by side; she kept her elbows on the desk and he sat erect in his chair, his back against its back, his eyes covered by the golden plate. They waited a moment in silence.

Suddenly Simon's body jumped. He thrust out his hands before him to touch the table, to reassure himself of its reality. Slowly he rose, whispering a few words

that the Translator repeated, "I'm seeing something
..." And then he shouted.

"I *see*! ... It's the Apocalypse! ... a huge plain ...
burning, rocks melting with the heat, armies dropping
out of the sky! Weapons spitting death at them, but
there are more of them coming down, like a plague of
locusts. They're burrowing into the ground. Now the
plain is splitting in two from one end of the horizon to
the other. The earth is heaving and falling back! Something huge is coming up out of the earth, a monstrous
machine, a disk of steel and glass! It's leaving the earth,
rising, spreading. It's filling the sky! Wait ... now all I
see is a man's face."

"Paikan!" Elea sobbed; she hid her face in her
hands.

The vision vanished from Simon's brain.

———

Coban knew.

He knew good and evil.

He knew the nature of the monstrous war machine
that filled the sky.

He knew how to create everything that men lack, to
draw food and shelter from the void.

Coban knew. But would he ever be able to communicate what he knew?

The physicians had found many lesions on the upper
body and arms: fewer on his lower body. They had assumed that these were the effect of cold, the man having manifested less tolerance for refrigeration than the
woman. But when they removed his mask, they discovered that every hair on his head, his eyebrows and his
eyelashes had been burned away to the skin. So it was

not the scars of freezing that covered his skin and his face, but those of burns. Or perhaps of both.

They asked Elea whether she knew how he had been burned. She did not know. When she fell asleep Coban was beside her, well and unharmed.

The doctors had wrapped him from head to foot in antinecrosis bandages that were supposed not only to prevent the skin from being destroyed when it returned to normal temperature but also to help it to grow again.

Coban knew. He was still nothing but a frozen mummy wrapped in yellow swaddling clothes, through which two transparent flexible tubes had been inserted in his nostrils. Wires of a dozen colours connected a battery of dials with the yellow tips inserted into various other parts of his body. Very slowly the physicians were allowing his body temperature to increase.

The sentinels on guard at the elevator were now backed up by a sensing device at the entrance to the sphere. This was wired to two of the mines that Lukos had brought back from his mission to Europe; anyone who approached the entrance would set them off. In order to enter the sphere, anyone arriving at the bottom of the shaft had to identify himself to the guards at the elevator. The guards would telephone the resuscitation room, where three physicians and a number of nurses and technicians were maintaining uninterrupted surveillance over Coban. One of them would throw a switch, and the mines would be disconnected. The visitor could then enter the sphere.

The Vignont family was lingering over fruit preserves at the half-moon table facing the television screen.

"That guy ought to go right back in the deep freeze," the daughter said. "The world can get along without him."

"Oh, come on, now," Mme Vignont said. "You can't

do that." Her voice had gone somewhat husky. She was thinking of the way she had seen him . . . and her husband, who was no longer exactly . . . A spasm of mourning sent tears to her eyes. She blew her nose. "I must have caught another cold."

"He can't be put back into his glacier after all the money that's been spent," Vignont, the father, said. "He represents a considerable investment."

"To hell with him," the son muttered. He was thinking of Elea stark naked. He dreamed of her at night, and when he could not sleep it was worse.

Elea, uncaring allowed the scientists to examine the gold circlets. Brivaux tried to find a circuit, a transmitter, something to explain their connection. There was nothing. The two circlets with their fixed plates at the temples and the movable forehead plates were made of solid metal with no visible substructure.

"Make no mistake about it," Brivaux insisted, "this is a product of molecular electronics. Each of these circlets is as complex as a TV transmitter and receiver in one, and as simple as a knitting needle. It's fantastic! When you put a circlet on your head it receives your brain waves and converts them into electromagnetic waves that you're sending to me, transforms them into brain waves and injects them into my brain. Do you follow me? If you ask me, we ought to hook this up with a television receiver."

"Huh?"

"It's not magic. Trap the waves while they're electromagnetic, amplify them, feed them into a TV receiver—that would certainly produce something. Maybe it won't be anything coherent, but we may as well try. Either it'll work or it won't. In any case, it isn't difficult."

Brivaux and his staff worked on it for barely half a

day. Then his assistant, Goncelin, put on the transmitting circlet. What came out were images lacking in sequence and coherence, an occasional precise shape, an unstable mental construct that shifted like dry sand in the hands of a child. Goncelin removed the circlet from his head in confusion.

"You mustn't try to 'think'," Elea counselled. "Thoughts are constantly forming and dissolving before they can be fixed in the mind. . . . You must try to recall images. Depend only on memory. The brain records everything, even if you aren't conscious of it. One must remember—recall a specific image at a specific moment. And then the rest will follow. . . ."

They tried again and succeeded.

In the second working session with the scientists Brivaux and his assistant, Goncelin, joined Leonova and Hoover who were sharing the platform with Elea and Simon. Brivaux was seated next to Elea. He was operating a complicated device no larger than a quarter-pound stick of butter, which was topped by a cluster of antennae about the length of a man's little finger and as intricate as the antennae of insects. This instrument was hooked up with a control panel placed in front of Goncelin. From the panel a cable led to Lanson's booth.

"The third war lasted for an hour," Elea said. "Then Enisor was frightened. So were we, probably. The fighting stopped. Eight hundred million people had been killed, the majority in Enisor. The population of Gondawa was smaller and it was well protected in its shelters. But absolutely nothing was left on the surface of the continent. The survivors had to stay underground because the lethal radiations contaminated the surface."

"Radiations? What weapons were used?"

"Earth bombs."

"Do you know how they worked?"

114

"No. Coban could tell you."

"Do you know anything at all about them?"

"They were made out of the metal taken out of the earth; they would poison an area long after the explosion itself."

Here the voice of the universal translator added, "The literal translation of the Gondawa words is 'earth bomb'. Hereafter, however, I will replace this term with its equivalent, 'atomic bomb'."

"I was born at Depth Five," Elea said. "I went up to the Surface for the first time when I was seven years old, just after my Selection. I hadn't been able to go up before because I had not yet received my key."

"Now then," Hoover demanded, "just what is this damned key? What can you use it for?"

Lanson trained his No. 2 camera on the key that Elea wore on her finger. The little pyramid appeared on the big screen and expanded to fill it. It was made of gold, visibly striated and etched with minuscule furrows and grooves in irregular shapes.

"The key is the key to everything," Elea said. "When a child is born the pattern of his key is fixed. All the keys look superficially the same, but they are as different as the individuals they belong to. The internal arrangement of their . . ."

"The last word does not appear in the vocabulary with which I have been programmed," the impersonal Translator announced.

"Shut up!" Hoover barked. "Tell us what you know and otherwise . . ." He stopped, surprised to find himself berating a computer. "Anyway, don't keep us in a sweat."

"I am a Translator," the Translator retorted: "I am not a Turkish bath."

The whole room roared with laughter. Hoover smiled and turned to Lukos. "Congratulations: your daughter has a brain in her head, but she's something of a hairsplitter, isn't she?"

"She is punctilious; it's her duty."

Elea listened without even trying to understand; these savages played with words as her people's children had played with shells on the subterranean beaches. Let them laugh or weep or lose their tempers—it was all the same to her. She was equally indifferent about continuing the session when they asked her to do so. She explained that the key contained all the individual's inherited characteristics inscribed in its substance. When a child was born his complete description was sent to the central computer, which designed his key, classified it and modified it every six months as the child grew. After seven years, the key was fully shaped, and the Selection took place.

"What was the selection?" Leonova asked.

"The central computer had the keys of all the living persons in Gondawa, and also genetic descriptions of our ancestors. The keys that we wear are only copies of the computer's original. It sorts the keys of all the seven-year-olds, knowing who they are and also who they will be. It searches among the boys for those who can and will fill my needs and my wishes. And among the boys there is one to whom I am perfectly suited, and I shall be for him what he needs and what he wishes.

"The boy and I are like a single pebble that had been broken in two and scattered among all the broken pebbles in the world. The computer finds the two halves and puts them together again."

"Then what's done with these two youngsters?" Leonova asked.

Still uninvolved, Elea spoke again, looking at no one. "They were brought up together, alternately by the boy's family and the girl's. Together they acquire the same tastes, the same habits. They learn to enjoy the same things together. They learn together what the world is like, what girls are, what boys are. When their sexual organs mature they join together and it is as though they become a single whole."

"Magnificent!" Hoover said. "And this always works? Your computer never makes a mistake?"

"The computer could not make a mistake. Occasionally a boy or a girl would develop in an unanticipated way. Then the pair were no longer suited to each other, and they would separate."

"And all those who remained together were happy?"

"Not everyone is capable of happiness. There were couples who were merely contented. There were those who were happy, and there were others who were very happy. And there were a few for whom the Selection is a complete success; *their* union might have been destined since the beginning of life in the world. The word *happiness* is not adequate to describe them. They are . . ."

In all the languages at its command the Translator's voice announced "There is no word in your language with which to translate the word that has just been uttered."

"You yourself," Hoover said, "were you content, happy, very happy, or . . . more than . . . what would you call it? . . . inexpressible?"

Elea's voice turned cold and hard as steel. "*I* was not. *We* were."

———————

Underwater detection devices off the coast of Alaska informed the American defence headquarters that twenty-three atomic submarines from Russia's polar fleet had passed through the Bering Strait. The submarines were heading south. There was no American reaction.

Russian intelligence informed Moscow that the American Seventh Strategic Satellite Flotilla had altered its orbit toward a more southerly course. There was no Russian reaction.

The European undersea aircraft carrier, *Neptune I,* which had been cruising the coast of western Africa on the surface, submerged and headed south.

China's shortwave transmitters began to scream, detailing these movements which all other news sources had ignored, denouncing the imperialist alliance which was converging on the Antarctic in order to smash mankind's greatest hope.

Alliance was not the most appropriate word; *understanding* would have been more accurate. Several of the richest countries had agreed among themselves to protect the threateningly unpredictable treasure against any attack by the poorer nations.

The secret understanding among the rich nations seeped down to the general staffs. A joint plan was prepared. Surface and submarine forces and aerial and space squadrons were converging on the southern Polar Circle in order to create a combined defence force—and, if necessary, an attack group—around Square 612.

The generals and admirals dismissed the scientists and their pitiful automatic weapons with contempt. But each nation's task force commander was under orders not to let Coban fall into their ally's hands. To that end, it was best that all the forces be brought together; it made it easier for each group to keep an eye on the others.

There were other, more secret, instructions, which

came neither from governments nor from general staffs. Universal energy—energy which could be found anywhere, cost nothing and could create anything—meant the end of monopolies in raw materials. *It meant the end of merchants.* The secret instructions had been issued not to military commanders but to a small number of unidentifiable individuals infiltrated into all the commands. These instructions, too, ordered that Coban must not be allowed to fall into an ally's hands. They added that he must not go anywhere.

"You're a boor!" Simon told Hoover. "Stop asking her personal questions!"

"All I did was ask her if she was happy. I had no idea—"

"Oh, yes, you did!" Leonova cried. "You just like to make trouble—"

"Would you have the courtesy to shut up?" Simon turned to Elea and asked her to go on.

"All right," she replied, clothed once more in her indifference. "I'm going to show you my Selection. The ceremony was performed once a year in the Tree-and-Mirror at each Depth. I was selected in Depth Five, where I was born." She picked up the golden circlet lying before her, and settled it on her hair.

Lanson cut off his cameras, activated the cable from the platform and hooked the sound channel into the Translator. Elea, her head between her hands, closed her eyes.

A violet wave surged over the big monitor screen, followed and replaced by an orange flame. Then there was a jumbled, indistinguishable image which seemed for a moment to become clear. Waves ripped it apart. The screen turned bright red and began to throb like a heart in panic with Elea's emotion. She raised her head without opening her eyes, took a deep breath and went back to her former posture.

Suddenly the screen held the image of two children. Their backs were to the screen, but their faces could be seen in a vast mirror that also reflected a tree. Between the mirror and the tree, as well as in and under the tree, there was a crowd of people. And facing the mirror, at intervals of a few yards, were some twenty pairs of children, naked from the waist up, decked with chaplets and wristlets of blue flowers and wearing short blue skirts and sandals. At each big toe, as well as at the lobe of each ear, a golden bird's feather, light and soft, had been placed.

The little girl in the foreground, the most beautiful of all, was Elea, recognizable yet different. The difference lay less in her age than in the peace and joy that shone in her face. She was looking at the boy standing beside her. He was blond like wheat ripened in the sun. His smooth hair fell straight to his slender shoulders, whose muscles were already outlining themselves beneath the skin. His hazel eyes were turned towards Elea's blue eyes in the mirror, smiling into them.

The adult Elea spoke, and the Translator translated, "When the Selection was perfect, the two children would recognize each other at once."

The child Elea and the boy were still looking at each other. They were happy and handsome. They recognized each other as if they had always been moving toward this meeting, without haste or impatience, with the certainty that they would come together. They were together, and now they were discovering each other: they were at peace yet marvelling.

Other children and their families were waiting behind them. The brown trunk of the tree was short but of tremendous thickness; its lowest branches almost touched the ground, and its highest formed a dense ceiling. Its thick leaves, bright green streaked with red, could have concealed a man from head to foot. Many people sat or lay stretched out at full length along its branches. Children were jumping from one branch to another like birds. The adults wore clothing of various colours; some of them were fully dressed, others, men and women alike, were clothed only from the waist to the knees. A few women were completely naked. Not all the faces in the crowd were beautiful, but all the bodies were healthy and graceful. They all had virtually the same complexion. There was somewhat more variety in hair colour, which ranged from pure gold to fawn and golden brown. Many of the adult couples were holding hands.

Deep in the mirror there appeared a man wearing a red robe that reached to the ground. He approached a pair of children, performed a brief ceremony and then dismissed them hand in hand. Another pair of children took their place. Other men in red came out of the depth of the mirror and followed his example with other waiting pairs of children.

One of the men in red stepped up to Elea. She looked at him in the mirror. He smiled at her, stood behind her, consulted a disc that he carried in his right hand, and placed his left hand on Elea's shoulder. "Your mother has given you the name of Elea," he said. "Today you have been Selected. Your number is 3-19-07-91. Repeat it."

"3-19-07-91," the child Elea said.

"Now you will receive your key. Hold out your hand in front of you." She put out her left hand, palm up and open. The tips of her fingers touched the tips of their reflection in the mirror. "Tell me who you are."

"I am Elea 3-19-07-91."

The reflection of the hand in the mirror trembled and opened, revealing an already vanishing point of light. An object fell into the outstretched palm. It was a ring—a ring for a child's finger, set with a truncated pyramid the volume of which was not more than a third of that of the pyramid worn by the adult Elea. The man in red took the ring and slipped it onto the middle finger of her right hand.

"Never take it off," he said. "It will grow with you. Grow with it."

Then he stood behind the boy. Elea watched the man and the boy with wide-open eyes, her solemn face alight with trust and strength.

The man looked at his disc, placed his left hand on the boy's left shoulder and said: "Your mother has given you the name of Paikan—"

A burst of redness flooded the screen, destroying the picture, overpowering the face of the child Elea and erasing the sky blue of her eyes, her hope and her joy. The screen went dark. Elea, on the stage, had just snatched the golden circlet from her head.

Hoover grumbled, "And we still don't know what the key is for."

I tried to bring you into our world. Even though—and perhaps even because—you had agreed to cooperate with us, I watched you retreating day by day farther into the past, nearer to the abyss. There was no bridge by which to cross the gulf. There was nothing left behind you but death.

I ordered cherries and peaches sent from South Af-

rica. I sent for a lamb, from which our cook made you chops served with some leaves of lettuce as soft as spring water. You looked at the chops in horror and said, "Is this something cut out of an animal?"

This had never come into my mind. In some embarrassment I answered, "Yes."

You looked at the meat and the salad and the fruit, and you said, "You eat animals! You eat grass! You eat what comes from trees!"

I attempted a smile, and I said, "We are barbarians."

I had roses shipped for you. You thought they were something else that we ate.

———

The key, Elea had said, was the key to everything. The scientists and correspondents crowded into the conference room were able to see for themselves in the sessions that followed. Having regained control of her emotions, Elea was able to show them the life that she had led with Paikan as they grew up together.

After the one-hour war the people of Gondawa remained underground. The shelters had proved their efficacy. In spite of the treaty of Lampa, no one dared to hope that war would never break out again. Wisdom again suggested that this reconstruction be carried out in a safe place.

The underground areas were dug down farther and also broadened. The work uncovered natural caverns, lakes and rivers below the surface of the earth. The employment of universal energy made it possible to exert unlimited power that could take any form. It was used for the re-creation beneath the earth of a richer and more beautiful vegetation than had been destroyed above ground. In light equal to daylight the buried cities became filled with flower beds and shrubs and forests. New species were brought into being, growing so quickly that the naked eye could observe the progress of a tree or a plant. Gentle, silent machinery made its way downward and laterally, causing earth and rock to vanish as it advanced. It levelled surfaces and left behind it polished ceilings and walls and floors that were harder than steel.

The surface now was no longer a place to live but it was put to good use. The small undamaged areas were cared for as preserves and equipped as recreation areas. In one place an area of forest was repopulated with animals; elsewhere there might be a river that had stayed within its own banks, a valley, an ocean beach. The new generation looked on surface expeditions as a great adventure.

Underground, life was orderly, rational and enjoyable. Everything that the people needed was produced by silent factories that produced no waste or pollution. And the basis of the distribution system was the key.

Each year every resident of Gondawa received a credit allocation based on equal division of the factories' output. This credit was recorded by the central computer. It was more than sufficient to enable him to subsist and to enjoy a considerable amount of luxury. Whenever a Gondawan wanted something new— clothes, a journey, goods—he paid with his key. When he pushed his key into a slot provided for the purpose, his account in the central computer was reduced by the price of whatever merchandise or service he had bought.

Certain distinguished citizens of superior status were given an extra credit allowance. But in practice this was of no use to them. Very few Gondawans could find ways of exhausting their annual incomes. Unused credits were automatically cancelled at the end of every year, preventing the accumulation of wealth in individual hands. There were no poor men; there were no rich men: The key system made it possible to distribute the national wealth without infringing the equal rights of all Gondawans or disregarding the disparities in their temperaments: each spent his credit as his needs and tastes dictated.

Once the factories had been erected and put into operation, they functioned without a labour force and with their own brains. But although the factories took care of production, there were still tasks of hand and intellect to be performed. Every Gondawan was required to work a half-day every five days, although his working time could be distributed any way he wished. He could work more than this if he wished. Or, if he preferred, he could work less or not at all. Work was not paid. Anyone who elected to work less than the required minimum suffered a reduction in his annual credit, but those who chose not to work at all still received slightly better than a subsistence income.

The factories were placed at the perimeters of the cities and at their greatest depths. They were all interconnected, forming an enormous super-factory that was constantly creating new sub-sections as it absorbed those that were worn out.

The goods manufactured by the factories were produced by synthesis, not by assembly. The basic raw material was always the same: universal energy. And out of the void the needs and pleasures of life poured into the underground city in a multiple and uninterrupted flow. What does not exist exists.

The key had a further equally important function: it prevented conception. In order to conceive a child, a man and woman had to remove their rings. Fertilization was impossible if either retained his ring, and a child could be born only if both parents wanted it.

Once he had received his ring on the solemn day of his Selection, no Gondawan was ever without it. It provided for all his needs as long as he lived. It was the key to his life, and, when his life was over, his ring remained on his finger as his body was returned to the universal energy. What does not exist exists.

Therefore, the moment when two spouses took off their rings before uniting in the creation of a child was endowed with a special emotion. They felt more than naked, as if they had taken off their skins as well as their rings. From toe to head they were in contact with each other's flesh and blood. They entered into a total communion. He penetrated into her and she fused him. The child was conceived in a single joy.

The key was sufficient to keep the population of Gondawa at a constant level. Enisor did not have the key and did not want it. Enisor was teeming. Enisor knew Zoran's equation and the utilization of universal energy, but she employed them for proliferation and not for balance. Gondawa organized, Enisor multiplied. And Enisor sought to expand its power beyond its own limits. Enisor's space vehicles were the first to land on the moon. Gondawa followed them immediately, so as not to be placed at a disadvantage. For ballistic reasons the eastern face of the moon was best suited for the launching of vehicles for the exploration of the solar system. Enisor built a base there and so did Gondawa. The third war broke out there because of an incident between the garrisons of the two bases. Enisor wanted to be alone on the moon.

But fear ended that war. The treaty of Lampa divided the moon into a Gondawan zone, an Enisorian zone and in the east an international zone. Enisor and Gondawa agreed to build a launching base there.

Other nations had no share in the moon. They sneered at it. Some were under the protection of Enisor, others of Gondawa. The cleverest nations received help from both antagonists, but the large nations had also dropped plenty of bombs on them during the third war, though fewer than on Gondawa and far fewer than on Enisor.

Enisor's population was far too large for any system of shelters to protect it. But in one generation its fertility had replaced all the war victims.

Under the treaty of Lampa, Enisor and Gondawa had pledged themselves never again to use "earth bombs". The bombs that had not been used were sent off into space to orbit around the sun, and the great powers had committed themselves never again to produce such powerful weapons.

But then Enisor began to manufacture individual weapons that made use of universal energy. A single weapon could produce only a limited shock wave, but nothing could stand against a group of them. Enisor's armies were growing larger every day as the density of her population reached and then surpassed its pre-war level.

At this point the Governing Council of Gondawa decided to sacrifice its central city, Gonda 1, for purposes of defence. The city was evacuated, its population resettled elsewhere, and machines went to work at what has been its subterranean site. The Governing Council of Gondawa let it be known that, if a new war with Enisor broke out, it would be *the last*.

Thus, in session after session, the scientists of the EPI became familiar with Elea's vanished world. But for Elea the sessions took on a different importance. She would recall the happiest, the most dramatic moments of her life in order to live them again. She abandoned herself endlessly to her memory and only the scarlet surges of emotion were occasionally able to tear her away from it. But little by little, in the background of her life with Paikan, the scientists discovered the world of Gondawa.

Astride her white horse, as shaggy as a Shetland and as lean as a greyhound, Elea galloped toward the Reprieved Forest as Paikan pursued her. She was laughing as she fled, anticipating the joy of letting him catch her.

Paikan had chosen a blue horse because its eyes were the colour of Elea's. He galloped close behind her, overtaking her gradually, prolonging the pleasure of the chase. His horse thrust its blue nostrils toward the flowing white tail of Elea's mount. The wind whipped the ends of its long silky hairs into the sensitive nostrils. Paikan's horse shook its long head, closed the gap somewhat more, seized a mouthful of the white tail in its teeth and pulled up alongside.

Elea's horse reared and whinnied. Elea was holding him by his mane, gripping him between her strong thighs. She laughed as he leaped and kicked in a dancing movement.

Now Paikan stroked the blue horse, gentling it, until

it let go of the other animal's tail. Side by side the two horses entered the forest at a walking pace, calm but cunning, watching each other cautiously. Elea and Paikan rode holding hands. The forest's trees, survivors of the third war, were like huge pillars armoured in brown bark. Far above the ground their interlaced fronds were a ceiling that the wind rearranged tirelessly, creating sunlit gaps that closed almost immediately with a distant rustle like the sound of many walking feet. Creeping ferns made a rough carpet over the earth. Spotted does raked it with their hooves in search of its tenderest leaves, which they then raised with the edges of their lips and tore away with a sharp twist of the neck. The warm air was rich with the smell of sap and mushrooms.

Elea and Paikan had reached the shore of a lake. They slid down from their horses, which galloped back into the forest chasing each other like schoolboys. There were few other people at the beach. A huge, weary tortoise, its shell cracked, was dragging its heavy body through the sand as a naked child rode its back.

In the distance, on the opposite shore, was the Mouth, a great cavity through which airborne vehicles looking like clusters of multicoloured bubbles entered and left the city of Gonda 7. Some flew quite low over the lake, with a sound like that of silk under a caressing hand.

Elea and Paikan started walking toward the elevators whose entrances emerged from the sand at the end of the beach. But before they had gone far they heard a metallic voice say, "Attention please!" The voice seemed to come simultaneously from the sky, the lake and the forest. It continued:

"Beginning tomorrow the G weapon and the Black Seed will be distributed to adult citizens of Gondawa through the regular mail. Classes in the use of the G weapon will be available in all recreation centres on the Surface and in the Depths."

As the metallic voice began to repeat its announcement, Elea and Paikan continued to walk toward the elevators, heading home. They lived in a Weather Tower above Gonda 7, their Tower and its many counterparts maintaining a system of controlled meteorological conditions over the continent, the purpose of which was to restore the climate that had been thrown out of balance by the war and enable the vegetation to grow again. Elea and Paikan had both become weather engineers so as to be able to live on the surface.

Now they could have summoned a vehicle but they preferred to return home through the city. They chose a two-place elevator, the green cone of which shone softly above the sand. When Paikan and Elea had thrust their keys into the control panel, the elevator opened like a ripe fruit. They entered its pink warmth. They emerged from it at Depth 1 of Gonda 7. Again they used their keys, opening the transparent gates that gave access to Avenue Twelve. The avenue was a mobile platform made of flowered lawn which moved at varying speeds. Low trees served as seats and offered the support of their branches for those travellers who preferred to stand. Flights of yellow birds, similar to gulls, pitted their speed against that of the central strip, singing with pleasure.

Elea and Paikan left the Avenue at the Lake Intersection and followed the path that led to the elevator of their tower. A little stream began at the intersection and flowed alongside the path.

Little light-coloured animals, no bigger than three-month-old kittens, with white bellies, short, flat tails and marsupial pouches, lolled in the grass or hid behind clumps of weeds to ambush the fish in the stream. Now and then a little head with soft, shrewd eyes and

perhaps a fishbone between its teeth would peep out from one of their pouches. They ran in and out among Elea's and Paikan's feet, coming close and then springing aside again just as the edge of a sandal threatened to crush a paw or a tail.

The subterranean Gonda 7 was situated beneath the ruins of the original Gonda 7 that had existed on the surface. All that was left of the old city was great heaps of ruins above which the Weather Tower rose like a flower on a slag heap. A circular terrace with trees, beds of grass, a pool and an anchorage arm in the lee of the wind was suspended at the apex of the long stem of the tower.

The living quarters were surrounded by the terrace. Curving partitions of different heights, broken at intervals, divided it into rooms that were variously circular or oval or irregular. The observatory dome above the living area crowned the tower with a transparent dome faintly tinted with blue. The entrance elevator from the city terminated in the middle room, near a small fountain.

As she entered, Elea opened all the windows; a light evening breeze blew into the apartment from the terrace. Marine plants of many colours swayed in the warm currents of the pool. Elea took off her clothes and slipped into the water. A school of needle-fish, some black, some red, swam around her and pricked at her skin; then, having recognized her, they wandered away.

Paikan, in the observatory, made certain that everything was in order. The dome itself was the apparatus, obedient to Paikan's gestures and operating without him when he so ordered. All was well, the sky was fair, and the dome hummed softly. Paikan undressed and joined Elea in the pool. When she saw him coming she laughed and dived. He caught her behind the rainbow-coloured concealment of a curtainfish that watched them uninterestedly out of a round eye.

They slept on the grass floor of their bedroom, as soft and silky as the fur of a cat's belly. A weightless white blanket, barely thrown over them, adjusted its shape and its temperature to the requirements of their slumber. Elea woke for a second, reached for Paikan's open hand and buried her own smaller one in it. Paikan's hand closed over hers: she sighed happily and went back to sleep.

The shriek of sirens frightened them into wakefulness.

Paikan thrust his key into the television switch. The wall facing them hollowed and brightened. An announcer's face appeared, ". . .—neral alarm. An unregistered satellite is heading toward Gondawa and has not replied to requests for identification. If it remains silent, our defence apparatus will go into action. All residents who are presently outside of the cities should return to the nearest city at once. Please extinguish light that would be visible from the air. Our surface broadcasts are now terminated. That is all." The picture in the wall became two-dimensional, clung a moment to the surface and vanished.

"Should we go down?" Elea asked.

"No. Come with me." Paikan wrapped Elea in the blanket and led her to the terrace. They slipped among the lower leaves of the silky palm tree and made themselves comfortable at the high railing that bordered the terrace.

The sky was black and moonless. The stars glowed brilliantly. The flying vehicles like luminescent bubbles in all their many colours, their size varying with their altitude, were converging toward the Mouth as though they were carried by a single air current.

On the ground the alarm had awakened the people in the flying resort houses moored on the plain, among the ruins and beside the lake. Their translucent shells adorned the night with coloured shapes—a goldfish, a blue flower, a red egg, a green spindle, a sphere, a star, a polyhedron, a teardrop. Some were taking off and heading for the Mouth. The others quickly went dark. A white snake was still illuminated, its light falling on a fragment of wall.

"What are they waiting for?" Elea muttered.

"In any case it's useless," Paikan said. "If the satellite is an attack weapon, it has plenty of other ways of finding its target."

"Do you think it is one?"

"That would be unlikely—" Suddenly a streak of light shot into the sky from the horizon. Then there were two more, then three, then four. "They're firing!" Paikan said.

He and Elea looked up toward the sky. Elea shivered, opened the blanket and pulled Paikan close to her. Suddenly, very high in the sky, they saw a new, gigantic star: it broke apart and spread out in a slow curtain of ionized pink light.

"That's it!" Paikan said. "They couldn't have missed it!"

"What do you think it was?"

"I don't know. Maybe a scout vehicle. Or just a poor unlucky freighter whose transmitters weren't working. Anyway, it's gone."

The sirens made them jump again, a horrible sound to which no one ever becomes accustomed. But now they were announcing the all-clear. The resort houses turned on their lights again. In the distance a bevy of vehicles rose out of the Mouth like a fountain of sparks.

The picture began to reappear on the bedroom wall,

but neither Elea nor Paikan wanted to leave the sheltering dark. Paikan placed his key in a panel on the railing. The picture left the bedroom wall and moved outdoors. Paikan guided it by turning the movable panel and settled it in the foliage of a tree. He sat down on the grass, his back to the rail, and held Elea close to him. Their faces were touched by a soft breeze that enveloped the tower from the west. Silky leaves rustled and undulated in the gentle current. Now the three-dimensional picture was bright and stable but it was impossible to understand a single word the announcer said. A black cube surged up at the bottom of the picture, then filled the whole receiver and blotted out the announcer. Inside the cube appeared the excited face of a very young man. His dark eyes were aflame with emotion; his flat, almost black hair did not fall farther than his ears.

"A student!" Elea said.

He was talking excitedly. ". . . peace! Preserve peace for us. There's never any justification for war! Ever! But war has never been more barbaric and absurd than it is today, just as man is about to win the fight against death! Are we going to slaughter one another for the moon? Mars? Ridiculous! Let Enisor nibble away at the solar system. She won't devour everything. Let her fight infinity! We are fighting a far more important battle here. Why does the Governing Council keep you in ignorance of Coban's work? I tell you, in the name of those who have worked with him for years, he has won! It is done! A fly has been living for 545 days in a test tube at the university: its normal life span is forty days! It's alive, it's healthy . . . A year and a half ago it was fed the first experimental dose of Coban's universal serum. Let Coban go on with his work! His serum has been perfected. Soon the machines will be able to manufacture it. Then no one will grow old any more! Death will be infinitely remote, unless someone kills you—unless there is a war! Demand that the Governing Council reject war and make peace with Enisor. That it let Coban continue his work. That—"

In a fraction of a second his image shrank and then disappeared. The regular announcer took his place, a transparent ghost at first and then a solid figure: "—forgive this pirate interruption—" He was swallowed again by the black cube, which once more opened on the vehement young man: "—bombs in orbit, but they have invented something worse! Can the Governing Council tell you what monstrous weapon is on the launching pad of Gonda 1? The Enisorians are men like ourselves! What will be left of the world if this—"

The cube turned black again, telescoped into two dimensions and was replaced by the head and shoulders of the regular announcer. "—chairman of the Governing Council will speak to you."

Chairman Lokan appeared. His thin face was serious and unhappy. His white hair fell to his shoulders, one of which, the left, was bare. His sensitive mouth and his very light blue eyes made an attempt to smile as he uttered words of reassurance. Yes, there had been incidents in the international zone on the moon; yes, the continent's defence apparatus had destroyed a suspicious satellite; yes, the Governing Council had had to take steps, but none of this was really serious. No one was more resolutely committed to peace than the men whose task it was to guide the destinies of Gondawa. Every effort would be made to avoid war.

"Coban," the chairman continued, "is my friend, almost my son. I am thoroughly familiar with his work. The Council is awaiting the results of his experiments on human beings and, if they are affirmative, it will immediately order the production of the universal serum. This is a great expectation, but it must not distract us from vigilance. As for the weapon that is on the launching pad at Gonda 1, Enisor knows what it is, and I will tell you only this: it is so terrifying a weapon that its mere existence should assure us of peace."

Paikan touched the control panel and the picture disappeared. Day was breaking. A bird not unlike a blackbird, except that its feathers were blue and its tail was curled, began to sing from the top of the tree. Birds of every colour replied from all the trees and shrubs on the terrace. For them there was no dread by day or by night. There were no hunters in Gondawa.

When they had eaten and bathed, Elea and Paikan walked up the short interior ramp to the working dome. Above the horizontal shelf that made a semicircle along the transparent wall, images of clouds in the process of formation were continually changing. Now one of these cloud-images began to worry Paikan, and he put in a call to the Weather Central. A new image appeared over the shelf, the tired face of Mikan, his superior. Mikan's long grey hair was lifeless and his eyes were red. After exchanging greetings with Paikan, he asked, "Were you at home last night?"

"Yes."

"You saw what went on? It brought back some sad memories. But we can't just let the bastards do as they like! Of course neither of you had been born then. . . . Why did you call me? Is something wrong?"

"This looks like the beginnings of a storm." Paikan spread three fingers and made a gesture; one of the cloud pictures was transmitted to Weather Central.

"I agree," Mikan said. "I don't like it. It can foul up our whole system if it's allowed to develop. What possibilities are open to us?"

"We can divert it or we can eliminate it completely."

"All right, eliminate it; I don't like it at all." Mikan signed off and his image vanished.

A mobile resort house in the shape of a blue cone changed course abreast of the dome, landing beside the wrecked superhighway whose twelve devastated lanes reared up defying the sky. The highways had never been repaired, for the factories were no longer making wheeled or treaded vehicles. Sub-surface transportation was provided by moving platforms and elevators; transportation above ground was entirely by air.

The young couples of the post-war generation who used the ground-level resort facilities neglected much of their potential. They no more dared to venture away from the Mouths than young kangaroos to wander out of sight of their mothers' pouches. That was why there were such concentrations of the mobile houses near the ruins of the old cities, which as a rule were directly above their underground successors.

When Elea looked to see whether the mail had come, the transparent box contained two G weapons and two tiny spheres, each of which held a Black Seed, as well as three message plaques, two of which were red—the colour of official messages. Elea opened the box with her key. She removed the weapons and the Seeds with revulsion, and laid them on a table. "Do you want to hear the mail?" she called to Paikan.

He left the weather dome to carry on its work unattended, frowning as he picked up the red plaques. One, marked with his name, bore the seal of the Defense Ministry; the other was addressed to Elea and bore the seal of the university.

But Elea had already slid the single green plaque into the slot of the reading machine. Elea's mother's face now materialized above the reading machine. It was hardly older than Elea's and looked very much like hers, though with something more frivolous about it.

"Hello, Elea," she said. "I hope you're well; I am. I'm leaving for Gonda 41. Your brother was mobilized in the middle of the night to lead a troop transport to the moon and we've heard nothing more from him for a week. Of course that's the way the military are. But Anea is all alone with her baby and she's worried. They could at least have waited a little while before they took off their keys! It's hardly been ten years since they were selected. Try not to be like them; you have plenty of time and this is hardly when you should be making children. Well, that's the way it is. I can't do anything about it, so I'm leaving. I'll get in touch with you. Spend a little time with your father—he can't come with me because he's been mobilized at his job. I think the Council and the military are all crazy. Anyway, go see your father and try to keep an eye on him; when he's alone he uses the food machine without thinking, he doesn't pay any attention to anything, he's just like a child. Good-bye Elea, I'll be getting in touch with you."

"Forkan mobilized, and your father too!" Paikan said. "It's unbelievable. What are they preparing for?" Apprehensively he inserted one of the red plates in the reading machine. The Defense Ministry's emblem appeared above it: a hedgehog rolled into a ball, his quills shooting flames.

"Attention, Paikan," an impersonal voice began. It recited an order mobilizing him at his post to continue his work.

When the other red plate was inserted in the reading machine, the university's seal appeared: the symbol for Zoran's equation. "Attention, Elea," a solemn voice said. "This is Coban."

"Coban!"

His face took the place of Zoran's equation. Every Gondawan knew his face; he was the most famous man on the continent. He had discovered a serum, rapidly put into universal use, which would make a man highly resistant to all diseases; another of his discoveries enabled its users to recover from exertion with such rapidity that the concept of fatigue was fading out of the Gondawan language.

Coban's face was thin and hollow-cheeked. His great black eyes were bright and piercing. He was known as a man who thought only of others, a student of Life itself, its wonders and its horrors. He worked with all his intelligence and all his strength. At the age of thirty-two he looked as young as his students, who idolized him and imitated the way he kept his black hair cut short.

"Attention, Elea," he repeated. "This is Coban speaking. I wanted to inform you of this personally. In the event of total mobilization, at my request, you will be assigned to a special position with me at the university. I don't know you and I would like to meet you. I would appreciate your coming to Laboratory 51 as soon as possible. Give your name and your number and you will be immediately brought into my office. I am expecting you."

Elea and Paikan looked at each other in bewilderment. There were two conflicting elements in this message: " . . . you will be assigned at my request . . ." and "I don't know you . . ." Now there was a danger that they would be mobilized in assignments that would keep them far apart. They had never been separated since their Selection; they found it beyond imagining.

"I'll go with you to see Coban," Paikan said. "If he really needs you, I'll ask him to take me too. Anyone can take over for me in the Tower."

It was simple; and it was possible, if Coban was amenable. The university was the prime force in the state. No administrative or military authority outranked it. It had its own independent budget, its own armed guard, its own broadcasting facilities; it did not have to account to anyone. As for Coban himself, although he held no political office, the Governing Council of Gondawa never made a major decision without consulting him.

In any case there was no hurry. The very notion of war was an absurd and improbable horror; one mustn't allow oneself to believe the official hysteria. The bureaucrats, sealed away as they were in their underground headquarters, had lost their sense of reality.

"They ought to come up here a little more often, look at what's on the surface," Elea said.

The morning sun was bathing the ruins, dominated in the west by an overturned, shattered stadium. To the east the twisted superhighway thrust into the glassy-smooth plain, where not a single blade of grass had been able to grow again.

Paikan put his arm around Elea's shoulders and held her close. "Let's go to the forest," he said.

He placed his key in the communication panel, called the Vehicle Pool at Depth 1 and asked for a taxi. The transparent bubble alighted on the anchorage arm of the tower a few minutes later. As he passed the table, Paikan picked up the two weapons. Then he called Weather Central. Now that he had been mobilized, he could no longer leave his post without notice.

———

"Have you noticed?" said Hoover to Leonova, "They're all left-handed." He was speaking in a low voice, covering his microphone with his hand. Leonova understood English very well.

What he had said was true. It was obvious now that he had called it to her attention, and she was annoyed that she had not realized it on her own. The weapons found in Elea's pedestal and in Coban's were in the form of gloves for the left hand. And at this very moment the picture on the big screen showed Elea and Paikan in a group of Gondawans being trained in the use of similar weapons. They were all shooting with their left hands at metal targets that sprang suddenly into the air. It was an exercise in skill and control, for the G weapon could bend a blade of grass or pulverize stone, disintegrate an adversary or merely knock him out, depending on the amount of pressure exerted by the three flexed fingers.

Suddenly an oval target appeared ten paces ahead of Paikan. It was blue: this meant that he must fire with minimal force. His left hand darted to the weapon, which was attached to his belt by a magnetic plate. He drew it, raised his arm and fired. The target made a sound like a harp string brushed by a finger and disappeared. Paikan broke into a laugh. He had come to terms with the weapon, and the training was now a pleasant game.

Almost immediately he was confronted with a red target; at the same time a green one appeared at Elea's left. She made a quarter turn and fired. Paikan, taken by surprise, had barely time to fire before the targets vanished. The red target echoed like thunder, the green one pealed like a bell. Everywhere targets were rising out of the ground, echoing with the impact of the weapons.

One of the university's aircraft appeared over the training ground and hovered for a moment before it landed quietly behind the marksmen. It was a fast machine, spearhead-shaped, with a transparent cabin that bore the sign of Zoran's equation.

Two university militiamen stepped out of it, wearing green breast plates and skirts. G weapons hung from the left side of their belts and S grenades at the right; oxygen masks were slung around their necks. They began to move among the marksmen, asking questions, while the marksmen looked at them in amazement and anxiety: they had never seen university guards so heavily armed.

The two guards were looking for Elea.

"I'm coming with her," Paikan said.

Since the guards had been given no conflicting instructions, they allowed him to come. Their vehicle shot like an arrow across the lake to the Mouth, where it dropped vertically through the channel leading to the university. It slowed down at the exit to the Vehicle Pool, hovered low over the central runway, took a feeder lane and arrived at the gate to the laboratories which opened to admit it and then closed behind it.

The simplicity of the university's streets and buildings stood out from the luxuriance of the rest of the city. Here there were only bare walls, roofs without a flower or leaf. There was no decoration on the trapezoidal doors, not even a tiny trickle of water on the surface of the white streets, not a bird in the air, not a startled deer, not a butterfly, not a white rabbit. The area was designed for the austerity of abstract knowledge; the moving platform here had manufactured seats and metal railings.

Elea and Paikan were struck by the abnormal activity that filled the street beneath them. University guards in battle dress, their hair pinned back and helmets on their heads, crowded the moving platforms. Different coloured signals blinked above doors, names and numbers re-echoed, laboratory workers in salmon-pink gowns rushed along, their long hair bound up inside hermetically sealed scarfs. This was not the Theoretical

Studies district; it was the Experiment and Research area. No student showed his bare feet and short hair here.

The vehicle came to rest on one point of a star-shaped intersection. Paikan followed as one of the guards conducted Elea to Laboratory 51, where they were shown into a bare room in which a man in a salmon-coloured gown was waiting for them. Zoran's equation, printed in red on the right side of his gown, identified him as a laboratory chief.

"Are you Elea?" he asked.

"Yes, I am."

"And who are you?"

"I am Paikan."

"What business do you have here?"

"I belong with Elea," Paikan said.

"And I belong with Paikan," said Elea.

The laboratory chief thought for a moment. "Paikan was not sent for," he said. "Coban wants to see Elea."

"I want to see Coban," Paikan replied.

"I will let him know that you are here. Please wait."

"I'm coming with Elea," Paikan said.

There was a silence, then the man repeated, "I will tell Coban. But before she sees him, Elea must have a medical examination. Please step into this booth, Elea." He opened a translucent door, and Elea recognized the standard booth in which every resident of Gondawa was placed at least once a year in order to check his physiological condition.

"Is this necessary?" she asked.

"It is," he said.

She went into the booth and sat down on the bench inside. The door closed automatically, and instruments came alight around her. Coloured lights flashed over her face, the analyzer buzzed, the synthesizer clicked. Then the examination was over. Elea rose and tried to open the door. It would not move. Astonished, she pushed harder, with no result.

"Paikan!" she called apprehensively.

She could hear his voice through the door. She tried again to open the door, becoming progressively more frightened. "Paikan! The door!" she shouted.

He rushed forward. She saw his profile crash into the translucent panel. The booth shuddered and broken instruments fell to the floor, but the door did not give. The wall of the booth behind Elea opened.

"Come in, Elea," Coban said.

Two women stood facing Coban. One was Elea. The other was a very beautiful brunette, more fully fleshed than Elea. While Elea argued and demanded that Paikan be allowed to come to her the other woman sat silent, watching her sympathetically.

"Wait, Elea," Coban said. "Wait until you know more." He was wearing a severe salmon-coloured laboratory gown on which Zoran's equation appeared in white. He paced up and down the room, barefoot like a student, moving silently among the desks, past the perforated wall that held thousands of reading reels. Elea was silent, too intelligent to persist in a futile endeavour. She waited for Coban to speak.

"The public doesn't know what has been done to the site of Gonda 1," he said, "but I'm going to tell you. Gonda 1 was converted to a launching site for the Solar Weapon. In spite of all my arguments, the Council has decided to use the Weapon if Enisor attacks us. And my contacts tell me that Enisor has decided to attack us in order to destroy it before we can use it. If we use the Weapon, it will be as if the sun itself had fallen on Enisor; the rocks will burn and melt; the entire earth will feel the shock. And I believe that the use of the weapon could mean the end of life on earth.

"But because of the enormous size and complexity of the Weapon, a half-day must elapse between the start of the launching procedure and the time when the Weapon leaves its site. What happens during that half-day will determine the fate of the world."

He had stopped his pacing while he spoke; now he began to move again, like a caged animal. "If the Enisorians succeed in preventing the launching of the Weapon," he continued, "they will destroy us. They outnumber us ten times over, and they are more aggressive. Our only defence against them has been to frighten them. But we've frightened them too much.

"They're going to attack with everything they have, and we have made them so angry and afraid that, if they win, they will leave none of us alive. That is why the Black Seed has been distributed to the residents of Gondawa. So that those who are captured may die by their own hands rather than by the executioners of Enisor—"

Elea rose belligerently. "This is absurd! It must be possible to prevent this war. Why don't you do something instead of whimpering? Destroy the Weapon! Go to Enisor, they'll listen to you!"

Coban stopped his pacing again and stood before her. He looked at her gravely and with satisfaction. "You have been well chosen," he said.

"Chosen for what?"

But he answered only her first question. "I *am* doing something. I have emissaries in Enisor, and I've made contact with the scientists of Enisor's Knowledge District. There are people in Enisor who understand the risks of such a war. If they can gain power they'll preserve the peace, but we have little time left. I'm going to try to persuade the Council to renounce the use of the Solar Weapon and to communicate the fact to Enisor. But I have the military against me, and

Mozran, the minister who sponsored the Weapon, *wants to see it operate!*

"In case all these methods fail I will have made other preparations. And that is why you have been chosen, both of you. I want to make sure Life is not destroyed.

"If the Solar Weapon operates even a few seconds more than is expected, the earth will be so shaken that the oceans will pour out of their beds and continents will be torn apart. No one knows where the disasters will stop. Mozran has never dared to test the Weapon, even on a small scale, but we may expect the worst."

"Attention, Coban," a voice said. "Here are the latest news reports: The Enisorian troops garrisoned on the moon have invaded the international zone. A military convoy on its way from Gonda 3 to our lunar zone has been intercepted by Enisorian forces before it could land. Our troops have destroyed part of the attacking force, and fighting is continuing. Our long-range observation has evidence that Enisor has recalled the nuclear bombs that she had placed in orbit around the sun. That is all."

"This is only the beginning," Coban murmured.

"I *insist* on going back to Paikan," Elea said. "If I must die I want to die with him."

"But listen to what I've done," Coban said. "I've constructed a shelter that can withstand almost anything. I have stocked it with seeds and fertilized ova which I can bring to life again in incubators. I've gathered over ten thousand knowledge reels, thousands of artifacts of our civilization, and all the tools one would need to build it up again. And in the heart of the shelter I will place a man and a woman. The central computer has selected five women for their physical and psychological fitness. Number One was killed yesterday in an accident. Number Four, who is travelling in Enisor, cannot get home. Number Five lives in Gonda 62 and although I've sent for her, I'm afraid that she won't be able to get here in time. Number Two, Lona, is you and Number Three is Elea."

He paused briefly, with a semblance of a weary smile, then turned to Lona. "Naturally there will be only one woman in the Shelter. It will be you, Lona." Lona rose, but, before she could say anything, a voice came into the room.

"Attention, Coban: the examination of Lona, Number Two, shows a slightly altered metabolism and a change in the hormonal balance. It appears that she is two weeks pregnant."

"Did you know this?" asked Coban.

"No," Lona said, "but I was hoping. We removed our keys on the third night of spring."

"I'm sorry for your sake," Coban said, spreading his hands. "This means that you are eliminated from the selection. The Shelter will keep its occupants in hibernation at a temperature of absolute zero, and it is conceivable that your pregnancy would threaten the success of the undertaking. I can't accept such a risk. Please go back to your home. Say nothing of what I have told you, even to your Chosen, for the next twenty-four hours. Within that time, everything will have been settled."

He gestured to the two guards at the door. They stood aside to allow Lona to leave, and Coban turned to Elea. "It will be you, then," he said.

Elea felt as though she were turning to stone. Then her blood began to roar through her veins and her face reddened. She forced herself to remain calm. Once more Coban began to speak. "The computer described you as balanced, quick-minded, strong-willed, aggressive."

Now she felt that she could speak again. "Why did

you keep Paikan outside? I won't go into your Shelter without him."

Coban shook his head. "The man who will emerge from the Shelter in a few years, or even perhaps a century or two, must be acquainted with all of the knowledge inscribed on the reels and, if possible, even more than that. He must be able to bring the world back to life. Paikan is intelligent, but there are limits to his knowledge. He wouldn't even be able to interpret Zoran's equation."

"Which man was chosen, then?"

"As with the women, the computer has chosen five."

"Who is the first choice?"

"I am."

"So America was Enisor," Leonova said to Hoover. "You were imperialists even then."

"My love," Hoover said, "we Americans are nothing but displaced Europeans, your distant travelling cousins. I really wish Elea would show us what those first Americans looked like. So far all we've seen has been Gondawans."

Elea showed them Enisorians. She and Paikan had made a trip to Diaydohu, the capital of central Enisor, for the Cloud Festival. She displayed her memories for the scientists.

With Elea they looked out of a long-distance aircraft to see a chain of immense mountains on the horizon. When they came closer they saw that mountain and city were one. Built of huge blocks of stone, the city clung to the mountain, covered it, outran it, used it as a base from which to thrust its tallest spire into the sky:

the monolith of the Temple, the summit of which was always hidden by clouds.

They saw the Enisorians at work and play. The needs of the population were so great that construction had to go on even on a holiday like this day of the Cloud Festival. Unceasingly the builders went on enlarging the city, carving streets and staircases and squares out of the still virgin flanks of the mountain, building retaining walls and new dwellings. On their breasts, hanging from golden collars, they wore the effigy of the fiery serpent, the Enisorian symbol of universal energy. It was not a symbol alone; it was a device allowing its wearer to control powerful natural forces. The EPI scientists watching the large screen saw Enisorian construction crews lift blocks of stone that must have weighed tons, place them one on another, align them, shape them, split them with the edge of a hand, polish them with a palm, as though they were modelling clay.

Foreigners who had been invited to attend the Cloud Festival were not allowed to land. Their vehicles remained hovering, ranked in curving tiers in the sky at the borders of Diaydohu like the varicoloured levels of a strange stadium floating in the void.

Facing them they could see the Temple, whose arrowlike spire—a single stone, soaring higher than the highest skyscrapers of modern America—buried its tip in the Cloud. A monumental stairway carved into the rock spiralled upward along its length. For hours a great crowd had been climbing this staircase toward the summit of the Temple. The massing of their colourful garments transformed them into an image of the fiery serpent along the stair. Its body followed, wrapping itself around the Spire as it moved. The crowd must have contained many hundreds of thousands of persons, perhaps more than a million. Through the aircraft's open windows the spectators could hear the mu-

sic of the serpent's movement. It was a harsh, slow
panting that seemed to come from the mountain itself
and merged with the deep sounds of the crowds on the
Spire, the masses of people that filled the other stairs
and the streets.

When the serpent's head finally arrived at the cloud,
the sun was setting behind the mountain: the serpent's
head entered the cloud in dim twilight. A few minutes
later it was completely dark. Searchlights throughout
the city were trained on the Spire. The rhythm of the
music and the chant became faster. *Then the Spire began to move.* Or perhaps the Cloud was moving. The
Spire thrust into the Cloud, the Cloud impaled itself on
the Spire, pulling back and thrusting again, the rhythm
becoming faster as in a supernatural coupling between
Heaven and Earth.

The panting of the music was faster and harder now;
the hovering aircraft rose and fell with the waves of
sound. On the ground the labourers had stopped their
work. In apartment buildings, houses and streets, men
and women approached each other at random. They
embraced; they lay down together wherever they were,
moving in unison with the single rhythms that shook
the mountain. The Spire plunged its whole length into
the cloud. The mountain fissured, the city rose, freed of
its weight and ready to thrust itself into the sky. The
Cloud burst into flame, erupted in thunderclaps; then it
darkened and receded. Once more the city weighed
down on the mountain. The Spire was naked, and the
crowd was gone from the great stone stair. The random
couples, wherever they lay, broke their embraces and
separated. Some got to their feet and moved off alone;
others fell asleep where they were. For a few fleeting,
stifling moments they had shared the same cosmic pleasure. And thus it came to pass once each year in all the
cities of Enisor.

The EPI scientists interrogated Elea. What had happened to the people on the stair?

"The Spire gave them to the Cloud," Elea said, "and the Cloud returned them to Universal Energy. But all those who climbed the Spire died willingly. Their fate had been decided for them since childhood, sometimes because they showed some defect of mind or body, and sometimes because they were more intelligent, stronger, more beautiful than the average Enisorian. They were brought up solely for the purpose of this sacrifice, and they learned to long for the day it would come to pass. Although they had the right to refuse it, only a very small number did. Enisor used the Cloud Festival to rid itself of genetic undesirables. But the number of people sacrificed could not compensate for the increase in population that the Festival caused. Twenty times as many Enisorians were conceived during the Cloud Festival as were killed on all the Spires on the continent."

"But all those good ladies must have given birth on the same day!" said Hoover.

"No," Elea explained, "the gestation period in Enisor ranged from one to three seasons, depending on the mother's preference and her age. There were no Selections, and hence no couples and no families. Men and women lived jumbled together in a state of absolute equality of rights and duties in communal apartment buildings or in individual houses. Children were brought up by the state. They never knew their parents."

Even though Elea's vehicle had hovered far above the ground, its magnifying window had enabled the scientists to see in detail a large number of faces in the crowd. The Enisorians had smooth black hair, slit eyes, prominent cheekbones. Their noses were hooked at the top and splayed at the bottom. They were unquestionably the shared ancestors of the Mayas, the Aztecs and

151

other American Indians and perhaps of the Japanese, the Chinese and all the Mongolian races as well.

"There are your imperialists!" Hoover muttered to Leonova.

———

"It's not mankind or civilization that you want to save: it's your own life," Elea said. "And you've had the Computer pick out the five most beautiful women on the continent so that you can choose one to be saved with you!"

"I'll show you someone I would have chosen to be saved with me," Coban said with sorrow, "if I had felt that I had the right." He activated a wave-cluster. The picture of a little girl who looked remarkably like Coban appeared above his desk. She knelt on a lawn beside a lake at Depth Nine, fondling a fawn with deep-set eyes. Long black hair, like a boy's, fell over her bare shoulders. Her graceful arms were around the animal's neck as it nuzzled at her ear.

"This is my daughter, Doa," Coban said. "She is twelve years old. All the other girls of her age have long since had companions. But she is alone because, like me, she is unselected. The Computer was never able to find a woman who could have tolerated me and wouldn't have irritated me with the slowness of her mind. You see, a certain quickness of the mental faculties can sentence one to solitude. Doa's mother was also unselected. She was a woman of great intelligence but her character was difficult. I asked her to bear me a child because of her intelligence and her beauty, and she agreed, on condition that she might remain with me so that we could bring up the child together. I thought it would be feasible. We took off our keys, but a few days later we had to separate. She was intelligent enough to recognize that she could never find happiness with anyone, even her own child. When it was born she sent it to me.

"Doa too, when her time came, was rejected by the Computer. She is a very affectionate girl, but her intelligence is superior to mine. She will never find her equal anywhere. If she lives . . ." Coban's voice died away, and he turned off the picture.

"Don't you think I love Doa at least as much as you love Paikan?" he resumed. "Don't you think I want to take her into the Shelter with me? Can't you imagine that I want to stay with her and let the next man in line take my place? But I know him; I know the worth of his knowledge and of my own. The Computer was right in choosing me. There is no question of love or feelings or self. We are confronted with a duty that transcends us. You and I must survive, to rebuild the world."

"Listen to me carefully, Coban," Elea said. "I don't care at all about the world, or mankind. Without Paikan I have no more world, and no more life. Let me take Paikan into the Shelter and I will bless you through all eternity!"

"No," Coban answered.

"Let me have Paikan! Stay with your daughter. Don't desert her!"

"I cannot," Coban said in a muffled voice. His face showed his resolution and his grief. He had come through a struggle that had left him shattered, but his decision had been made once and for all. Coban had been unable to build a larger shelter. The government had shown no interest in Coban's project; it had allowed him to go ahead but it had refused to help him. The university had created the Shelter with its wealth of energy, the resources of its machines and its laboratories, but its wealth had only sufficed to provide shelter space for two. A third would condemn all three to perish. Even a small third, even Doa.

"Take some other woman!" Elea cried. "There are millions."

"No," Coban said, "there are not millions. There were five, and now there is only you. Let's not discuss it any further, I beg you; the decision is made."

"I hate you," Elea said.

"I don't love you either. That doesn't matter very much."

"Attention, Coban," a voice called. "Chairman Lokan wishes to speak to you."

Lokan's image appeared in a corner of the room and Coban shifted it so that it faced him across his desk. Lokan was almost in a state of panic. "Listen, Coban, have you been able to contact your associates in the Knowledge District of Enisor?"

"I'm expecting a report any minute."

"It's impossible to wait any longer! The Enisorians are bombarding our lunar and Martian bases with nuclear bombs. We have reinforcements on the way and we're going to retaliate. But that isn't the worst that's happening ... An Enisorian invasion army is forming up on its launching pads, and it will be dropping on Gondawa in a few hours! When I hear that the first troops have taken off, I'll activate the launch mechanism of the Solar Weapon—but I'm like you, Coban: the Solar Weapon frightens me. Perhaps there's still time to save the peace. The Enisorian government knows that attacking us will mean the destruction of its people. But either it doesn't care or it expects to be able to destroy the Weapon before we can launch it. Only the Knowledge District people might be able to stop the attack. There's not even half a second left to lose, Coban! I implore you: try to reach them!"

"I can't reach them directly. I'll call Partao in Lamoss."

Chairman Lokan's image vanished. Coban thrust his key into a panel. "Attention," he snapped. "Get me Partao in Lamoss."

"Lamoss plans to remain neutral," Coban explained to Elea. "But in this war neutrality will be no protection. Partao is the head of the Lamossian university. He's my contact with the Knowledge District people."

Partao's image appeared where Chairman Lokan's had been. Partao had just spoken with Professor Sutaku in the District. "He can't do anything more," Partao said, "and he's beside himself. He's going to try to call you directly."

A pale image appeared beside Partao's. It was Sutaku, in the gown and the round hat of an academician. He seemed bewildered and he gestured as he spoke, striking himself on the chest and pointing his outstretched finger at something invisible in the distance. But what he was saying was inaudible; an interflow of coloured surfaces sliced his image into sections, vibrated, blended, separated. Then he disappeared.

"I have nothing more to tell you," Partao said. "I wish you good luck."

Coban replied, "This time there will be no luck for anyone."

He called Lokan and brought him up to date, promising to attend the Council meeting that was about to begin. Then he turned to Elea, who had been watching him in silence.

"There you are," he said in a voice like ice. "Now you know where we stand. You and I will enter the Shelter tonight; my assistants will prepare you for it. Among other things, you will receive the only existing dose of a serum that I have been synthesizing in my private laboratory, molecule by molecule, over the past six months. I was the experimental subject for the first dose. If by some miracle war doesn't break out, you will still have become the first woman to enjoy perpetual youth. And I promise you that if that is the case the next batch will be given to Paikan. The serum will make it possible for us to survive absolute zero without danger. Now I'm going to turn you over to my staff."

Elea jumped up and ran towards the door. Her left fist struck one guard a dreadful blow. The man dropped. His colleague grabbed Elea's wrist and twisted it behind her back.

"Let her go!" Coban shouted. "I forbid you to touch her."

The guard released her and she rushed for the door again. But it wouldn't open.

"Elea," Coban said, "if you will submit to the treatment without struggling I will let you see Paikan again before you enter the Shelter. My assistants have told him what has happened to you, and they have taken him back home. He's waiting to hear from you. If you protest, if you struggle and thus risk flaws in your preparation, I will put you to sleep and you will never see him again."

Elea looked at Coban silently and took a deep breath. "You can have your men sent in," she said. "I won't move."

Coban pressed a button. Part of a wall slid away, giving access to a laboratory filled with guards and technicians, among whom Elea recognized the laboratory chief who had greeted her and Paikan. He pointed to a seat in front of him. "Come here, Elea," he said.

Elea started towards the laboratory but suddenly she turned back to face Coban. "I hate you," she wailed.

"When we come out of the Shelter to the dead earth," he replied, "hate and love will no longer matter."

Hoi-To had gone down into the egg with some new photographic equipment, hoping to illuminate the area below the egg's transparent floor sufficiently well to be able to photograph it. He surveyed the area around him while his assistants were arranging the floodlights on low tripods. The surface of the walls seemed strangely irregular. He ran the tips of his long sensitive fingers over the surface, and then his fingernails. They caught.

He ordered a floodlight trained on the wall at close range, and improvised a microscope with several of his lenses. The surface of the wall was etched with innumerable ridges. And each of these ridges was a line of Gondawan script. The wall of the egg, completely covered with microscopic symbols, contained the equivalent of a respectable library.

Hoi-To hurriedly made a few photographs of various points on the wall. An hour later, they were being viewed on the big screen. Lukos identified fragments of a historical narrative, a scientific treatise, a poem, a dialogue that might have been either part of a play or a philosophical discussion. The wall of the egg was a veritable encyclopedia of Gondawan culture.

One of Hoi-To's photographs contained a number of isolated items that Lukos recognized as mathematical symbols. They surrounded the symbol of Zoran's equation.

They had examined her from head to foot, weighed her almost to the last microgram, fed, irrigated, massaged, balanced, lulled her into total passivity. Then they explained to her the mechanism by which the Shelter could be opened and closed; and finally they gave her the universal serum. She felt a new energy infusing her body; she was strong, serene, at peace. She relaxed and felt herself drifting into sleep.

When she awakened she was lying on a fur coverlet laid on a soft, warm couch that floated in the void. She opened her eyes to find that she was in a bare, round room. A guard was sitting beside its one door, watching her. Something made of thin tubes of glass interwoven in complex swirling patterns dangled between his fingers. The frail tubes were filled with a green liquid.

"Now that you're not asleep any longer," the guard said, "let me warn you: if you try to force your way out of here, I'll drop this thing on the floor. When the glass breaks, it'll release a vapour that will put you right to sleep."

Elea made no answer; she only continued to look at him.

The guard was tall, broad-shouldered and barrel-chested. His pinned-back hair was the colour of newly cast bronze. He was bareheaded and, except for the glass object, unarmed. His thick neck was almost as broad as his heavy face; his hands and arms were incredibly muscular.

"Attention, Elea," a voice said. "Paikan requests to speak to you. We have granted him permission."

The image of Paikan appeared between her and the guard. Elea leaped up and cried his name. He was standing in the dome where he worked; she could see part of a shelf and the image of a cloud beside him.

"Where are you, Elea? Why did you leave me?"

"I refused to leave you, Paikan. I belong with you. Coban forced me! They're keeping me here."

"I'll come and find you. I'll kill them!" He shook his left hand, buried in the weapon.

"You can't. You don't know where I am. Wait for me! I'll come back to you."

"I'll be waiting for you." Paikan's image vanished.

An express vehicle from the university was waiting on the anchorage arm at the Tower. The university guards it had carried were searching the living quarters and the dome. On the terrace, near the tree, Coban was talking to Paikan. He had just told Paikan of Elea's flight and explained why he needed her.

"She destroyed whatever tried to stop her: men, doors, walls!" Coban said. "We could follow her trail as far as the street, but there we lost track of her."

The guards interrupted Coban to report that Elea was not in the apartment or the dome. He ordered them to search the terrace and turned back to Paikan. "I doubt very much whether she's here," he told Paikan. "She knows this is the first place I would look for her. But I know that she has only one desire, and that is to be with you. Eventually she will let you know where she is, and then we will be able to pick her up. That is inevitable. But it will make us lose a great deal of time. If she calls you, make her understand that she must go back to the university."

"No."

Coban stared at him sombrely and sadly. "You are

159

no genius, Paikan, but you're intelligent. Do you belong with Elea?"

"I do."

"If she comes into the Shelter with me she will live. If she does not, she will die. Elea is intelligent and strong-willed; it may be that, in spite of all our vigilance, she will succeed in rejoining you. Then it is your job to persuade her to return to me. With me she will live; with you she will die. The Shelter means life. Which do you prefer? That she live without you or that she die with you?"

Furious, Paikan shouted, "Why don't you choose some other woman?"

"That is no longer possible. Elea has been given the only available batch of universal serum. Without it, no human organism could endure absolute zero without suffering serious damage."

The guards returned to say that Elea was nowhere on the terrace. "She must be somewhere nearby," Coban said, "waiting for us to leave. The Tower will be kept under surveillance. You two cannot meet without our knowing it. But, if by some miracle you do manage to do so, remember that you must choose whether she is to live or die."

Coban and the guards boarded their vehicle, which rose a few inches above the anchorage arm, turned in its own diameter and departed at maximum acceleration. Then Paikan went to the railing and looked up. A vehicle marked with Zoran's equation was lazily circling above the Tower. He switched on the close-vision screen and turned it to the flying resort houses moored on the ground all around the Tower. Everywhere he saw the faces of guards who were watching him on their own screens.

He went into the apartment and opened the elevator. A guard was standing inside. Paikan closed the door again in a rage, and went up into the dome. Standing in the middle of the transparent room, looking up at the clear sky where the university's aircraft was still flying in its lazy circles, he raised his crossed arms with his fingers spread and began to make the storm-calling gestures.

Above him, though rather high, a puffy little white cloud took shape in the blue sky. Everywhere the sky around the Tower began to be dotted with delightful little clouds that transformed the blue into a great flowering field. Then the clouds grew larger and merged, forming a single mass that thickened and darkened and began to seethe with rumbles of captive thunder. The wind bent the trees on the terrace, swept over the ground, howled as it cut through the ruins and rocked the moored resort houses.

The face of Paikan's superior appeared on the screen. "Paikan, what's going on there? What's this tornado? What are you doing?"

"I'm not doing anything," Paikan said. "The dome is malfunctioning. I'm trying to repair it now, but I'll need help. Send a repair crew, quickly!"

His superior spat out an oath and his image disappeared.

The rotating cloud had become green shot through with sudden flashes of purple and violet. It rang with a fearsome, unremitting din and the crash of a thousand thunderclaps. The cloud flickered with lightning. A lightning bolt struck the university's hovering aircraft, which crashed in flames. In the clamour and commotion that followed, Paikan ran down to the apartment, onto the terrace, and dived straight into the pool.

Elea was lying hidden in the sand at the bottom of the pool, concealed by marine plants, her face covered by the oxygen mask. When she saw Paikan motion to her, she left her refuge and rose to the surface with him. Outside cascades of water were pouring from the cloud, borne on an eddying wind that shook the resort houses as they strained at their moorings. A gust wrapped itself around the tower as if seeking to rip it out of the ground. The Tower creaked but it held. The wind carried off the silken tree, which soared dishevelled towards the cloud and vanished into a black void.

Paikan and Elea hurried into the dome. The bottom of the cloud had just reached it and surrounded the vault with a chaos of howling wind, rain and hail, punctuated by a series of lightning flashes. They were just fastening their weapon belts when they saw the repair craft arrive. It thrust its nose against the pane of the dome, which Paikan opened. Two repair men jumped down into the Tower, accompanied by the artillery of the storm. "What's happening?" one of them asked.

Instead of replying, Paikan thrust his hand into his weapon and fired at the Soul of the Dome, which rang, groaned, and collapsed. He seized Elea, thrust her into the opened nose of the repair vehicle, leaped in after her. They took off at once, while Elea was still trying to close the conical nose. The vehicle disappeared into the maze of the storm.

It was a heavy, slow craft, not very manoeuvrable but stable and resistant to the buffeting of the wind. Paikan smashed the transmitter that continuously signalled the craft's position. He manoeuvred the vehicle into the centre of the cloud that crackled around them. They moved westward, following the impetus that he had given it. Now that Paikan's Dome had been destroyed, action by other Towers would be required in order to neutralize the tornado. This would allow enough time to complete the first part of the plan that Paikan now described to Elea.

The only solution was for them to leave Gondawa

and reach Lamoss, the neutral nation. But the repair vehicle could not make the trip. To find a long-distance vehicle they had to go to one of the vehicle pools in the underground city.

The university's vehicles would not venture into the storm lest it damage their anti-gravity field. But they were certainly maintaining a tight vigil outside the storm. Elea and Paikan would have to reach an elevator terminus while remaining camouflaged by the cloud.

Paikan brought the repair ship down to the lower edge of the cloud. Swept by the torrential rain, the great vitrified plain glistened and flashed in the lightning only sixty feet below. The last elevators of Gonda 7 must not be far away. Then Elea saw one of them looming up out of the fog and Paikan put the repair ship down hard. It had barely touched the ground when they leaped out of it at a run and fired their weapons at it simultaneously. The wind carried away its dust.

The elevator was an express that ran directly to Depth Five. That didn't matter: each Depth had its own vehicle parks. They paid with their keys and took the special-services elevator. When it opened to allow them to leave they were washed, dried, combed and brushed.

The crowds on the moving avenue seemed both excited and tired. Images leaped out of the air everywhere to announce the latest news; but one had to insert one's key in a sound slot in order to hear the words. Sitting on the high-speed moving platform, Elea and Paikan listened to Chairman Lokan making reassuring pronouncements. No, there was no war. Not yet. The Council would do everything conceivable to prevent it. But the men and women of Gondawa were requested not to leave their mobilization posts. Most of the people on the avenue were wearing the Weapon on their belts, and no doubt they had the Black Seed concealed somewhere on their persons.

The birds had not heard the news, and they continued to frolic, chirping and soaring above the central lane. Elea smiled. She extended her left arm over her head, and a yellow bird braked hard in full flight to perch on her outstretched hand. Elea lowered it to the level of her face and rubbed her cheek against it. It was soft and warm. She felt its heart beating so fast that it was almost a continuous vibration. Elea hummed a few words of affection for the bird. It answered with a shrill whistle, leaped from Elea's finger to her head, pecked at her hair a few times, flapped its wings and flew away. Elea took Paikan's hand.

They left the avenue at the vehicle pool. This was a fan-shaped forest; the branches of its trees arched above rows of parked vehicles, and runways converged on the ramp of its exit channel. Paikan selected a fast long-distance two-seater. He and Elea inserted their keys into the control panel, waiting for a blue light in the panel to begin to blink before requesting their destination. The light remained dark.

"It's not working," Paikan said. "Quick, let's find another."

As they moved to leave their seats they heard a voice from the vehicle's loudspeaker. The voice froze them: it was Coban's. "Elea and Paikan, we know where you are. Now listen to me. I have had your accounts closed out at the central computer. Your keys are no good to you now. If you try to use them, they will only reveal where you are. Stay where you are and I'll send someone to fetch you."

Elea and Paikan leaped out of the vehicle and fled quickly. Hand in hand they ran across a runway, then they plunged into the trees. Thousands of birds were singing in the green and purple foliage; the whispers of

idling motors made a soothing *obbligato* that tempted
one to do nothing, to be merged into the joy of the
birds and the leaves. In the green and gold light Elea
and Paikan reached the beginning of another row of
long-distance aircraft. The nearest one had barely landed, and a traveller was coming out of it. Paikan raised
his weapon and fired at low intensity. The man was
tossed some distance and then fell to the ground,
unconscious. Paikan ran up to him, grabbed him under
the arms, moved him under a low branch and knelt
down beside him. He found it immeasurably difficult to
remove the man's ring: he was fat and the ring had
sunk into his flesh. Paikan had to spit on the finger in
order to lubricate the ring's passage. When at last the
key yielded, Paikan was ready to cut off the man's finger or his head or do anything else to be able to get
Elea away from Coban and the war.

They boarded the vehicle, which was still hot, and
Paikan inserted the stolen key in the control panel. Instead of the blue warning light, a yellow one began to
flash. The vehicle's door slammed shut and the loudspeaker began to yell, "Stolen key! Stolen key!" Outside
the vehicle an alarm began to whine.

Paikan tugged at the door. They leaped out and ran
into the refuge of the trees. Behind them the alarm was
still sending out its blood-chilling howl.

The other travellers paid them little attention. A
huge image of the battle on the moon hung above the
entrance to the Thirteen Streets. Both Enisor and Gondawa were attacking the satellite with their nuclear
bombs, creating gigantic craters, breaking apart its continents, vaporizing its seas, scattering its atmosphere
into space. Passers-by stopped, watched for a moment
and then hurried on their way. It was a rare family that
did not have a relative in the garrisons on the moon
and Mars.

The street was filled with agitated crowds. Groups formed in front of the official images that were broadcasting the news. Now and then someone turned on a sound channel with his key and once more the chairman uttered the same soothing words, "There is no war as yet."

"What more do they need?" a thin, bare-chested, short-haired boy shouted. "This is war now, if you let it happen. Say no! with the students! *No* to war!" He tried to start the crowd chanting but his protest evoked no reaction. The people who were near him moved on, knowing that shouting *no* or *yes* could do no good at all.

Elea and Paikan hurried toward the entrance to the public elevator, hoping to hide in the crowd long enough to reach the surface. Once they were outside they would make a new plan. But a triple line of university guards was already stationed across the end of the street. They began to move forward, check each individual's identity. The crowd was growing apprehensive and edgy.

"What are they looking for?"

"A spy! ... An Enisorian ... There's an Enisorian at Depth Five! ... A whole command of Enisorians—saboteurs!"

"Attention, please. Listen to me!" Coban's image leaped out above the middle of the street. It was repeated every fifty paces, dominating the crowd and the trees, repeating the same gesture and the same words. "Listen to me! I am Coban. I am looking for Elea 3-19-07-91. This is her picture."

A picture of Elea, taken a few hours earlier in the laboratory, appeared in place of Coban. In the crowd, Elea turned to Paikan and buried her face against his chest. "Don't be afraid," he said gently.

He stroked her cheek, slipped a hand beneath her

arm, loosened the end of her breast cloth, uncovered one shoulder and, with the part of the cloth that he had thus released, covered her neck, her chin, her forehead and her hair. This was a style that was occasionally adopted by both men and women: it would considerably reduce the likelihood of her being recognized.

"I am looking for this woman for her own good." This was Coban's voice again. "If you know where she is, inform the university at once. But do not touch her ... Listen Elea! I know that you can hear me. Signal with your key in any panel at all. Listen to me, Gondawans. I am looking for the woman Elea 3-19-07-91."

There was a man leaning against a wall between two climbing vines, lounging beneath the machines for the distribution of water, food and the thousand other necessities and luxuries which a key could obtain. He was keyless; the machines were of no use to him. He was a pariah with no further credit, living only by begging. He would hold out his hand, and the people who came to buy in the forest of many-coloured machines would give him the dregs of a glass or a bit of food. A black ribbon around the knuckle of his ringless middle finger concealed its disgraceful nakedness.

The man had recognized Elea. He had seen her bury her face on Paikan's chest and Paikan rearrange her clothing to conceal her identity. But when she raised her head to look at Paikan, the keyless man had seen her strikingly blue eyes and recognized them as the blue eyes of the image.

The university guards were drawing closer. Each person questioned inserted his key in a panel attached to a guard's wrist. The key of anyone who was being sought would remain locked in the panel, thus holding him prisoner. Elea and Paikan started moving in the other direction. The keyless man followed them.

They had never before taken the public elevator, used principally by those who had been less favourably selected, those who did not hold each other's hands and who needed the company of third persons. Now Elea and Paikan saw that this means of escape was closed to them: the pivot-hung doors would admit a person only after he had inserted his key. They could not take this elevator or any other, or the moving avenues, nor would they be able to buy food or drink.

A gigantic image of Elea suddenly filled the whole width of the street. A voice said, "The university is looking for this woman, Elea 3-19-07-91. If you see her, do-not-seize-her-do-not-even-touch-her. Follow her and report her. Attention, Elea: I know you hear me. Report yourself with your key."

"They're looking at me!" Elea whispered.

"No," Paikan replied, "they can't recognize you."

"You can recognize her by her eyes, regardless of what disguise she may be wearing," the voice of authority said. "Look for this woman's eyes. We are seeking her for her own good."

"Keep your eyes on the ground," Paikan ordered.

A triple line of guards appeared at the intersection of the eleventh street and the Transverse, moving forward to join the others. There was no way out now. Paikan looked around desperately.

"Look for this woman's eyes . . ." Each of the eyes in the image was enormous, and the blue of the iris was a gate opened in the night sky, where golden sparks shone like fire. The image turned slowly so that it could be seen from all angles.

Elea bowed her head, hunched her shoulders and tightened her grip on Paikan's hand as he led her toward the gates of the Avenue. The impalpable image barred their path. Elea stopped and raised her head.

From the gigantically enlarged image of her face, enormous eyes looked into her own.

"Come," Paikan said gently. He drew her close and she resumed walking, wrapped in a mist of a thousand shivering colours: she and Paikan had now entered the image. They emerged from it at the entrance to the Avenue, as the gates suddenly opened under the pressure of a crowd of students. Boys and girls alike, they were naked from the waist up, and extremely thin. Since the beginning of their campaign they had been fasting every other day and on the second day eating only the basic energy ration. They had become as hard and light as arrows.

"*Pao!*" they chanted as they ran. This means *no* in both the languages of Gondawa. Paikan and Elea forced their way into the crowd, trying to get through the gates before they closed. The chant of "*Pao!*" grew louder. The students jostled them and pushed them back; they started forward again, Paikan cutting through the crowd like the prow of a ship. The students crowded them, flowed past them on both sides as if they did not even see them.

Finally Elea and Paikan reached the gate. But it was blocked by armed men in a wedge formation—white guards belonging to the Council Police, advancing elbow to elbow, G weapons on their left hands.

The White Police was never called out as a mere gesture. Its members were chosen by the Computer even before the age of Selection. They received no keys, they had no credit accounts and they were brought up and trained in a special camp below Depth Nine, farther down even than the industrial complex. They never went up to the Surface and only seldom higher than the industrial level. Their universe was that of the Great Wild Lake, whose waters disappeared into the shadows of an unexplorable cavern. On its mineral-laden shores

they engaged in merciless battles with one another.
They fought, slept, and ate; their unused sexual energy
was channelled into aggressive activity. They wore
clinging uniforms of a leatherlike substance that covered their whole bodies, even their heads and their feet,
leaving only their faces exposed. They carried two G
weapons, also white: one on the left hand, the other on
the right side of the belt. They were the only Gondawans allowed to carry two of the weapons. And now
the Council had unleashed them against the city to liq-
uidate the students' revolt.

"Pao! . . . Pao! . . . Pao! . . . Pao! . . ."

The wedge of white guards continued through the
Avenue's gates and advanced on the students, whose
many-coloured skirts were swirling in the streets and
soon appeared in the trees. The students had a premoni-
tion of what was coming and fled towards every available exit. Blocked by the university guards at either
end of the street, they fell back towards the entrances
to the elevators and the Avenue. A new image of Chairman Lokan appeared in the sky, horizontal and running the whole length of the street; it spoke from this
prone position. An image that spoke without the intervention of a key was so out of the ordinary that everyone, even the guards, stood still to listen.

"Attention, please! The Governing Council has decided to send its International Friendship Councillor to
Lamoss and to request that the government of Enisor
send a comparable representative to meet with him
there. We intend to try to limit the war to the external
territories and to prevent it from spreading to the earth.
Peace can still be saved! . . . All citizens in Categories I
to 26 should immediately report to their mobilization
posts."

The image made a 180-degree turn and began to repeat its message. "Attention, please! The Governing Council has decided . . ."

"Pao! Pao! Pao! Pao!" The students had formed a human pyramid, at the top of which a girl stood with her arms upraised. She screamed. "Don't listen to him! Don't go to your posts! Refuse the government's war! Say *no*! Force the Council to declare peace!"

A white guard fired and the girl disintegrated in the cheek of Elea's image. "We are looking for this woman . . ."

The guards charged, firing as they advanced. *"Pao! Pao! Pao! Pao!"* The pyramid flew apart into shreds of flesh.

Paikan reached his hand toward his weapon, but it was no longer on his belt. The dense white surge of the guards was coming closer, the crowd was fleeing, the students were shouting their slogan of revolt. Paikan threw Elea to the ground and himself over her. A white guard stepped over them as he ran. As he did so, Paikan grabbed him by one foot. The ankle broke and the man fell without a sound. Paikan smashed his knee into the guard's cervical vertebrae and yanked the man's head back with both hands. The vertebrae broke. Paikan raised the inert left hand encased in its weapon and bent the fingers all the way to the palm. A squadron of guards were flung into the air and smashed against a wall, which disintegrated into a cloud of dust. Through the gap that was left, the Avenue's moving platforms were clearly visible. The crowd overran them, shouting, as the white guards proceeded with their job of extermination.

Elea and Paikan left the Avenue at the Vehicle Park Traffic Circle. The Vehicle Park was their only possible way out now that Paikan had thought of another way of taking over a vehicle.

The twelve trunks of a Red Tree rose out of the centre of the circle. They opened out in a corolla, joined at the base, their branches intertwined like children holding hands in a circle. Far above, their purple leaves hid the roof of the city and quivered with the sound and motion of countless invisible birds. A little stream ran around the base of the trees. Gasping with thirst, Elea knelt beside the stream and drank its water from her cupped hands. She spat it out in revulsion.

"It comes from the lake at Depth One," Paikan said. "You knew that."

She knew it, but she had been thirsty. The beautifully clear water was bitter, salty, and tepid; it was undrinkable. Paikan gently helped Elea to her feet and held her close. He too was thirsty, and he was hungry; indeed, since he had not received the universal serum, he was more drained than she. The branches above their heads were hung with a thousand machines that offered them, in a thousand shimmering colours, food and drink, sport and pleasure. Paikan knew that even breaking into one of them would do no good, for there would be nothing inside. Each of them created what it dispensed out of the void. Without a key . . .

"Come," he said gently. Hand in hand they approached the entrance to the Vehicle Park, but they found it blocked by three rows of university guards. In each of the streets that led into the circle the guards were advancing, pressing back the growing crowd. Paikan thrust his hand into his stolen weapon. He turned toward the entrance to the Vehicle Park and raised the weapon.

"Don't," Elea said. "They have gas grenades."

In each guard's belt there was a transparent, brittle grenade filled with green liquid. Even one of them would be enough to plunge the whole crowd into unconsciousness. Elea still had the oxygen mask that had enabled her to escape from the university, but Paikan had none.

"Put on your mask," he said. "I can hold my breath long enough to get through the gas. As soon as I fire, you start running."

A picture of Elea suddenly glowed out of the circle of the Red Tree's trunk and Coban's voice said: "Elea and Paikan, you cannot get out of the city. Every exit is guarded. I know you can hear me, Elea, wherever you are. You can report with your key. Paikan, think of her and not of yourself. With me she has life, with you death. Save her."

Paikan inhaled deeply and fired at medium intensity. The guards collapsed; a green fog from their shattered grenades filled the area from street to roof. The crowd of people were seized simultaneously with unconsciousness; they sank to their knees, tottered and lay flat. Tens of thousand of birds fell from the leafy ceiling like snowflakes of a thousand colours. Paikan had already got hold of Elea and was rushing her into the Vehicle Park. Running, stepping over fallen bodies, little by little he was releasing the air with which he had filled his lungs. He bumped into an upraised knee, exclaimed involuntarily, inhaled in spite of himself and was immediately asleep. His momentum threw him forward and his head fell on some other sleeper's belly.

Elea rolled him over, grabbed him under the arms and began dragging him.

"You'll never make it alone," said a nasal voice.

The keyless man stood beside her, his face hidden in an old-style gas mask that showed signs of having been mended many times. He bent down and lifted Paikan's feet. "Come with me," he said.

He guided Elea towards the wall. In a space between two climbing vines they set Paikan down, and the man looked around. There was not another living being on his feet as far as the eye could see. Then he took a shaped piece of wire out of his pouch, thrust it into a hole in the wall and turned it. The area of wall between the two vines opened before him like a door.

"Hurry up!" he urged, as a university vehicle landed at the entrance to the Vehicle Park. They picked up Paikan and went with him into the black doorway.

As soon as Paikan was out of the influence of the green fog, he awakened as suddenly as he had lost consciousness. He opened his eyes and saw Elea on her knees beside him, watching him in anguish.

Around them was greyness: grey walls, grey floor, grey vault above, and opposite, a grey stairway. Broad enough to accommodate huge crowds, it rose before him, empty, bare, endless, disappearing in greyness and silence.

Another equally broad and empty stairway spiralled downward into the greyness to the left. Narrower flights of stairs and sloping corridors were cut in the walls in all directions; a thick layer of dust formed a grey cloak over everything.

"The Stairway!" Paikan said. "I'd forgotten about it."

"Everyone has," said the keyless man.

Paikan stood up to look at him. He too was grey. His clothes and hair were grey, and his skin was a greyed pink. "Was it you who brought me here?" Paikan asked.

"Yes, with her. She's the one they're looking for, isn't she?" The keyless man's voice was low, devoid of expression or character.

"Yes," Elea said. "I am."

"They won't think of the Stairway right away. It's been out of use for such a long time that all its doors have been sealed up and camouflaged. They'll have trouble finding them.

"If you want to go up to the Surface," the keyless man said in a voice that was barely—just barely—loud enough to be heard, "there are thirty thousand steps. It will take you a day or two."

Automatically Paikan muted his own voice when he replied. "We want to get to a Vehicle Park," he said.

"The one at Depth Five is filled with guards so you'd have to go up or down one depth. It would be easier to go down."

The keyless man thrust his hand into the pouch he wore at his waist and brought out some of the tiny food spheres and offered them to Elea and Paikan. While they were letting the spheres melt in their mouths their benefactor used the edge of his palm to wipe away the dust from a pipe that ran along the wall at eye level. He cut into it at two points with a knife and two streams of water began to flow.

Open-mouthed, Elea rushed under the tiny transparent waterfall. Choking, coughing, sneezing, she laughed with joy. Paikan cupped his hands and drank. They had barely relieved their thirst when the flow of water dwindled and stopped: the pipe had sealed its leaks.

"You can drink again farther on," the keyless man said. "Let's hurry: we have to go down three hundred stories to reach Depth Six."

Hand in hand Elea and Paikan followed him, plunging into the dense greyness. Now and then they saw other silent keyless persons, who moved without haste, alone or in small groups. The Stairway complex was their universe. They had unsealed forgotten doors through which they sneaked into the world of sound and colour just long enough to beg or steal the things they needed. Then they went back to their grey sanctuary. Dust absorbed the sound of their voices and their footsteps and the silence they inhaled made them silent too.

Running and leaping down the stairs in a daze, Elea and Paikan followed their guide as he hurried on ahead. He spoke to them in grudged words, bits of half-broken phrases—his words were hardly more than whispered. He told of the famine that came when the people in the world of colour refused to give alms. Then the keyless men were reduced to eating round-birds. He pointed out a roundbird that was fleeing ahead of them. It was as thick as a fist, grey, and it had no wings. When it had to cross a landing it ran as fast as it could on its skinny legs. Then, reaching the top of a flight of stairs, it jumped, hiding its head and feet in its feathers, and rolled to the bottom like a ball.

Elea felt no diminution in her strength but Paikan had to stop. They rested briefly, seated at the bottom of a flight of stairs. In a cranny of the landing three crouching, silent men were cooking roundbirds, which they held by the feet over a fire. The revolting stench of the burning flesh was inescapable, and it gave Paikan new energy. "Let's go on," he said.

Just as he was getting to his feet there were loud sounds from one of the walls. The three silent men fled, taking along their half-cooked victims. A section of the wall shattered to the ground.

"Quick!" the keyless man said. "That's an old door. They've found it!"

He thrust Elea and Paikan in front of him and started them back up the stairs. They took the steps four at a time. On the landing behind them the wall collapsed and university guards rushed in.

The three fugitives veered off into a sloping corridor, frightening a flock of roundbirds which scurried off faster and faster, without a single utterance of fright—round, silent, grey. Coban's voice rose from the end of the corridor ahead of the fugitives. It was muffled by layers of dust; it seemed both very near to them and as diluted as though it were coming from the end of the world.

"Attention, Elea," Coban said. "We know where you are. If you continue to run away from us you're going to lose your way. Stay where you are and we will come for you. I repeat, stay where you are. Time is running out."

The guards' heavy footsteps were audible ahead of them, behind them, above them. The keyless man stopped running. "They're everywhere," he hissed. Paikan thrust his hand into his weapon, but the keyless man ordered him to wait. He knelt, scooped dust with his hands until the floor was exposed, and pressed his ear against it. Then he leaped up again. "Aim there," he whispered. Hiding behind Paikan, he pointed to the area that he had cleared.

Paikan fired, and the floor shook. Mats of dust, torn from walls and floor, flew through the corridor. "Harder!" whispered the keyless man. Paikan fired again, and with a roar the ground opened in front of them. "Follow me," their guide ordered.

He leaped into the hole and Elea and Paikan followed him, falling into bitter, tepid water, where strong currents tugged at their bodies. The water was very slightly phosphorescent, brightening in its eddies and little whirlpools. Elea bobbed to the surface. Then she saw Paikan's face coming up out of the depths. His hair was glistening with a green light. He smiled to her and reached out his hand. In front of them the sloping ceiling plunged into the water, and a whirlpool spun where the river flowed out through the drain. In the centre of the whirlpool they could see a shining bubble: the keyless man's head. He raised his hand, indicated that he was about to dive and disappeared. Elea and

177

Paikan swam closer to him and felt themselves being drawn into the depths. Hand in hand, weightless, letting their legs hang idle, they were engulfed in the throbbing, warm, aqueous vortex. They fell at incredible speed, spun around on the axis of their clasped hands, swept around corners where they were thrown against walls cushioned by billions of tiny roots, thrust their heads out of the water at the apex of a curve, inhaled and sailed on again, constantly drawn and pulled still lower. The water tasted of rot and of chemical salts. This was the major stream that flowed out of the lake at Depth One. As it left the lake it flowed through a device that infused it with the nutrients needed by plants. Then it flowed down, level by level, below walls and floors, and irrigated the roots of all the vegetation in the underground city.

A vertical drop ended in a sweeping curve and an upsurge that hurled Elea and Paikan into a geyser of phosphorescent bubbles. They breathed air again at the surface of a lake that moved leisurely towards a dark portico. A host of spiral columns, some as thick as ten men's bodies, others as slender as a woman's wrist, swooped down from the ceiling into the water, a glistening nation of roots. The keyless man was sitting on one of them, scowling. "Climb up out of the water! Fast!" he shouted.

Elea pulled herself up to an almost horizontal section of a root and dragged Paikan after her: he was exhausted. They clung there, motionless. A pale light rose from the water, cold and viscous and green. Then, from every part of the lake, little circles of bright pink light poured into the eddies left by the three fugitives. Soon there was a seething surface of pink light beneath them. From time to time some of these living drops leaped out of the water like sparks and tried to attach themselves to the naked legs that hung beyond their reach.

"The bitterfish," the keyless man explained. "If they so much as get a taste of you, they'll finish you off completely—even your bones."

Elea shuddered. "But what do they eat ordinarily?"

"Dead roots and whatever rubbish comes down with the current. They're scavengers. And when they can't find anything else, they eat one another."

Then the keyless man turned toward Paikan, struck his fist against the low ceiling that his head was already touching, and said, "The Vehicle Park of Depth Six is above us."

———————

Paikan drew his weapon and aimed between two rows of roots. He fired. A section of ceiling fell away. A gigantic tree sank into the lake through the gap. In its branches was an aircraft in which two bright silhouetted figures were caught. The branches of the tree trapped the craft and held it under water. In a glare of pink the millions of lenticular fish swarmed over its occupants—White Police—and attacked their unprotected faces, driving through their eyes into their brains and through their noses into their chests and abdomens. The water that filled the vehicle was stained with red.

Followed by the keyless man, Elea and Paikan climbed along roots and branches until they reached the surface of the Vehicle Park. There the students were still waging a hopeless battle against the White Guards. They had found gold ingots and prefabricated machinery in a cargo vehicle immobilized by the war and dodging in and out among the trees and aircraft, they were using these to bombard the police. They were pitiable weapons. Occasionally one of them found its target and a skull was split with a flash of gold, but more often they fell short.

The police forces were weaving among the trees like white snakes and firing at whatever moved. They caught the students in mid-run and flung them against the trees like shapeless sacks. Trees were splitting and falling, vehicles were exploding in bits. All the birds in the Vehicle Park had left the trees and were spinning, screaming, in panic-stricken circles through the upper air. An image of the Military Councillor with his bound black hair was announcing the Enisorian government's refusal to send a minister to Lamoss, ordering Gondawan citizens to report to their assigned mobilization posts.

Above the entrance to the Twelve Streets hung an image of Elea. "The University is looking for this woman: Elea 3-19-07-91. You will be able to recognize her by her bright blue eyes. Please report her whereabouts to the University. We are seeking her for her own good. Elea, report yourself with your key. . . ."

Near the departure channel a crowd swarmed around a rectangular vehicle strange to Gondawa. They seized the Lamossian national who was inside and dragged him violently into their midst. He was shouting that he was not an Enisorian, not a spy, not an enemy. But the crowd didn't understand Lamossian. It saw only the strange garments, the closely cropped hair. People began beating the man. Students rushed to his rescue, followed by the White Guards, but the Lamossian was already lying beaten, slashed, trampled beneath the feet of the mob. The students began screaming in rage at the horror and the stupidity of what happened, and the crowd yelled back, "Kill the students! Kill the traitors!"

Then the White Guards fired to clear the area, annihilating everyone within range.

With a melancholy smile the keyless man went off toward the Twelve Streets. Elea and Paikan ran for a safer part of the Vehicle Park. They stopped at the second row of long-distance vehicles. The area was almost deserted, and very peaceful. An aircraft had just arrived and was being jockeyed into its place. It settled to the ground; its door opened and a man emerged who paused in surprise at the sound of shouts and explosions of weapons. He hurried the few steps to Paikan, asking, "What's going on?"

By way of reply Paikan raised his left hand in its white weapon-glove. He snatched the other man's weapon away with his right hand and threw it far out of reach. "Get back inside! Fast!"

Still more bewildered, the man obeyed. Paikan made him sit down, took his hand and thrust his key into the elastic panel. The moment of silence that followed was endless. Then suddenly, the communication screen began to vibrate.

"Destination?" the loudspeaker asked.

"Lamoss, first Vehicle Park."

There was a brief hum followed by a light clap. "Credit good. Destination noted. Remove your key. Prepare for takeoff."

Paikan jerked the man out of the seat and pushed him from the vehicle, calling out thanks and apologies. The door slammed, the vehicle rose, turned on its own axis and headed out towards the runway. It moved into the exit line. The loudspeaker on board began to speak: "The university is looking for Elea 3-19-07-91. Elea, report your whereabouts with your key."

The mechanism of the exit channel caught the vehicle and hurled it upward. It soared out of the Mouth and climbed into the night. Lying hand in hand on the couch in the vehicle, Elea and Paikan allowed themselves to blend into infinite softness and silence.

Presently the loudspeaker announced, "We are about to initiate horizontal flight towards Lamoss. Permissible speeds are from nine to seventeen. What speed do you prefer?"

"The maximum," Paikan said.

"Maximum: Speed Seventeen—recorded. Prepare for acceleration."

In spite of the warning, the horizontal thrust pressed Elea against one wall of the vehicle and threw Paikan on top of her. She started to laugh, seized his long blond hair with both hands and began to nibble at his nose, his cheeks, his lips. Now they had forgotten the danger they were in; they had put their sufferings aside. They were heading towards safety, though it might turn out to be brief, and the present was a moment for joy.

Their joy was aborted by the howl of alarm sirens in the loudspeaker. Frozen, Elea and Paikan sat up. A red light started blinking on the control panel. "This is a general alarm," the loudspeaker said. "All flights are hereby cancelled. We are returning you to the Vehicle Park by the shortest route. Please report at once to your mobilization posts."

The aircraft changed course and began a steep and swift descent. Elea and Paikan could see the ground through the transparent cabin. They watched the madman's ballet of mobile resort houses rushing towards the Mouth; they saw the funnel of the Mouth inhaling the luminous bubbles that hovered around it awaiting their turns.

Then their own vehicle slowed to take its place in the carrousel.

"If we go back to the city, we'll be trapped," Elea said. "We'll have to jump!"

At that moment they were flying at reduced speed

above the lake, low enough so that they might have jumped to safety. But the aircraft doors would not open during flight. Now they had left the lake behind and were moving above a compact mass of trees. Paikan fired into the control panel. The vehicle rolled, started upward, turned downward, rose again, rocking unevenly, then lost altitude again: it fell like a leaf in autumn. It skimmed the treetops, rose a little, dropped again, crashed into the summit of a huge tree crowned with palm leaves. There it stayed, impaled like an apple on a stick.

――――――――

They lay on the grass side by side, just above the sand of the lake shore. Elea's hand was in Paikan's and their wide open eyes watched the empty night. The Mouth had drawn in the last of the laggards; the sky had nothing left to display but its stars. Elea and Paikan could see nothing else. In the midst of the stars, in the immeasurable, impersonal peace of space, they resumed their interrupted journey of hope.

In front of them, as if from the opposite side of the lake, they saw the moon rising. It looked bloated and misshapen. Purple flashes played over its darker parts and sometimes its whole surface glared with a fleeting sunlike brilliance. This was the soundless testimonial to man's destruction of a world.

Without another movement, without even looking toward each other, Elea and Paikan interwove their fingers and their palms clung to each other. In the forest behind them a horse whinnied softly, as if in pain. A bird, its sleep broken, chirped briefly and was silent again. A breeze brushed their faces.

"We could try to find the horse," Paikan suggested.

"And go where? There's nowhere left to go. It's all over." She smiled in the night. She was with him. No matter what happened, it would happen to them together.

The whinny came closer now, and there was a soft sound of the horse's hoofs on the grass. They rose. White as the moon, the horse approached them, stopped and shook its head. Elea buried her hand in its long hair and felt it trembling. "It's afraid," she said.

"It should be." She saw the silhouette of Paikan's arm swing in a broad arc, indicating the bright flashes that flickered in the night like distant storms. "They're fighting at Gonda 17, Gonda 41, Enawa. The Enisorians must have landed everywhere."

Now a deep rumbling began to be audible after each flash. It became a continuous thunder, surrounding them. They could feel the ground shake beneath their feet.

The animals in the forest were awakening. The birds flew off, frantic to see that it was still night, and then tried to go back to their nests, bumping into branches and leaves. The spotted does emerged from the forest and congregated around the human couple. The blue horse, invisible in the night, was there too, with the slowly moving white-chested little tree bears and the short-eared black rabbits whose tails wagged at ground level behind them.

"Before the night is over," Paikan said, "nothing living will remain here—not an animal, not a blade of grass. And those who think they're protected down below are just having a few days of grace, perhaps only a few hours. Elea, I want you to go into the Shelter. I want you to live."

"Live? Without you?" She leaned her body on his and lifted her head. "I won't be alone in the Shelter.

Coban will be there. Have you thought of that?" He shook his head as if to reject the idea. "When we are awakened I shall have to bear his children. I haven't yet had yours, I've been waiting. . . . Doesn't the idea of Coban inside me, making children, mean anything to you?"

He pulled her to him roughly, then he forced himself to be calm. "I'll be dead, long dead."

A huge, disembodied voice sent the birds into a panic again. All the loudspeakers in the forest were speaking with Coban's voice. It echoed and expanded over the surface of the water. "Elea. Listen to me, Elea. I know you're on the surface. You are in danger there. The invasion army is landing in waves, and it will soon occupy the entire surface. Go to the nearest elevator, Elea. Signal with your key; we will come to find you, wherever you are. Don't delay any longer. Listen, Paikan, think of her! Elea, this is my last call. Before the night is over the Shelter will be sealed, with you or without you."

Then there was silence.

"I belong with Paikan," Elea said in a low, solemn voice. She clung to his neck.

A massive explosion made the ground tremble. Part of the forest suddenly burst into flame. Paikan raised his head and looked at Elea's face below him in the flickering light. She lay on the grass, her whole body completely relaxed, barely breathing. She was beyond waking and sleeping. She was happy in all her being, and she knew it. Without opening her eyes, she asked very softly, "Are you looking at me?"

"You're beautiful," he replied.

Slowly her mouth and unopened eyes became a smile.

The sky pulsed and was riven. With a savage howl a horde of half-naked Enisorian soldiers, painted red and sitting astride their iron cars as if they were horses, poured down out of the heights of the fiery night and veered off obliquely above the lake toward the Mouth. Defensive weapons fired from all the outlets. The airborne army was slaughtered, scattered, exterminated, thrown back to the stars in the form of thousands of shattered corpses that plunged into the lake and the forest. The animals fled in every direction, threw themselves into the water, ran back to the shore, pranced in panic around the couple on the ground. A succession of terrifying explosions picked up the burning forest and scattered it everywhere. A flaming branch fell on a doe, which made a grotesque leap and dived into the lake. Horses in flames galloped and neighed. A new army was coming down from the sky and howling as it came.

Then Paikan wanted to raise himself from her, but she held him close. She opened her eyes and looked at him happily. "We're going to die together," she said.

He slipped his hand into the G weapon that he had placed near them on the grass. He went out of her and stood up. She barely had enough time to see him train the weapon on her and she cried out.

"You're going to live," he said. And he fired.

———————

What happened afterward was as new to Elea as it was to the EPI scientists. Although Paikan's weapon had knocked her unconscious, her senses had continued to function and her subconscious memory had gone on recording what they felt.

Her ears had heard, her not-quite-closed eyes had seen Paikan cover her with a few garments, take her into his arms and walk to the elevators in the centre of the flaming Vehicle Park. He had thrust his key into the panel but no car had come. He shouted, "Coban! This is Paikan! I'm bringing you Elea!"

There was silence. Again he shouted Coban's name and Elea's. A green light began to flash above the door, and Coban's voice came through blurred and interrupted. ". . . very late. The enemy . . . inside Gonda 7. Your elevator complex is cut off . . . I repeat, bring her down . . . sending a patrol . . . signal . . . your ring . . . I repeat. . . ."

The elevator car arrived. As it opened its doors the ground heaved with a frightening explosion. The top of the elevator terminus was disintegrated. Elea was torn out of Paikan's arms and both of them were thrown violently in to the air. Elea's unconscious eyes saw the red sky, the hordes of red painted Enisorian troops descending on the land. Her ears heard their howls filling the fiery night.

Her body sensed Paikan's presence. Her eyes saw his anguished face bending over her. She saw his wounded forehead and the bloodstains in his blond hair. She heard his voice speaking to her, "Elea, I'm here. I'm taking you . . . to the Shelter. You're going to live."

He picked her up and slung her over his shoulder, so that her head and upper body hung toward his back. Now her eyes saw nothing. She heard Paikan's voice among the explosions and the crackling of the burning forest. "I'm going to take you down the elevator shaft on the emergency ladder. . . . Don't be afraid of anything . . . I'm with you."

At the desk on the platform in the conference room, her eyes closed and her head in her hands, Elea let her memory recall what it had recorded. The amplifiers shuddered with explosions and unearthly cries. The visual circuit relayed cascades of colour, eruptions of shadow, a shattered world's return to the chaos that preceded creation.

Then came a series of dull, muffled strokes. The sounds grew stronger and more frequent. Elea seemed confused, distracted. She snatched off the golden circlet and opened her eyes. The screen went dark.

The sound continued. Suddenly the sound system carried the voice of Lebeau, who was not in the conference room, shouting "Do you hear? *It's his heart!* We've done it!"

Hoover leaped from his chair with a shout and began to applaud. Everyone else followed his example. They cheered all the louder to purge the embarrassment that they felt at having watched Elea's and Paikan's lovemaking. They were profoundly disturbed by it both in spirit and in flesh. They were ashamed—ashamed of their prudishness and ashamed of their shame. Elea's innocence showed them the extent to which, since St. Paul, not since Christ, Christian civilization had perverted with shame the most beautiful pleasures that God had given to man.

Coban's heart pulsed, stopped, and started again, irregular and precarious. When the pauses grew too long, the electrodes of a stimulator attached to his chest shocked his heart back into motion.

The doctors clustering around the resuscitation table wore apprehensive expressions. Suddenly Coban's respiration became difficult, and his bandages showed red stains at the mouth.

"Coagulant! Serum! Turn him over on to his side. Get his mouth free."

His lungs were bleeding. If the haemorrhage did not stop, it would be because the burns in the pulmonary tissue were too severe for scar tissue to form. In that case it would be necessary to transplant new lungs. The physicians consulted over Coban's inert body.

OBJECTIONS: The time that would be required for the arrival of new lungs (three pairs as a matter of insurance) from the International Organ Bank: radio message, packing, shipment from bank to airport, Geneva-to-Sydney flight, transshipment. Sydney-to-EPI flight: a minimum of twenty hours.

"Don't forget all the red tape. Customs documents."

"Surely they wouldn't—"

"Anything is possible. Double the time estimate."

"Forty hours."

How to keep Coban alive during the interval: Blood needed for transfusions. Blood-group test for Coban immediately. Red group and sub-group, white group and sub-group. A nurse uncovered Coban's left hand and arm. When surgery began blood would be needed in quantity. Have twice as much in reserve.

Another problem with the operation: a surgical team specializing in organ transplants.

Moissov: "We have—"

Forster: "We can—"

Zabrec: "In our work—"

Lebeau: "Out of the question. Too risky. No new hands here. Especially when those hands hold knives. We will operate ourselves, in telecommunication with the French, American and South African experts. We can do it. Lungs aren't black magic."

Artificial lung to oxygenate the bloodstream during the operation. There was one in the infirmary.

"Why not use it now, give Coban's lungs a rest and a chance to form a scar tissue?"

"They won't heal if they don't get blood. They have to go on functioning. Either they'll heal or they won't heal; that's the way it is."

Blood-test results: groups and sub-groups unknown. The tested blood (Coban's) coagulated all the blood samples.

This was amazing.

"But don't forget how far back he comes from. It's reasonable that new blood groups would have developed in nine hundred thousand years."

"No blood, no operation. That simplifies things. Either he gets better or he dies."

"There's still the girl."

"What girl?"

"Elea. Her blood might be suitable."

"Never in enough quantity for an operation! She'd have to be bled white, and it still wouldn't be enough."

"Perhaps. If we ligatured everything, very quickly ... With the artificial lung hooked in right from the start—"

"Look, we aren't going to murder that girl!"

"She might survive it. You saw what recuperative powers she has ..."

"I'm against it! You know damn well she couldn't manufacture fresh blood fast enough. You're asking that she be sacrificed. I won't permit it!"

"She's a beauty, unquestionably, but in comparison with this guy's mind she doesn't even count."

"Beautiful or not has nothing to do with it: she's alive. We're doctors, not vampires."

"Her blood could still be tested against Coban's. That doesn't commit us to anything. Undoubtedly we'll need some blood from her if he doesn't stop bleeding. Not to mention surgery."

"O.K., that's all right, completely O.K."

When Elea returned to her memories, an image of Chairman Lokan was speaking to Coban, and Paikan was bending over her.

Lokan seemed nearly crushed by exhaustion. "They've captured all the cities in the Centre," he was saying, "and Gonda 7 down to Depth Two. Nothing can stop them. Their losses have been fantastic, but their number is beyond our imagination. Now they're converging on Gonda 7 and on the Solar Weapon. We've blown up all the accesses leading to the Weapon, but they're still coming in by the million and each man is digging his own little tunnel. I can't accelerate the launching. In all frankness I can't say whether we'll succeed in holding them off long enough or whether they'll reach the Weapon before it is launched."

"I hope they do!" Coban said. "If Gondawa is going to be destroyed, at least let the rest of mankind live. Why must the whole earth die with us?"

"You are a pessimist, Coban. It won't be so bad . . ."

"It will be worse than anything you can imagine; you know that quite well!"

"I don't imagine anything any longer. I've done what I had to do in my capacity as the chief executive of Gondawa. Now no one can do anything to change what will happen. I'm exhausted."

"It's the burden of a murdered world that's crushing you."

"That's easy for you to say, Coban! You didn't have to make the decisions. But take care of yourself: the Enisorians have just launched a new army against Gonda 7, and the university is one of their most important targets. I can't help you at all; I need all the troops available to me. You have the university guard . . ."

"It's in battle now. We're holding them off."

"Good-bye, Coban."

Lokan's image disappeared and Coban stepped to Elea's side. He gestured toward someone she couldn't see.

"Listen, Elea," Coban said. "If you can hear me, do

not be frightened. We're going to give you a tranquilizing drug that will put your mind to sleep and relax your body so that not a single cell will shiver when the cold grips it."

"Elea, I'm here with you," Paikan said.

Elea's body was aware that a flexible tube was being inserted into her mouth. It moved through her throat into her stomach, and a liquid was poured down it. Her revulsion was so strong that it restored her to consciousness. She wanted to sit up and protest. But suddenly she felt no more need to do so. She was at peace, everything was as it should be. She had no wish even to speak.

"Are you happy?" Coban asked. She didn't even look at him; she knew that he knew. "You're going to go to sleep, Elea, a deep peaceful sleep. It won't be a long sleep. Even if you sleep for a few centuries, it will be no longer than a night."

"Did you hear?" Paikan added. "No more than a night ... And when you awaken, I'll have been dead so long that it won't cause you any suffering.... I'm with you, Elea, I'm beside you."

"Undress her and wash her," Coban ordered his assistants.

"Don't touch her!" Paikan roared. He bent over her and removed the shreds of clothing that she still wore. Then he poured warm water over her and washed her tenderly. She felt his beloved hands on her, she was happy.

She saw the whole room around her, narrow and low-ceilinged, with a convex golden wall broken by a round door. She could hear the sounds of battle coming closer through the thickness of the earth. The image of the commander of the guard appeared, drenched with blood.

"They've broken through at Depth Three!" he cried. "They're moving toward the Shelter . . ."

"Concentrate all your forces around the Shelter," Coban ordered. "Abandon all the rest." The commander's image disappeared. The earth was trembling. "Pick her up, Paikan," Coban said, "and come with me."

Everything was right when she was in Paikan's arms. In his arms she was carried down a golden staircase and through a golden door. Then he carried her down a few more steps.

"Put her down there, her head toward me," Coban said. "Arrange her arms on her chest. Good . . . Attention, Moissan can you hear me?"

"I hear you."

"Let me see the image of Gonda 1. I want to keep informed to the very end."

The concave ceiling of the Shelter became a vast plain. The Enisorian warriors were dropping out of a fiery sky. The defence weapons killed many of them but more and more troops plunged from the sky. Those that reached the ground were swept by the crossfire of concealed weapons. The survivors dug into the earth in their war vehicles which carved the passage for them. The surface fought back, exploded, hurled its dismembered attackers into the air amid the shards of its own flesh.

Elea saw the plain split open from one end of the horizon to the other. A gigantic, fantastic flower of glass and metal rose out of the earth and climbed into the sky. The Enisorian troops were brushed out of the way. The incredible flower climbed steadily, growing larger, and its petals, of every imaginable colour, opened around it to reveal a core more transparent than the clearest water. It filled the sky. It continued to rise, beginning now to spin slowly, then faster ... It was all miraculously right. Elea was falling asleep.

Coban said, "I'm going to put the mask on her. Say goodbye to her now."

Paikan's face blocked out the flower and the sky, looking down at her. He was beautiful. Paikan. There was only Paikan. She belonged with him.

"Elea, go to sleep now ... I'm with you."

She closed her eyes and felt the mask being placed over her face, an air tube inserted between her lips. She could still hear Paikan's voice. "I won't give her to you, Coban! She will never belong to you! ... Elea, my life, be patient. ... Only a night. ... I'm with you ... for eternity."

She heard and felt nothing more. Her consciousness was submerged. Now she was nothing but a mist of golden light, without shape or weight or boundaries, a fading light. ...

———

Elea had removed the golden circlet and she sat bolt upright in her chair, silent and unmoving as a stone statue; her expression was so tragic that no one wanted to stir, to utter a syllable, to break her silence with a cough or the creaking of a chair.

It was Simon who finally stood up. He moved behind her, put his hands on her shoulders and said softly, "Elea." She didn't move. "Elea," he repeated. He felt her shoulders tremble beneath his hands. "Elea, come ..." The warmth of his voice and the warmth of his hands broke through the barriers of horror " ... and rest."

She rose, turned toward him and looked at him as if

194

he were the only living being in a city of the dead. He offered her his hand. She studied that outstretched hand, hesitated a second, then placed her own in it. Hand in hand they left the stage and walked through the auditorium. Henckel sitting in the last row, rose and opened the door for them.

As soon as Simon and Elea had left, a clamour of voices filled the hall. The last images had been the same scene that had been shown to Simon when he had put on the receiving circlet. And those who had seen it guessed what must have happened afterward: Paikan leaving the Shelter, Coban drinking a sleeping potion, undressing and lying down on his pedestal, pulling the golden mask down over his face. Then the Shelter closing, the refrigerating motor beginning to work. . . .

During this time the Solar Weapon had continued on its course toward Enisor and gone into action. What exactly was its effect? That could only be conjectured. "As if the sun itself were to fall on Enisor," Coban had said.

What Coban feared had come to pass: the shock had been so tremendous that it had affected the whole mass of the earth. The earth had lost its equilibrium and wavered like a child's rocking top before it found its balance on a new axis. There had been earthquakes and volcanic eruptions everywhere, the beds of the oceans had been emptied as their waters drowned and despoiled the land. And the new equilibrium of the earth had shifted Gondawa to the new South Pole. Cold had gripped the continent and the snow that fell on its surface during the years, the centuries and the millennia that followed was transformed into ice by its own weight.

Coban had not anticipated this. His shelter was supposed to reopen automatically when circumstances would permit life on the surface. But circumstances had never turned favourable, and the shelter had remained a seed lost in the pit of the cold.

Hoover rose. "I propose," he said, "that in a solemn declaration we pay tribute to the intuition, the intelligence and the determination of our friends in the French Polar Expeditions. They were able not only to interpret correctly the unprecedented findings of their instruments but also to shake the apathy and inertia of the nations to such a point that they made up their minds to send us here!"

The assembled scientists stood up and cheered.

"Tribute must also be paid," Leonova said, "to Coban's genius and to his pessimism, which together caused him to construct a shelter that could last through eternity."

"O.K., little sister," Hoover conceded. "But Lokan was right: Coban was *too* pessimistic. The Solar Weapon didn't destroy *all* life on earth, because we are still here! There were survivors: vegetable, animal and human. The houses, the factories, the bottled energy, everything that had kept them alive was destroyed, and the survivors were left to exist as well as they could. Perhaps there were a few dozen of them scattered over the five continents! And they'd forgotten how to use their hands. What can I do with my bare hands—me, Mr. Hoover, the big brain? Nothing, aside from lighting cigarettes and patting girls' bottoms. Nothing at all. Can you picture me trying to catch a rabbit on the run? If *I'd* been in the survivors' place I'd have eaten insects, and fruits when it was the season, and dead animals when I was lucky enough to stumble on any. And that's what they must have done. That's what they were reduced to. They started out from below the bottom rung on the ladder, and they made the whole climb all over again, falling back a rung now and then along the way, picking themselves up, missing more rungs, and

still pigheadedly shoving their noses in the air and starting their climb again every time. And they made it!
They're us! They've repopulated the world, and now
they've achieved the same state of idiocy they were in
before, ready to blow themselves up all over again.
Great, isn't it? That's the human race!"

It was a marvellous day, full of sunshine and rejoicing.
Outdoors the surface wind had dropped to its minimum
velocity, not more than seventy-five miles an hour, with
occasional moments of total calm. Very far above the
earth, the wind was purging the sky of the slightest
taint of cloud, the tiniest dust-grain of mist, making it
shine with an intense, brand-new, joyful blue. And the
snow and ice were almost as blue as the sky.

The assemblage in the conference room was full of
excitement. Leonova had suggested that the scientists
swear a solemn oath; that they dedicate their lives to
the struggle against war and stupidity and the latter's
most savage forms: political stupidity and nationalist
stupidity.

"Kiss me, little Red sister," Hoover cried. "And let's
include ideological stupidity." He hugged her; she began to weep. The scientists stood up and swore the oath
in all their various languages and the Translator had
multiplied their oath.

Then Hoi-To gave a report on the work that was
being done on deciphering the writings engraved on the
wall of the Shelter. The group had just finished working
on one document photographed on the first day. Its
title was: *Treatise on the Universal Laws,* and it
seemed to be the explanation of Zoran's equation. In
the light of its importance, Lukos himself was going to
undertake the projection of the twelve hundred photographs on the Translator's analytic screen. This was
news of exceptional importance. Even if Coban died it

was possible that the *Treatise* would be deciphered and the equation understood.

The scientists were laughing, hugging one another, slapping backs. Then Lebeau's voice came out of all the loudspeakers.

He said that Coban's lungs had stopped bleeding. Coban was very weak and still unconscious, his heart beat was irregular, but now there was hope that he might be saved. It was truly a wonderful day.

Hoover asked Hoi-To whether he knew how much time Lukos would need to complete feeding the photographs of the *Treatise of Universal Laws* into the translation machine. "A few hours," Hoi-To replied.

"So then in a few hours we'll be able to know what Zoran's equation means in seventeen different languages?"

"I think not," Hoi-To said with a thin smile. "We will have translations of the introductory matter, the argumentation and the commentary, but the significance of the mathematical and physical symbols will still elude us for a time. But even without Coban's help, I think that we shall be able to discover their meanings."

"I suggest," said Hoover, "that we use Trio to alert universities and research centres to what we have found; we can suggest that they record our initial translation of the *Treatise*, plus the original in Gondawan, which we'll broadcast tomorrow. That way, no one will be able to get a monopoly of the information, and they'll forget about trying to assassinate Coban. And we'll be able to tell that aggregation of military hardware that's been spying on us under the pretext of protecting us to go crawl back into its respective holes."

Hoover's proposal was approved by acclamation. It was a great day, a long day without a night and without clouds, with a golden sun that paraded its optimism along the whole circumference of the horizon. When at last the sun hid behind the ice mountain, the scientists and technicians kept their euphoria alive in the bar and restaurant of EPI 2. Serious inroads were made that evening on the expedition's reserves of champagne and vodka. Scotch and bourbon, akvavit and slivovitz poured their infusions of optimism into the bubbling cauldron of general rejoicing.

"Little sister," Hoover informed Leonova, "I am a disgusting fat bachelor and you are a horrible skinny Marxist egghead. I won't say I love you because it would be ludicrous. But if you agree to be my wife, I promise you I would get rid of my belly and I'd even go so far as to read *Das Kapital*."

"You're loathsome," Leonova sobbed on his shoulder; "you're horrid."

She had been drinking champagne and she was not used to it.

Simon had not joined the general jubilation. He had taken Elea back to the infirmary and stayed with her. When she reached her room, she went directly to the food machine. She tapped three white keys and the machine gave her a small blood-red sphere that she swallowed with a glass of water. Then, with her customary indifference to the presence of others, she undressed, busied herself, stark naked, with her preparations for the night. Still naked, she went to bed already half asleep, probably as a result of the red sphere. She hadn't said a word since she had removed the golden circlet.

The nurse had seen Elea's memories projected in the conference room, and she looked at Elea now with pity.

"The poor thing," the nurse said. "Maybe I ought to put her pyjamas on her: she might catch cold."

"Don't touch her," Simon said in a low voice. "She's

asleep and at peace. Cover her well and keep an eye on her while I get a little sleep. I'll relieve you at midnight."

He adjusted the thermostat for a slightly higher temperature and lay down fully clothed on his narrow bed. But as soon as he closed his eyes, a parade of visions began behind his eyelids. Elea and Paikan; Elea naked; the sky on fire; the heaving piles of soldiers' corpses; Elea naked; Elea without Paikan; the earth parting; the plain slashed open; the Weapon filling the sky; Elea; and again Elea.

He sat up, knowing that he wouldn't be able to fall asleep. A sleeping pill? The food machine was there within reach of his hand. He tapped the three white keys. The drawer opened and offered him a red sphere.

"Are you going to eat that?" the nurse demanded, looking at him reproachfully. "It could be poisonous!"

He did not reply. If it was poison, Elea had taken it and, if Elea died, he would have no more desire to live. But he did not believe that it was poison. He picked up the sphere with his thumb and his index finger and put it in his mouth. It burst between his teeth like a cherry without a pit. It seemed to him that the whole inside of his mouth, his nose and his throat was filled with an unpleasant softness. It was not sweet to the taste—there was no taste; it was like a liquid velvet, a contact, a sensation of infinite softness that spread and penetrated within the flesh, ran through cheeks and neck and finally reached the skin, invaded the inside of his skull and when he swallowed it, entered and filled his entire body. He lay down again easily. He wasn't aware of feeling sleepy. It seemed to him that he could walk to the Himalayas and skip merrily up to their peaks.

"Doctor! Quick! Get up right away!" The nurse was shaking him.

"What? What is it?" He looked at the luminous dial of his watch. It was thirty-seven minutes after eleven.

"I told you it was poison! Here, drink this, right away—it's ipecac."

He thrust aside the glass she was offering. He had never felt so well, so euphoric, as rested as if he had slept ten hours.

"Well," the nurse said, "if it's not poison, what's wrong with her?"

Elea was awake now, her eyes open, her jaw set. Her whole body shook with sudden attacks of trembling. Simon uncovered her and palpated the muscles of her arms and thighs. They were hard and tense, as if paralyzed by tetanus. He moved his hand back and forth before her eyes. She didn't blink. It was difficult to find her pulse beneath the hardened muscles of her wrist. Finally he felt it, strong and rapid.

"What is it doctor?" the nurse asked. "What's wrong with her?"

"Nothing," Simon said softly, covering Elea again. "Nothing . . . except despair."

"The poor thing. What can we do for her?"

"Nothing. Nothing."

He was still holding Elea's icy hand in both of his. He began to massage it gently, and then to massage her rigid arm. "I'll help you," the nurse said. She walked around to the other side of the bed and took Elea's other hand. But Elea jerked her arm away.

"Leave her alone," Simon said. "I'll take over from you now. Please leave us alone."

The nurse gathered her belongings and with a long, suspicious glance at Simon, she left the room. He didn't notice her. He was watching Elea, her frozen face, her staring eyes, which reflected the lights of the room in two pools of static tears. "Elea," he whispered. "Elea . . . I'm with you."

Suddenly it occurred to him that it was not his voice but the voice of the Translator that she heard. His real voice reached her as a jumble of foreign sounds. He removed her earphones very carefully. Now there were no machines between them.

"Elea I'm with you—completely alone with you for the first time. And you don't understand what I'm saying to you. Elea, my love, my dearest, I want to be beside you, to reassure you, to warm you, to calm you, to console you. I love you."

In his hands he felt her hand soften, he saw her face lose its rigidity and her bosom rise and fall more calmly. He saw her eyelids drop very slowly over her tragic eyes, and at last the tears came.

"Elea, Elea, my love."

He felt Elea's hand clasp his, he saw her other hand grope for the sheet, pull it up to cover her naked breasts.

He stopped speaking. She spoke, and in French, "I understand you, Simon." She paused briefly. "I belong with Paikan."

From her closed eyes the tears were still running.

———————

You understood me, you had understood perhaps not all the words, but enough of them to know how much, how very much I loved you. You had understood. How could this have been possible? None of us had reckoned with the remarkable capacities of your intelligence. In spite of all the accomplishments of Gondawa that you had shown us, it never entered our minds that you might be superior to us. Your successes could have been no more than coincidence. You were inferior to us because you came before us.

This conviction that man-as-a-species improves with time no doubt derives from an unconscious confusion with man-as-an-individual. Man is a child before he becomes an adult. We—modern man—are adults. Those who lived before us could have been nothing but children.

But perhaps it is time to ask ourselves whether perfection is not in childhood, whether the adult is not a child but has already begun to decline.

You, the childhood of mankind, you who were new, who were pure, who were not worn out or weary or drained of life, what was impossible to you, with your intelligence?

For weeks you had been hearing words and sentences of an unknown language—mine—in my voice that spoke to you all day long, beside you from morning until night. In the other ear you heard translations of my words, and your miraculous intelligence compared and classified and translated and understood.

You understood me.

I too, my love, I understood. I knew. You belonged with Paikan.

Lukos had finished. The Translator had devoured and digested the test of Zoran's *Treatise* and processed it in seventeen languages. But it was retaining the translations in its memory bank for printing or distribution later, on demand. It had put only the English and French texts on magnetic film, and these films were locked in a safe, waiting to be released to the world.

An engineer named Murad, Lukos' deputy, guided the press through the intricacies of the machine, since Lukos was still busy inside the egg, working with Hoi-To on the photographic reproduction of the etched texts. Hoover had insisted on going along with the correspondents, and Leonova had accompanied him. Sometimes he would engulf her tiny hand in his enormous paw, or she would twine her slender fingers over his thick ones. And so they proceeded through the chamber and passages of the Translator, hand in hand like two Gondawan lovers.

"This apparatus makes it possible to transfer the images to the films," Murad said. "Lines of text appear on this screen in luminous characters. This television camera sees them, analyzes them and converts them into electromagnetic signals that it inscribes on the film. As you see, it is quite simple: it's the old system of the magnetoscope. What is less simple is the way in which the Translator goes about creating the luminous letter. It is . . ." Murad broke off in mid-sentence and whispered something into Hoover's ear. Hoover indicated by gestures that he did not understand, and Murad took Hoover by the sleeve and showed him something behind the recording television camera—something that Hoover understood immediately and that the nearest journalists, who were looking at the same time, did not understand.

"Gentlemen," Hoover said, turning to them, "I need to have a private talk with Murad. Since we don't have a language in common, we can talk only through the intermediary of the Translator. I do not wish you to hear our conversation. I request that you be good enough to let me have your earphones and then leave the room."

There was an explosion of protest from the newsmen. Cut off from the information just when something sensational seemed to be happening? Not a chance! Nothing doing! What did he take them for?

Hoover turned purple with rage. "You're making me waste time!" he shouted. "If you keep on arguing I'll have you all sent back to Sydney. Let's have 'em!" He held out his two cupped hands. Such vehemence from the normally easygoing man convinced the press that this was an important matter. "I promise you," Hoover added more quietly, "that I'll bring you up to date as soon as I've found out what's what."

One by one they filed past him and surrendered their earphones, variously coloured buttons still warm from the heat of their ears. Leonova closed the door after the last of them and turned to Hoover with excited curiosity. "What is it? What's happening?"

He and Murad were already peering into the viscera of the camera. "The camera's been bugged," Hoover told her. "See that wire there? That's not the magnetoscope wire. It's been added on."

Taped to the magnetoscope wire, almost indistinguishable from it, the illicit wire ran with it into a hole in the metallic case. Murad quickly removed four Phillips-head screws and pulled out the polished aluminium plate allowing the entrails of the magnetoscope to be examined. The intruding object was obvious: a tobacco-coloured, average-sized briefcase of artificial leather. The extra wire terminated inside it and another led out of it, followed a crevice of the wall to the ceiling, and disappeared there, undoubtedly to be connected through some shrewd contrivance with an external antenna.

"What is it?" Leonova asked again, embarrassed by her lack of technological knowledge.

"A transmitter," Hoover told her. He was already opening the briefcase.

Against his will he had to admire the exceptional

skill that had condensed such a complicated device into so small a space. It was not dependent on the general electrical supply; instead, a storage battery and a transformer provided it with the power that it needed. But this limited both its life and its range. It would not have been able to carry beyond a radius of six hundred twenty-five miles—a thousand kilometres.

Hoover checked the transmitter battery, which was almost dead. Doubtless it had already sent out a reproduction of the *Treatise* to some receiver on the Antarctic continent or not far off its coasts.

This was preposterous. Why obtain translations secretly when in a few hours they were going to be released to the whole world? Logic compelled a frightening reply.

If a group of men wanted exclusive control over Zoran's equation, they would have to make it impossible for anyone else to see the *Treatise on Universal Laws*. To that end, those who had installed a transmitter and dispatched pictures of the treatise to some unknown point would be obliged to destroy the magnetic films on which these pictures had been recorded; destroy the original films on which the etched text had been photographed; destroy the engraved text itself; destroy the memory chambers of the Translator that contained its seventeen translations, *and kill Coban.*

"Nom de Dieu!" Hoover cried. "Where do you keep the films?"

Murad quickly took Hoover and Leonova into the record room, opened the aluminium safe and grabbed one of those double-pie-pan containers that have always been used as receptacles and storage places for films. Like everyone else who has ever handled such a thing, Murad found it extremely difficult to open; he broke a fingernail and swore in Turkish, and he swore again when he finally succeeded and saw what was inside: a slimy mass that gave off a few lazy fumes.

Acid had been poured into every one of the film cans. Original and magnetic film alike were now nothing but a stinking paste that was beginning to drip through the holes in the metal that the acid had made.

The Translator's memory bank was a corridor a hundred feet long; its left-hand wall was a metal grill studded with apertures each one-ten-thousandth of a millimetre square. Each was a memory cell. There were ten billion of them.

Murad, Hoover and Leonova entered the corridor at a run. They found that four round tins, quite similar in appearance to film cans—four mines like those that protected the entrance to the spheres—had been planted on the metal wall of the corridor. They adhered to it magnetically and they would pulverize the whole Translator if anyone tried to pull them off.

"My God," Hoover said. "Have you got a revolver, Murad?" When the engineer said that he had none, Hoover turned to Leonova. "Give him yours."

"But—"

"Give it! Good Christ! Do you think this is any time to argue?" Leonova handed her gun to Murad. Hoover said, "Murad, you close the door. Mount guard outside it, don't let anyone in and, if anyone insists, shoot."

"And suppose the mines blow up?"

"Then you'll go up with them, and you won't be the only one! Where's Lukos?"

"In the egg."

"Come on, sister!" He pulled Leonova with him as he rushed away. Outside the storm had risen just when the sun was highest on the horizon. Green clouds had engulfed the sun and spread out to cover the entire sky. The wind whipped the snow off the ground and mixed it with the fresh snow, filling the air with a vicious abrasive. The wind swept away rubble, waste, abandoned packing cases, oil drums, jeeps—it swept the surface clear.

The guard at the door wouldn't allow Leonova and Hoover to go out. A step outdoors without protection was certain death. The wind would blind them, asphyxiate them, carry them off. They would be lost in the lethal whiteness.

Hoover snatched away the guard's headgear and pushed it down on Leonova's head; he took the man's goggles, his gloves and his padded coat, and wrapped the young woman in them. He lifted her onto an electric truck loaded with barrels of beer and aimed his revolver at the guard. "Open that door!"

The frightened man threw the switch and the door slid away. The howling wind sent a whirling volley of snow to the very end of the corridor. The slow, all-enduring electric truck moved out into the storm.

"But what about you?" Leonova shrilled above the wind. "You have no protection!"

Hoover's voice roared back at her. "I have my belly!"

White surrounded them. The truck thrust its nose into a white, roaring ocean. Hoover felt the sharp crystals of snow embedding themselves in his face, freezing his ears and nose. The elevator terminus for the sphere was straight ahead, a hundred feet away. Thirty times the distance needed to lose one's way and be devoured by the wind. Hoover thought of nothing but holding the truck to a straight-line course. He forgot his cheeks and his ears and his nose, and his scalp beginning to freeze under his ice-helmeted hair. The wind was blowing from the right and must be throwing them off course. He braced himself against it.

They still could not see the door of the elevator turret. Was it just ahead of them, hidden in the driven snow? Or had they missed it?

Suddenly Hoover was convinced that they had overshot their goal and that if they went on, even a foot or two, they were doomed. He pressed on the tiller and forced the truck into the wind.

The storm swept under the truck with all its force and lifted it off the ground. But the weight of the beer barrels and Hoover's belly forced it back to earth. Leonova cried out with fright and Hoover grabbed her and held her against him. Left to itself, the truck turned tail, its back now to the wind. The wind thrust its shoulders under the driverless vehicle, and overturned it. Hoover and Leonova were thrown out onto the ice. They clung together. Rolling over and over, the truck was blown about as if it were a leaf; and Hoover and Leonova, wrapped in each other's arms, were thrown about ruthlessly. But suddenly they crashed into a vertical red surface: the door to the elevator turret.

The elevator was heated and the snow and ice that filled every fold of their clothing began to melt. Leonova took off her gloves. Her hands were warm. Hoover blew on his. They remained motionless and pale. Very soon he would have to act, and he knew that he wouldn't be able to do anything. He groped for his revolver. It fell to the floor.

He looked at Leonova.

"Pick it up," he said. "I can't."

Anxiety showed in her eyes. "Your hands . . . ?"

"My hands can wait. Pick up that damn thing! Know how to use it?"

"What do you think I am?" She handled the weapon with confidence. It was a heavy-calibre professional killer's gun.

"Release the safety catch," Hoover said.

"Do you think—"

"I'm worried. . . . Everything may depend on a tenth of a second."

The elevator braked in its final few yards and then stopped. The door opened.

Heath and another man were standing guard over the mines outside the elevator. They looked on in amazement as the soaked, dishevelled Hoover emerged, his hands hanging like useless bundles at the ends of his arms. Leonova walked beside him brandishing the huge black revolver.

"What's the matter?" Heath asked.

"There isn't time to explain. Get me the resuscitation room, fast!"

Heath had already recovered his composure. He called the resuscitation room. "Mr. Hoover and Miss Leonova want to come in—"

"Wait!" Hoover cried. He tried to grab the telephone but his useless hands dropped it. Leonova picked it up and held it for him. "Hello? Hoover speaking. Who is this?"

"Moissov speaking," a voice replied in French.

"Tell me: is Coban alive?"

"Yes, he's alive."

"Don't take your eyes off him! Watch everyone in the room! *Someone's trying to kill Coban!*"

"But—"

"I can't even trust you. Let me talk to Forster." Hoover repeated his warning to Forster and then to Lebeau. Then he asked, "What's happening in the egg?"

"I don't know," Lebeau replied. "The camera broke down."

"Broke down? Like hell! Deactivate the mines, fast!"

Leonova handed the telephone back to Heath. The red light stopped flashing, showing that the minefield had been deactivated.

They moved toward the staircase that connected the bottom of the shaft with the entrance to the sphere. "We'll go down now," Hoover said. "Heath, you're not to let anyone else in, you understand? No one."

"But what's—"

"Later."

Holding his arms away from his body so that his tortured hands would not touch anything, Hoover was already starting down the stairway, and Leonova was following him.

In the egg there was one man prostrate and one man still on his feet. The prostrate man had an ice-knife in his chest. His blood was forming a little pool on the ground. The other man was wearing a welder's helmet that concealed his face and pressed down on his shoulders. He held the barrel of the plaser in both hands, directing its flame at the etched wall, where the gold was melting and running off to the floor.

Leonova had the revolver in her right hand. She was afraid that she might not be holding it firmly enough. She added her left hand and fired.

The first three shots tore the plaser out of the man's hands and the fourth shattered his wrist, almost severing the hand. The shock sent him sprawling and his feet entered the plaser's flame. He screamed. Hoover rushed forward and switched off the current with his elbow.

The man with the knife in his chest was Hoi-To.

The other man was Lukos. Hoover kicked off the welder's helmet, revealing Lukos' sweating face, his rolled-back eyes. The unspeakable pain of his charred foot had caused Lukos to faint.

"Simon, you're his friend: you try!"

Simon tried. He leaned over Lukos, who was lying

in a room in the infirmary, and begged him to tell how the mines connected with the Translator's memory bank could be defused, for *whom* he had done this senseless thing. Lukos did not reply.

He had been questioned without a break by Hoover, Evoli, Henckel, Heath and Leonova since he had regained consciousness. He had confirmed that the mines would go off if anyone touched them and that they would eventually go off if no one touched them. But he had refused to say what the timing was. He would reply to no other questions. Bending over him, Simon studied that intelligent face with its prominent bones and its black eyes that looked at him steadily without fear or shame or defiance.

"Why, Lukos? For whom did you do it?" Lukos looked at him and said nothing. "It wasn't for money, was it? You're not a fanatic? Well?" Lukos said nothing.

Simon thought back to the battle against time that Lukos had fought, trying to decipher the three small words that would make it possible to save Elea. How, after that exhausting, inspired labour, that totally selfless devotion, could he have murdered one man and plotted against all mankind? Why? For whom? Lukos looked at Simon and said nothing.

"We're wasting time," Hoover said. "Give him a shot of pentothal. He'll tell everything he knows very nicely and without pain."

Simon stood up. Just as he was about to leave the bedside, Lukos thrust out his good hand, snatched the revolver out of the holster at Simon's belt, and fired at his own head. The bullet followed an oblique trajectory: the top of Lukos' skull burst open and half his brain spattered against the wall.

Suppressing their repugnance, the leaders of EPI decided to appeal to the international force on patrol duty off the coasts to seek out, capture and/or destroy whoever might have received the clandestine broadcast. It was possible that a midget submarine or an amphibious plane could have slipped through the mesh of the defence network. But, even if it were an element of the International Force that had slipped away to receive the transmission only that Force could find it. The scientists of the EPI would have to hope that national rivalries would intensify the hunters' zeal.

Rochefoux and Admiral Huston, who was the highest ranking officer on duty, conferred by radio; Huston alerted all his planes and ships. But the planes could do nothing in the storm that was still raging. The aircraft carriers were armoured in ice. The submarine *Neptune I* had taken refuge beneath the surface, and there was no possibility that she might come up again during the storm. It was with the utmost anguish that Huston admitted to himself that the only effective instrument left to him was the flotilla of Soviet submarines. If Lukos had been working for *them,* what a joke it would be to send them on the hunt. But if he had been an agent of the FBI of whom the Pentagon knew nothing, was it not appalling to send the Russian wolfhounds against the defenders of the West and its civilization?

But suppose he had been working for the Chinese? the Indians? the Blacks? the Jews? the Turks? Suppose ... suppose ...

A soldier, regardless how high his rank, can always seek solace in discipline. Huston stopped putting questions to himself, stopped thinking, and set the prescribed plan in motion. He awakened his colleague, the Russian Admiral Voltov, and informed him of the new development. Voltov did not hesitate for an instant. He issued alert orders at once. The twenty-three atomic submarines and their hundred fifteen patrol boats set a course for the south, sailed in even closer to shore than prudence would permit, and covered every yard of underwater rock and ice with a battery of electronic detection devices.

There was a gap in the storm. The wind continued to blow but the clouds and the snow vanished into the depths of the blue sky. And *Neptune I* was ordered to go into action. Her bow thrust out of the waves. The first two helicopters brought out of her holds were tossed into the sea even before their rotors could be started. Then Admiral Wentz of Germany, the commander of *Neptune*, called on his ultimate instrument: the two rocket planes ensconced in their tubes. Each carried a rosary of miniature H-bombs and under its nose the two eyes of a stereoscopic transmitting camera. They leaped into the wind like bullets. Their cameras sent back to the *Neptune*'s receivers two ribbons of coloured, three-dimensional pictures.

All the senior officers of *Neptune* were in the observation post. The Admirals Huston and Voltov had risked their lives to be there, to keep watch on each other. They were no more competent than any other of the officers present to recognize whatever might appear in the pictures that flowed over the two screens or to tell the difference between a king penguin and a pregnant whale. But there were electronic detectors that could tell the difference. And suddenly two white arrows appeared on the right-hand screen. The two arrows were converging on each other at a right angle and designating the same point, moving with it and with the image from the left of the screen to the right.

"Stop!" Wentz cried. "Maximum enlargement."

A horizontal screen began to glow on the table in front of him. He looked through a stereoscopic loupe, seeing a fragment of shoreline become larger and larger. In a battered cove at the far end of a bay, a few yards below the surface of the clear, bubbling water, he saw an oval shape, too regular and too motionless to be a fish.

Two men were jammed against each other in the miniature submarine, in a musty odour of sweat and urine. No sanitary facilities had been provided for them. They had no choice but to contain themselves, but the storm had kept them under almost twenty feet of water for twelve hours. In order to get out of the cove they would have to rise enough to cross a reef barely six feet below the surface: they would just make it if they showed a minimum of their craft above water. In such a wind this was a desperate manoeuvre: they were as likely to succeed as a tossed coin was to land on edge. Even hugging the most luxuriant growth along the shoreline the little submarine was not safe. It bumped against rocks, scraped bottom, creaked and groaned. The precious television receiver that had recorded the Translator's confidences occupied a third of the submarine's space. The two men, one of whom was piloting the submarine while the other operated the receiver, had no room even to make a quarter-turn on their own axis. Thirst was licking their throats dry, sweat had soaked their clothes, the salt of their urine stung their thighs. Their oxygen tank was hissing softly. When there was only two hours supply of oxygen left, they decided to get out of this trap regardless of consequences.

There were no mine-clearance personnel on board any of the ships of the International Force. An appeal relayed by Trio had alerted the experts in the Russian, American and European armies, and they were rushing by jet toward the EPI. Since their planes were too large to land at the EPI's facilities, they had to stop in Sydney and transfer to smaller jets. But even these planes faced terrible difficulties because of the storm. Perhaps they would be able to land, perhaps not. And how long would it take? Very long. Too long.

The chief engineer of the atomic pile that supplied light and power to the base was named Maxwell. He was thirty-one years old and his hair was grey. He drank nothing but water—American water, which was flown in frozen into twenty-five-pound blocks of ice: the United States was shipping ice to the South Pole, sterilized, filled with vitamins, fluoridated, enriched with oligoacids and spiced with a touch of mild euphoric drug. It was consumed in great quantities by Maxwell and the other Americans in the EPI, both for drinking and for brushing their teeth. They were willing to accept melted polar ice for external use. Maxwell was six feet tall and weighed one hundred fifty-two pounds, stripped. He held himself extremely erect and looked other human beings up and down through the lower level of his eyeglasses without the slightest disdain even when they were shorter than he. His opinions were the more valued because they were not often voiced.

He paid a visit to Heath, who had made the journey to Europe with Lukos .to purchase arms, and asked unemotional questions about the explosive force of the mines attached to the Translator. Heath could tell him nothing, for it had been Lukos who had made the deal with a Belgian trader. But Lukos had told Heath that each of these mines contained three kilograms—six and-a-half pounds—of PNK.

Maxwell whistled. He had heard of this new American explosive, a thousand times more powerful than TNT. The three mines were the equivalent of nine tons

216

of TNT. If a nine-ton bomb exploded inside the Translator, how would it affect the neighbouring atomic pile? In theory its thick concrete armour protected by several dozen yards of ice should be able to take the shock, but there was a possibility that the shock wave would disturb the architecture of the pile, cause fissures and leaks of radioactive liquids and gasses and perhaps set off an uncontrollable reaction in the uranium.

"EPI 2 and 3 must be evacuated," Maxwell said without raising his voice. "In fact, it would be wise to evacuate the entire base."

A few minutes later the urgent-alarm sirens, which had never gone off before, shrieked through all three EPI's. Loudspeakers and earphones announced "Emergency evacuation. Prepare to evacuate immediately."

To give the order and prepare for evacuation were obviously something. But evacuate *how*?

———

Outside, the storm was still raging. The sky was bright, and the wind was blowing at one hundred thirty-two miles an hour. But it was carrying snow only at ground level, where it was picking up whatever it could and making grenades of it.

Lebeau had left the resuscitation room barely an hour earlier. He had just fallen asleep when Henckel rushed in to drag him out of bed and tell him what was happening. Disheveled and haggard with exhaustion, Lebeau telephoned the operating room. At the other end of the wire, Moissov swore in Russian and then said in French, "Impossible! You know that perfectly well. What are you asking of me? It's impossible!"

Yes, Lebeau was quite well aware. In Coban's

present state, taking him out of the resuscitation apparatus meant killing him as effectively as by cutting his throat. Twelve hundred yards of ice guaranteed his safety against any explosion, but if the surface facilities were destroyed he would be dead in ten minutes.

Then both Moissov and Lebeau had the same inspiration. Coban might be saved by a blood transfusion. The test of Elea's blood had come out positive.

When Coban's condition had begun to improve the doctors had decided to use this step only in case of a relapse or some extreme emergency. Now an emergency had arisen. If the transfusion were undertaken without delay, Coban could be moved in an hour or two.

"And what if the atomic pile blows up first?" Moissov cried. "The mines might go off any minute!"

"Let them go off!" Lebeau shouted back. "I'm going to get the girl's consent."

He and the rest of the resuscitation team had been living in the infirmary, where it was only a few steps to Elea's room. Her terrified nurse was frantically packing.

"So much the better," Simon was saying to Elea. "It was a shame to keep you here. Now you're going to get to know our world at last. It's not ice, our modern age. I don't mean that it's Paradise, but—"

"Paradise?"

"Paradise is—it would take too long to explain, it's too involved. But anyway, I'm not taking you to Paradise. I'm taking you to Paris! Let them say what they like, I'm taking you to Paris. That's . . ."

He was not thinking of the danger; he didn't believe it existed. He knew only that he would take Elea far from her icy tomb, into the world of life. He wanted to sing. He talked of Paris with exuberant gestures.

"It's . . . You'll see, it's Paris! There aren't any flowers except behind glass in the shops, but then there are hats that are flowers, dresses that are flowers, the shops are gardens. . . . The bright-coloured stockings are flowers, nylon slacks, the rainbow-coloured shoes, the dresses are daisies. Paris is the loveliest garden in the world for a woman: she can become a flower herself, a flower among other flowers—that's the miracle of Paris, and that's where I'm taking you!"

"I don't understand."

"You don't have to understand, you have to see. Paris will heal you. *Paris will cure you of the past!*"

It was at this point that Lebeau arrived. "Would you be willing to give a little of your blood to Coban?" he asked Elea. "You're the only one who can save him. The procedure isn't painful. If you agree, we'll be able to move him safely when we evacuate the base. If you refuse, he'll die. Giving blood won't do you any harm."

Simon exploded. It was out of the question! He forbade it! It was monstrous! Let Coban die. Not one drop of blood, not one second more: Elea was going to leave on the first helicopter, the first jet, the first anything, but the first. She should have left already, she would not go down the shaft again. Lebeau was a monster, he had no heart, he—

"I'm willing," Elea said.

The two men trapped in the pocket submarine were playing all or nothing. If they stayed where they were and the oxygen tank gave out, they were caught. And eventually they would tell everything. Even if I refuse—pentothal. Even without pentothal, they'll make me talk, a heel ground into my toes and I'll scream, I'll curse them—I can't go forever without talking, then they'll know where I come from, they'll know . . .

They had to move.

There were two hours supply of oxygen left. Five

mortal minutes to get over the reef, then there would still be an hour and fifty-five minutes of submersion. It was a slim chance. Perhaps the big submarine would suck them in. Or the big plane would pick them up. If they missed, maybe the storm would stop and the tiny submarine could surface. No choice: move.

They moved. A wave threw them against a rock. They bounced off, rebounded against another rock, fell back to the bottom. The impact was so brutal that the man whose head was facing the stern had all four of his lower incisors broken. He howled with pain, spitting out his teeth and his blood. The other man heard nothing. In his television eyeglasses he was watching horror unchained. The wind snatched up the surface of the sea and hurled it gleaming white into the sky. Just as the waterspouts began to subside the man clenched both his hands on the accelerator control. The stern of the battered steel cigar spat out a huge jet of fire and the craft leaped into the waves.

But the crashes against the rocks had damaged the ejection pipe. The jet veered off to the left and roared as it corkscrewed. The submarine began to spiral, gluing the two men to its walls; it swung a hundred degrees and hurled itself against a wall of ice, burying itself a yard deep. The ice crashed down on it and smashed it. Wind and sea snatched away a red spume of flesh and metal.

The cameras of the *Neptune*'s two rocket planes recorded and transmitted pictures of the disintegration.

The base was swarming with activity. Scientists, technicians, cooks, nurses, had hastily tumbled their possessions into bulging suitcases, and now they were fleeing from EPI 2 and 3. Snowdogs waited outside the buildings to carry them to the entrances of EPI 1. Once there, in the heart of the ice mountain, they caught their breath again, their hearts slowed, and they believed they were safe.

Maxwell knew that this wasn't so. Even if the atomic pile didn't explode, if its thick shell was cracked and its lethal gases and liquids leaked to the surface, the wind would begin to shift these about. It would carry them as far as the ice mountain, and they would accumulate at its base. Here the wind would blow, as it always did, from the centre of the continent to the coast, from EPI 2 to EPI 1. Those who had taken refuge in EPI 1 would be trapped there, unable to leave the tunnels inside the mountain. And soon the radiation would begin to seep through the ventilation system into their shelter.

"It's very simple," Maxwell said again as he had said before. "We must evacuate."

How? No helicopters could take off. In an emergency the snowdogs could charge into the storm. There were seventeen of them, of which three would have to be kept for Coban, Elea and the resuscitation teams.

"Better say four. And they'll be jammed full."

"All the better: that'll keep people warm."

"So then there are thirteen left."

"An unlucky number."

"Let's not be idiotic."

"Thirteen—let's say fourteen, with ten people each—"

"There'll be twenty people on each!"

"All right, twenty. Twenty times fourteen—that's ... how many is that?"

"Two hundred eighty."

"Now that the worst of the job is over, the total base staff is down to 1749 persons. How many trips does that mean? Seventeen hundred forty-nine divided by two hundred eight—"

"Seven or eight trips—but let's say ten."

"All right, it can be done. Set up a shuttle convoy

system: the snowdogs will drop off their passengers and keep coming back for more."

"Drop them off where? The nearest shelter is the Scott base. That's three hundred seventy-five miles from here. If everything goes without a hitch, the trip will take two weeks each way. And if we set the people down outside a shelter, they'll freeze to death. Unless the wind drops."

"So?"

"So we'll have to wait and see."

"Wait! When the damn thing can go off . . ."

"How do we know it will? Lukos said that the mines would explode even if no one touched them. But do we have any proof that he was telling the truth? Maybe they'll go off only if they're jarred. So let's not touch them! Even if they do go off, are we sure there'll be any damage to the atomic pile? Can you say so categorically, Maxwell?"

"Of course not. But I can state categorically that I'm afraid of what might happen. And I think we have to get out."

"It might not do anything, that pile of yours! Can't you do something! Put more protection around it? Remove the uranium? Cut off the circuits?"

Maxwell looked at Rochefoux as if the Frenchman had asked him whether he could spit on the moon without leaving his chair.

"All right, all right," Rochefoux yielded. "You can't. Well, then, we'll have to wait. . . . But if the mine clearance squads get here in time . . . Or if the wind dropped . . ."

"Where the hell are those goddamned mine experts?"

"The nearest is three hours away. But if the wind continues. how is he going to land?"

Elea waited tranquilly lying alongside the bandage-wrapped man, her eyes closed. Her left arm was bare, and a small area of the man's arm had been exposed for the transfusion. His skin had the redness of burns in the process of forming scar tissue.

The entire resuscitation team was there—the six experts, their assistants, the nurses, the technicians and Simon. Not one of them had been tempted to take refuge in the ice mountain. They had come from every part of the world to restore life to this man and this woman. They had succeeded with the woman, and now they were attempting a last-chance operation, working against time limitations that were unknown to save the man. Perhaps they still had a few hours, perhaps a few minutes; they didn't know which. They couldn't waste a second, nor could they jeopardize Coban's life by hurrying.

"Elea, listen to me," Forster said. "Relax, I'm going to prick you slightly, but it won't hurt."

He swabbed the inside of her elbow with cotton soaked in ether, then stabbed the hollow needle into the vein that had been swollen by a tourniquet. Elea didn't move. Forster removed the tourniquet and Moissov set the transfusion apparatus going. Elea's blood ran bright red through the plastic tube. Simon shuddered and felt his skin crawl. His legs grew weak, there was a roaring in his ears and everything he saw turned white. He exerted an immeasurable effort of self-control to remain erect and not give way. Then his eyes regained their sight, his heart returned to its normal rhythm.

The public-address system crackled and then announced in French, "This is Rochefoux. There's good news: the wind is dropping. The latest gust was timed at one hundred thirty miles an hour. How far have you got?"

"Just beginning," Lebeau replied. "Coban will be getting the first drops of blood in a couple of seconds."

As he spoke, he was removing the mummylike wrappings from the man's temples. He cleaned the burned skin very gently and placed one of Elea's golden circlets on Coban's head, handing the other to Simon.

"As soon as his brain starts functioning again, you'll know it," Lebeau said. "The subconscious will awaken before the conscious, probably in the form of memory. The pre-waking dream won't come until later. Tell me as soon as you have an image."

Simon sat down on an iron chair. Before he pulled the frontal plate of the circlet down over his eyes, he looked at Elea.

She had opened her eyes and was watching him. And in her look there was what might have been a message, a warmth, a communication that he had never seen in her. It wasn't pity; perhaps it was compassion. Yes, that was it. Pity can be uninvolved, it can even coexist with hatred. Compassion requires a kind of love. Elea seemed to want to comfort him. Why such a look at such a time?

"Well?" Lebeau said roughly.

The last thing that Simon saw before he lowered the forehead plate was Elea's hand opening and resting on the food machine which had been placed within reach so that she might draw on it to restore her strength.

"Well?" Lebeau repeated.

"Nothing so far," Simon said.

"The wind is now down to one hundred fourteen miles an hour," the public-address system said. "If it drops a little more, the evacuation will begin. Where do you stand now?"

Moissov said, "We should very much appreciate it if you would refrain from disturbing us."

"Still nothing," Simon said.

"Heart?"

"Thirty-one."

"Temperature?"

"Ninety-four point one."

"Still nothing," Simon said.

The first helicopter departed. The wind had dropped to ninety miles an hour, and sometimes it went as low as seventy-five. At the same time a helicopter left the Scott base to meet the EPI machine at the halfway point. But the Scott base could serve as no more than a relay point. It had not been designed to house a large number of persons. But every component of the International Force that could come close to shore without too much risk was heading for the continent. The American aircraft carrier and the *Neptune* launched their vertical-take-off planes, which headed for the EPI. Three helicopter-carrying Russian cargo submarines surfaced off the Scott base.

"Heart forty-one."

"Temperature ninety-five."

"Still nothing," Simon said.

The first group of mine-clearance experts had landed at Sydney and changed planes. These were the best, the English.

"Now!" Simon shouted. "Images!"

He heard Moissov shout back angrily, and in his other ear the Translator told him not to shout. At the same time he heard within his brain, transmitted to it directly without the intervention of auditory nerves, a heavy rumbling, blows, explosions and blurred voices.

The images that he saw were fluid, unstable, continually distorted; it was as though he were seeing them through a wall of water tinged with milk. But, since he had already seen the places involved, he recognized them: the shelter, the heart of the shelter, the egg. He tried to describe what he saw.

"We don't care what you see!" Moissov retorted. "All you have to say is: 'Not clear,' or 'Clear,' and then shut up until the next dream comes. When things get frantic and excited, memory has stopped being passive and gone crazy: that's the dream. It'll come just before he awakens. Announce it. Do you understand?"

"Yes."

"You'll say 'Not clear', then 'Clear', then 'Dream'. That's enough. Understand?"

"I understand," Simon assured him. And a few seconds later he said, "Clear."

He saw and heard clearly. He did not understand, because no Translator circuit had been inserted between the two golden circlets and the two men whom he saw were speaking Gondawan. But there was no need to understand the words.

In the foreground he saw Elea lying naked on the pedestal, her face covered by the mask of gold; Paikan was bending over her and Coban was tapping Paikan's shoulder and evidently telling him that it was time to leave. Paikan turned around and gave Coban a shove that hurled him a considerable distance. Then Paikan bent over Elea again and softly brushed his lips on her hand, her fingers—elongated, relaxed, pale golden petals. Then Paikan began to weep, and his tears dropped on the golden, silken belly, and the savage roars of the war that was shattering the earth around the shelter came in through the open door and flowed over him; and he did not hear them.

Coban rose from the floor and returned to stand beside Paikan, spoke to him and pointed to the door. Paikan paid no attention.

Coban grasped him at the armpits and pulled him erect; he pointed to the image of the Solar Weapon that almost covered the ceiling of the egg. The noise of war filled the egg. It was a sound without end, cutting its way through the earth. And it was time, more than time, to close the shelter. Coban began to push Paikan toward the golden stairway. Paikan struck his arm aside and freed himself. As Coban watched him, he opened his key, swinging its pyramid around on the pivot of one of its sides. In Simon's brain there was a gigantic close-up of the opened ring. And in the base of the ring, in a little rectangular receptacle, he saw a black sphere. The Black Seed.

Again Coban pushed Paikan toward the stairs. His hand was on Paikan's elbow, the pill leaped out of the ring, swelled huge in Simon's brain, filled the whole field of his inner vision, shrank again to almost nothing, then it vanished.

Robbed of Elea, robbed of his own death, Paikan was at the extreme of desperation. In an uncontrollable rage he swung his hand through the air like an axe and struck; then he struck with the edge of the other hand; then with both fists; then with his head. Coban collapsed.

The noise of the war had grown louder. Paikan looked up. The door of the egg was open, and at the top of the stairs was the open door of the sphere. Flames were leaping just beyond the golden aperture, as a battle was raging in the laboratory. He had to close the shelter to save Elea, and she had given him the means to do so. Coban had explained the operation of the shelter to her, the golden circlets had allowed her to share the memory with Paikan. He knew how to close the golden door.

Made almost weightless by his fury, he flew to the stairs. As he reached the last few steps he saw a red warrior appear in the doorway. Paikan fired. At almost the same instant the red enemy saw him and fired his own weapon. But the infinitesimal time difference was enough to save Paikan. The red warrior's weapon had released pure thermal energy. But as he pressed the trigger, his finger had already become a shred that disintegrated with his shattered body. The air around Paikan started to become incandescent and in the same moment the heat projection was extinguished. Paikan's eyelashes, brows, hair and clothes were burned away. A thousandth of a second more and nothing would have been left of him. He was not yet conscious of the pain in his skin as he manipulated the controls of the door. Then he tumbled down the stairs. The passage cut through nine and a half feet of gold closed its thousand simultaneous eyelids.

Simon heard the tremendous explosion which the closing of the door had triggered. Coban's laboratories and everything else within several miles of the shelter were destroyed. Attackers and defenders alike were disintegrated and their bodies were merged with the avalanche of melted rock.

He also heard the voice of the doctors and technicians, who had become suddenly anxious.

"Heart forty."

"Temperature ninety-four point six."

"Arterial pressure?"

"Eight-three, eight-two, seven-two, six-one—"

"My God, what's happening? He's losing his grip again! He's giving out on us!"

"Still getting images, Simon?" Lebeau asked.

"Yes."

"Clear?"

Simon nodded.

Clearly he saw Paikan go down into the egg again, bend over Coban, shake him without result, listen to his heart. Coban was dead. And Simon saw Paikan drag Coban's lifeless body up the stairs and push him out of the egg. Now Simon felt in his mind the indescribable pain of Paikan's burned skin. He saw Paikan go down the stairs again, stagger to the empty pedestal and stretch out on it. He saw the egg filled with a green light. The door began to drop slowly as the hanging ring became visible beneath the transparent floor. He saw Paikan, with a final effort, pull the metal mask down over his face.

"Elea!" Simon cried, ripping the golden circlet from his head. Moissov cursed him in Russian.

"What's got into you?" Lebeau asked angrily.

Simon didn't reply. He thought of Elea's hand, beautiful as a flower, graceful as a bird, poised over the food machine. The golden pyramid of her ring was lying on one side, and the little rectangular cavity was empty. Her Black Seed was gone; she had swallowed it with the little pellets of food from the machine.

She had wanted to poison Coban by giving him her poisoned blood. But it was Paikan whom she was killing.

You could still hear, Elea. You could still have known. You no longer had the strength to keep your eyes open, your temples seemed to be growing hollow, your fingers were turning white, your hand slipped and fell away from the food machine, but you could still have heard me. I could have shouted the truth; before you died you would have known that Paikan was beside you and you were dying together as you had wished. But what would you have felt when you learned that you might have continued to live together!

I had called your name. I was going to shout "It's Paikan!" But then I saw your opened key, the sweat on your temples, death already poised upon you.

If I had spoken . . .

If you had known that the man next to you was Paikan, would you have died in despair? Or could you still have saved your own life and his as well? Didn't you know some remedy, couldn't you, with your miraculous food machine, have manufactured some antidote? Or would you still have had strength enough?

All these questions I asked of myself in an instant as brief and as long as the sleep from which we had aroused you. And then, finally, I called out again. But I did not say Paikan's name. I called to the men who were watching both of you die and who were in a panic. I shouted to them "Don't you see she's poisoned herself?" I insulted them, I grabbed whoever was nearest—I don't remember now who it was—and shook him. But they had seen nothing, they had paid no attention to you, they were idiots, blind imbeciles. . . .

And they couldn't understand me. Each one an-

swered me in his own language and I did not understand them. Only Lebeau understood me, and he wrenched the needle out of Coban's arm. He too was shouting, giving orders; and the rest did not understand.

You and Paikan, unmoving and at peace, were the centre of a panic of voices and gestures, a ballet of green and yellow surgical gowns. Everyone was screaming at all the others, pointing, yelling and failing to understand. Babel had come back to earth: the Translator had blown up.

———

Moissov, when he saw Lebeau snatch the needle out of the patient's arm, thought that the Frenchman either had gone mad or was trying to kill Coban. He grabbed Lebeau with one hand and hit him with the other. "Poison, poison!" Lebeau shouted as he tried to defend himself.

Forster understood and shouted at Moissov in English, forcing him to let go of Lebeau. Zabrec shut off the transfusion apparatus. Elea's blood stopped running over Paikan's bandages. After several minutes of total confusion the truth broke through the language barriers and the resuscitation team concentrated their efforts on saving Elea and the man whom everyone except Simon still thought to be Coban.

But both had already gone too far on their journey; already they were almost at the horizon. Simon took Elea's hand and placed it in Paikan's. The others watched in amazement but no one had anything further to say. The chemist was analyzing the poisoned blood.

Then, hand in hand, Elea and Paikan completed

their journey. Their two hearts stopped at the same time. A moment later, Simon gestured toward the man who lay beside Elea and told his colleagues, "The man is Paikan."

It was at this instant that the lights went out. The public-address system had begun speaking in French, but it cut off after a few syllables. The screen of the television set that showed the interior of the egg closed its grey eye. The operating room, twelve hundred yards below the surface of the ice, was filled with absolute darkness and silence. Those in the room stood as if paralyzed. Each man could hear the sound of his own heart, his neighbours' breathing, the rustle of garments and the stifled exclamations. And the sound of Simon's voice echoed in their minds: "Paikan".

Elea and Paikan. Their tragic story had been dragged out for millennia until fate had struck them down for the second time. Night had reunited them at the bottom of the icy tomb. And now it was enveloping the living and the dead alike; it would bury them together until the very end of time and space.

The lights went on again, pale and yellow and flickering; they went out again and returned somewhat brighter. The people in the room looked at one another and began to breathe again, but they knew that they were no longer the same. Henceforth they were all brothers to Orpheus.

"The Translator's blown up! The whole EPI 2's been blown open; you could run a highway through the hangar wall!" Brivaux shouted. He was on guard duty at the top of the elevator shaft. "The electricity's out—the atomic pile must have been hit. I've hooked you into the emergency generators in the shaft. You'd better get back up on the surface fast. But don't rely on the elevator: there isn't enough power. You'll have to go up

232

the ladders. How are you doing with the two freaks? Can they be moved?"

"The two freaks are dead," Lebeau replied with the composure of a man who had just seen his wife, his children, his fortune and his faith destroyed by a cataclysm.

"Well, worry about yourselves now. And get a move on before the atomic pile decides to cause trouble."

Forster translated into English for those who had not understood the French, and those others who understood neither language understood his gestures. For the last time Forster deactivated the mines at the entrance. Some technicians were already going up toward the entrance of the sphere.

But the doctors could not resign themselves to leaving Elea and Paikan. Moissov indicated by sign language that they could be carried on a couple of men's backs, and he added a few words in an appalling English that Forster translated as meaning "Everyone will take a turn." Twelve hundred yards of ladder-climbing, carrying two dead bodies.

"The atomic pile has cracked open!" the loudspeakers cried. "It's splitting and smoking all over. This is a disaster evacuation! Hurry!"

Then Rochefoux came on the speaker. "As you come out of the shaft, head south so that you have your backs to the site of EPI 2. The wind is carrying the radiation in the other direction. Helicopters will come to pick you up. I'm leaving a group here to wait for you, but if the thing blows up first and you get out, don't forget: due south. I'm going to take care of the others now. Make it fast."

Van Houcke said something in Dutch, but no one understood. Then he repeated, in French, that Elea and Paikan must be left behind. With this, he headed for the door.

"The least we could do," Simon said, "would be to put them back where we found them."

"I think so too," Lebeau said. He quickly explained to Forster and Moissov in English, and they agreed.

First they placed Paikan on their shoulders and carried him back down the path up which they had borne him with hope, and they laid him on his pedestal. Then it was Elea's turn. Four of them carried her: Lebeau, Forster, Moissov and Simon. They placed her on the other pedestal, beside the man next to whom she had slept for nine hundred thousand years.

When the full weight of her body came to rest on the pedestal, a dazzling blue flash shot up from below the transparent floor, filled the egg and the sphere and picked out the men and women clinging to the ladders. The hanging ring resumed its motionless turning, the motor began again to generate cold.

Swiftly, for the cold was already gripping them, Simon removed some of the bandages from Paikan's head so that his face would be bare. He was now very beautiful. The burns could hardly be seen. The universal serum carried by Elea's body had healed his flesh even as the poison was robbing it of its life. Both Elea and Paikan seemed unbelievably beautiful and at peace. A frozen mist began to fill the shelter. Stray words in the nasal twang of the public-address system came down from the resuscitation room: "Hello! Hello! Anyone still there? Hurry up!"

They could linger no longer. Simon was the last to leave the egg, going up the stairs backward and turning off the floodlight. At first he had an impression of profound darkness, but then his eyes became accustomed to the blue light that once again bathed the interior of the egg in its nightlike clarity. A barely perceptible transparent sheath began to form over the two uncovered faces, which glowed like two stars. Simon went out and closed the door behind him.

———————

A relay had been set up to link the aircraft carriers, the submarines, the nearest bases and the approaches to the EPI. Without a break, helicopters landed, loaded and took off. The site of EPI was marked by a jagged bell-shaped crater, filled with wreckage and gleaming with shards of ice. Little wreaths of smoke kept rising from it, and the raging wind seized them at ground level and whipped them off to the north.

Little by little the entire staff was evacuated, and the group in the shaft emerged in its turn and was removed without loss.

Hoover and Leonova were aboard the last helicopter flight with the resuscitation team. Standing at a porthole, Hoover wrapped his arms tightly around Leonova, who was trembling with grief. He looked in horror at the ruined base and said in a low, hoarse voice: "What a shame! My God, what a shame!"

There was no one left on the ground, and there was no one aloft except for a few planes that circled at prudent altitudes, keeping EPI 2 within range of their cameras. Once more the wind was howling in a furious storm. It swept away the wreckage of the base, carrying its multicoloured fragments toward unguessable horizons.

The atomic pile exploded.

The cameras saw the colossal mushroom picked up by the wind, twisted, overturned, torn apart, ripped to the red of its hellish heart and then carried out to the ocean and to distant lands. New Zealand, Australia and the Pacific islands were endangered, but the worst threat was to the components of the International Force. The planes returned to their carriers, the submarines dived and the surface ships put on full speed across the wind.

Simon, aboard the *Neptune*, told the scientists and reporters who were on the ship what he had seen during the transfusion and how Paikan had taken Coban's place.

The Vignont family was dining at its half-moon-shaped table and watching the mushroom with its helmet of gorgon's snakes that was the last trace of a gallant adventure. Mme Vignont had opened a large tin of ravioli with tomato sauce and heated it in a double boiler. She was serving it right from the tin because, she said, it stayed hotter that way. But actually, it was quicker, it meant fewer dirty dishes and, between you and me, who cares about amenities? The picture of the explosion was followed by that of a man who assumed a suitably melancholy expression while he uttered a few words of regret and who then went on to the rest of the news. Unfortunately it was not so good. On the Manchurian front it was expected that . . . A new offensive in Malaysia by . . . Bombing attacks by blacks in South Africa . . . The starvation caused by the Berlin blockade . . . In the Pacific both fleets . . . The oilwell fires in Kuwait . . . In South America . . . The Middle East . . .

Every government was attempting the impossible in order to avert the intolerable. Special envoys and mediators were crossing paths at all altitudes and directions. There was hope, there was a great deal of hope. The young were restless just about everywhere. It was impossible to guess what they wanted. Probably they didn't know either. The students, the young workers, the young peasants, were combining, storming the streets of capital cities, blocking traffic and attacking the police with shouts of "No! No! No! No!" All of them were shouting it; one thing they did know was what they did not want. It was not quite clear who was the first to adopt the Gondawan students' version of *no,* but within a few hours the young people in the streets were all shouting *"Pao! Pao! Pao! Pao!"*

In Peiping, in Tokyo, in Washington, in Moscow, in Prague, in Rome, in Algiers, in Cairo: *"Pao! Pao! Pao! Pao!"* in Paris, under the Vignonts' windows: *"Pao! Pao! Pao! Pao!"*

"If it were up to me, I'd shove those young bastards into jobs," Vignont-the-father said.

"The government is making every effort—" the face on the screen began. Vignont-the-son stood up, grabbed his plate with both hands and threw it at the television set.

"You damn fool!" he screamed. "You let them die with your goddamn stupidity!"

Tomato sauce was running down the unbreakable screen. The sad face of the announcer went on talking.

Father and mother, completely amazed, stared at their transfigured son.

"We'll go back there!" he was shouting. "We'll save them! We'll find an antidote. I'm just a jerk, but there are others who know things. We want no death! We want no war!"

"Pao! Pao! Pao! Pao!" The shouts in the street were growing louder and louder. So were the whistles of the police and the muffled explosions of the tear-gas grenades.

"The demonstrations—" the face behind the tomato

sauce said. Vignont-the-son threw the whole tin of ravioli at it.

"Pao! Pao!" he shouted as he slammed the door. For a while they could hear him on the stairs, and then his voice was lost among the others.